TAINTED GROUND

TAINTED GROUND

Margaret Duffy

This first world edition published in Great Britain 2006 by
SEVERN HOUSE PUBLISHERS LTD of
9–15 High Street, Sutton, Surrey SM1 1DF.
This first world edition published in the USA 2006 by
SEVERN HOUSE PUBLISHERS INC of
595 Madison Avenue, New York, N.Y. 10022.

British Library Cataloguing in Publication Data

Duffy, Margaret
    Tainted ground
    1. Langley, Ingrid (Fictitious character) - Fiction
    2. Gillard, Patrick (Fictitious character) - Fiction
    3. Women novelists - Fiction
    4. Detective and mystery stories
    I. Title
    823.9'14 [F]

ISBN-13: 978-0-7278-6435-2
ISBN-10: 0-7278-6435-1

All Severn House titles are printed on acid-free paper.

Typeset by Palimpsest Book Production Ltd.,
Polmont, Stirlingshire, Scotland.
Printed and bound in Great Britain by
MPG Books Ltd., Bodmin, Cornwall.

The three who would shortly be hung by their heels and have their throats slit were still walking and talking and fearfully peering over their shoulders for unwelcome faces intruding into their new lives . . . .

One

D ark days.
   They would continue: all the while the raw February days promising only more misery and darkness. Looking professionally and critically at that sentence – I am a writer by trade – it seems over the top and excessively dramatic. But, reflecting on that time when bitterly cold mist saturated everything, dripping from every branch and twig in our Dartmoor garden, and within the cottage feverish and fretful children cried and coughed, and in a not-so-distant field a man took up a captive-bolt pistol to shoot an old, much-loved horse . . .

Dark days.

On that day when Polar Bear had to be put down my husband Patrick could not be described as having reached rock bottom but he had been writing off for jobs for weeks (he had recently resigned his army commission), mostly dead-end jobs that he did not really want, and having received no useful replies his mood was already grim.

'He *was* around thirty years old,' he said, matter-of-factly, reseating himself at the dining-room table and making a play of resuming letter writing.

Patrick and I had been taking it in turns to look after the animals. Katie was still too poorly to help and that morning I had let them out of the stable and into the field, the big grey retired hunter and Katie's pony Fudge, and given them hay. All had seemed well. Later, the owner of the field, whose house overlooked it, had phoned to tell us that Polar Bear seemed to have rolled, as horses enjoy doing, but was unable to rise. Old horses do sometimes get cast, as it is referred

1

to, when they become stiff in the joints, but when Patrick had arrived with a farmer friend shortly afterwards and they had, by dint of encouragement and their own muscle-power got Polar Bear back on his feet, he had promptly collapsed again. The vet had diagnosed progressive heart failure and the decision that had then been made was the only one possible.

I sat down at the table and put a hand on Patrick's arm. 'I'm really sorry. But he had a couple of really happy years with us after you rescued him.'

Word in a small village gets around at a speed that seems to defy even modern electronic communications. The phone rang and it was a friend offering to take Fudge off our hands for a while on the grounds that he would be lonely. Gratefully, I agreed.

'He'd have been dead by tomorrow morning but you can't just leave them like that . . .' Patrick whispered after I had relayed the information to him, his voice trailing away and giving no indication that he had heard a word I said.

Katie came into the room and I was shocked at how pale she was after suffering from a bad chest infection. Her brother Matthew had had it too, to a lesser extent, but had now recovered and was able to go back to school. They are Patrick's brother Larry's children and we adopted them when he was killed. Nothing had been said about Polar Bear in Katie's hearing other than that he was having trouble getting up but, gazing at her, I knew that she had guessed the worst.

'Is he—?' she began, lips quivering.

Patrick pushed back his chair and held out his arms to her. 'Please come and give me a cuddle,' he requested softly.

I found this psychology quite magnificent and took myself off, my own lips quivering, to attend to Justin, just turned four, our eldest, who was wailing, spluttering and revoltingly messy with tears and a bad cold, having, I discovered, just tripped over one of the sea of toys on his bedroom floor and hit his head on something. Our youngest, Victoria, mercifully too young to know anything about dead horses, had merely just started crying because she was teething and Justin had woken her from her afternoon nap. Oh, and their nanny, Carrie, was at home with her mother in Plymouth, with the flu.

As to the deadline for the delivery of the shooting script of *A Man Called Celeste* – what shooting script?

I was fully aware that after an eventful career working for Special Operations units and then D12, a department of MI5, during part of which time I too had been involved and we had operated as a team, Patrick must be feeling that his life had run into a wall. In his mid-forties and with a young family to support he was too young and his army pension not sufficiently generous to enable him to devote the rest of his working life to charity even if that appealed to him, which it did not. Not yet. I supposed that if my writing earnings were added in we could manage but most of this was being squirreled away into investments for the children's university fees.

Here then was a man who had given up his career (danger had come far too close to home as a result of the MI5 work to make carrying on an option), whose old regiment, the Devon and Dorset, had just been axed and who had this very day had to watch his horse being destroyed.

Mid-morning the following day Patrick's mother, Elspeth, phoned from the rectory at Hinton Littlemoor in Somerset to tell us that John, his father, had been rushed into hospital after being taken ill with chest pains during the Communion service at which he had been officiating. I spoke to her initially and then handed over to Patrick, numbly dreading even worse news to come.

'I'm going up there,' Patrick announced afterwards when he found me in the kitchen. 'Now. Mother's fantastic but he's never had a sick day in his life and she's a bit thrown by it all. I can act as a buffer between her and the parish duties and organize things. Can you manage here?'

Well, of course I could. I put my arms around him and drew him close. 'Please drive carefully.'

The following days tended to merge one with another and

I put writing to the back of my mind and threw myself into cooking the kind of meals that would put colour back into the children's cheeks now they had their appetites back. They all love roasts. So we had mountainous roasts and Yorkshire puddings, almost every day. I made soups with dumplings and all the nourishing and hearty things I could think of. I unashamedly bribed them with extra pocket money to eat more fruit and vegetables and after almost a week, with a wan Carrie back at work and well enough to look after Vicky, took the three eldest into Plymouth on the Saturday for a river trip and plenty of sea air. Looking at them, running about on the Hoe afterwards, I knew they were well on the mend.

Patrick rang every evening. John was still having tests but the enforced rest had done him good. Then, shortly after we arrived back from the outing to Plymouth, Patrick rang again with the more sombre news that his father needed a triple-bypass operation and it would take place the following Monday.

'Is it at all possible for you to come here?' he went on to ask. 'I think Mum would enjoy female company and I'm having to go out quite a bit – flying the flag at local events.'

I found myself wondering if he was attending Mothers' Union meetings and undertaking other such parish duties and said, after consulting with Carrie and aware that Katie was now fit for school and Justin for playgroup, that I would set off with my laptop the next morning.

'We're taking Mum out to lunch,' Patrick said after giving me a quick kiss. He had met me at Bath station as he had the car. 'She's popped into Sainsbury's. I said we'd pick her up there.'

'I've brought your post.'

'Anything interesting?'

'I haven't *opened* them.'

'You could have done.'

'But I never have and I'm not going to start now. How are they both?'

'Mum's OK but, understandably, will be going through hell on Monday. Dad's actually quite a lot better. He was suffering from total exhaustion as well as the heart problem.'

'I thought he looked really tired the last time I saw him – when James was shot.'

'Yes, well, we were all wrung out then.'

Detective Chief Inspector James Carrick, a friend of ours, had had three months off work after the attack that had almost ended in his death. He was now back at work and I knew we would call in at the Manvers Street police station to see him.

Elspeth, a little thinner in the face than I remembered, enjoyed our lunch at the restaurant. Over coffee she transferred her worries from husband to son.

'Nothing in the job line yet? Heavens, it must be awful for you – you've never been unemployed before.'

Patrick said, 'Well, if nothing else I've established that it'll mean carrying on commuting to London, or at least the Home Counties. There's nothing with the right sort of money in the West Country, although I don't mind doing most things in the short term.'

Elspeth's lips pursed. She cannot be described as a snob but would nevertheless not be enchanted if her firstborn went from lieutenant colonel one moment to supermarket cleaner the next, even temporarily. 'You could always move to cut down on the travel,' she said.

'That'll be the last resort,' Patrick told her, not adding, 'Over Ingrid's dead body,' a state of affairs of which I had made him aware.

'That reminds me,' I said, rummaging in my bag. 'One of your letters is from the Home Office. I didn't know you'd applied for any government jobs.' I gave him the thick white envelope.

'I haven't,' Patrick said. 'Perhaps they've decided I ought to be in prison after all.'

He read in silence for a while – there was a lot of it – once glancing up fleetingly at the pair of us, eyes rather round, read on, gazed out of the window for a few seconds and then, when Elspeth and I were practically bursting with impatience, whistled softly.

'Well?' I shrieked at him, causing a few nearby heads to turn.

Patrick cleared his throat. 'Tell me – do I want to be a policeman?'

'A policeman?' Elspeth and I chorused in unison.

We got into a huddle around the coffee pot in order to cease making an exhibition of ourselves and he read the whole thing out to us. Well boiled down, it was this. Following proposals set out in a government White Paper by the previous Home Secretary it had been decided to run pilot schemes allowing retired army officers and others in comparable services – Customs and Excise and the probation service – and jobs such as financial crime investigators and business executives with particular management skills to join the police at senior ranks. If the scheme was eventually formally adopted, police recruits would not necessarily have to start as constable and spend specified lengths of time at lower ranks before promotion.

There would be intensive training and, eventually, examinations. Candidates would have to show good aptitude: a previous senior position did not even guarantee a place on the pilot scheme, which would run initially for twelve months, following a probationary period of three. The writer of the letter was unusually frank and pointed out that not all senior police officers were convinced it was a good idea and the final decision would probably rest with them.

I ran my eye down the pay scales. 'You'd be getting practically the same salary, even during the trial, as you were before.' I studied Patrick. '*Do* you want to be a policeman?'

'Not if it's a desk job.'

'You might have to not be fussy and settle for that,' Elspeth said, uncharacteristically brutal.

'OK,' said Patrick, after due thought. 'I'll go for it if I can do the probationary period somewhere in the West Country, preferably not far from here. You'll need a hand while Dad's ill.'

'You mustn't run your life around your father and me,' Elspeth said.

He smiled upon her. 'I can't keep travelling the length and breadth of the UK if they send me to Cumbria or East Anglia either. Those are my terms and I shall make them very clear,' he added regally, refolding the letter and putting it back in the envelope.

'Didn't you join the police when you left school?' I asked. 'And left because it wasn't exciting enough?'

'When we lived near Plymouth just after John was ordained,' Elspeth said. 'That's right. I have a photo of you in uniform standing next to a double-decker bus at the training school looking about fifteen. I must show it to the children.'

Patrick sighed.

Later, back at the rectory, he filled in the application form, enclosed a copy of his CV, which fortunately he had with him, and was going out to post it when he paused and said, 'Why me, though? Why did this land on *my* doormat?'

'Commander John Brinkley,' I said, looking up from the book I was reading.

'Brinkley?'

'He was the liaison officer between the Met and MI5 when you worked for D12, wasn't he? Not only that, I've thought for some time – after certain things had been smoothed out in odd ways – that your name is still wafting around favourably in the upper regions of New Scotland Yard. They want you. But you won't be working here, not after the initial period, and if it comes about at all, you'll be in London.'

Patrick gazed around. 'Where the hell do you keep this crystal ball?'

When he had left the room Elspeth said, 'What certain things sorted out, if you don't mind my asking?'

'Oh, dead bodies in the course of our work and when we were helping James Carrick – things like that,' I replied lightly.

She stared at me. 'Sometimes, Ingrid, I simply don't know whether the pair of you are having me on or not.'

* * *

7

One of the things uppermost in both Patrick's mind and mine was that if, due to his ill health, John had to retire soon, as obviously he must do eventually anyway, where would they live? The rectory came with the job; the stipend was modest so they could not have accrued sufficient savings with which to buy a retirement home now. It looked as though my desire to stay in the Devon cottage might just have to go out of the window in order that we could buy a larger house with an annexe or granny flat for them. *That* was if Patrick made a go of the job.

I forced myself out of this somewhat negative reverie with an effort. I would deal with one problem at a time.

John had his operation and on the Tuesday evening was well enough to receive more than his wife by way of visitors. Patrick had waved to him through the glass doorway when he had accompanied Elspeth late the previous day – she can drive but had obviously been glad of his support.

'Everything's absolutely fine,' Patrick told his father. 'A retired lay reader from Frome has volunteered to take Matins and a ditto Bishop of Plymouth who now lives in Norton St Philip is doing the rest. Members of the PCC are organizing nearly everything else.'

'That's good of them,' John said, speaking very quietly as he was still weak. 'Sorry about the old horse,' he went on. 'Your mother told me.' There was the hint of a twinkle in his eyes. 'I think she's quite relieved in a way, never liked horses – too big and dangerous.'

As we were leaving another visitor arrived.

'James!' I exclaimed and kissed his cheek.

'Thought I'd return the favour being as John practically lived at my hospital bedside for a week not all that long ago,' he said.

'So you're fully fit?' Patrick enquired, a hand on the other's shoulder in man-to-man fashion.

'Absolutely,' Carrick replied with a grin. 'And back at work terrorizing the ungodly in this lovely city of ours. Is your father well enough to see folk?'

'Yes, but he's tired so we didn't stay very long,' I said.

'Know the feeling,' he said and with another smile for us both was gone.

'What did you think about James?' I asked Patrick when we were in the car.

'I'm not at all happy about him. Scots are only jolly like that when they're putting a brave face on things. I have an idea he's finding it a struggle to regain fitness.'

A reply to Patrick's application for a place on the pilot scheme came very quickly, almost uncannily so, making me wonder if my suspicions were correct. His own conditions or no, he was told to present himself, the day after next, at an address in London for a week-long course that would amount to a suitability test. Elspeth would have none of his reservations about leaving us, for as she said, John would be in hospital for at least another week after that and meantime she and I would have a ball. She ended up, when the time came, by practically shooing him out of the door.

This too, of course, was brave talk for John was not a young man and by no means yet out of danger. During the next few days there were a couple of scares, one complication suffi- ciently serious to necessitate us having to go to the hospital during the night. But John weathered the storm and following a request from Elspeth I played down the seriousness of the temporary setbacks when I spoke to Patrick on the phone.

'He'd only have come rushing back, and to what purpose?' she rightly said, garden herbs in her hand as she prepared to make chicken soup to take in to the patient.

In a quiet moment I wondered which duties Patrick would be given, assuming he passed the preliminary aptitude tests. I almost wrote 'attitude tests', for that would be where any pitfalls would lie. He was never the archetypal army officer, although such a thing might not exist in today's modern armed services. He is a man who has never posed, never yearned for the accessories of some of his colleagues, a couple of black Labradors and a Filofax; never drunk gin and tonic, preferring instead to have a beer and play darts

in the public bar with the locals. He was in trouble count-
less times for doing things his own way – insubordination,
they called it – and as he himself once said there were few
carpets upon which he had not spent time. That he had
reached the rank of lieutenant colonel had a lot to do with
possessing the kind of charisma that ensured he could lead
men into a black bog and safely out the other side, win the
war and come home again, not to mention a downright scary
ability to be instantly at home with whichever weapon was
placed in his hands. And hey, hadn't James and Joanna
Carrick bought him a Swedish throwing axe for Christmas
as a joke only to have him fall on their necks with grati-
tude as he had always wanted one and would now be able
to go to Sweden and take everyone on as it was a sort of
national sport there?

I have not even touched on his proficiency in mimicry,
almost essential when working undercover and the smile that
would charm Sauron clean out of his tower.

I surmised that if he got his own way as to where he would
be stationed for the probationary period he would have to
report to Avon and Somerset Police HQ at Portishead in
Bristol and take a turn in various departments savouring all
aspects of the work. It occurred to me that no one had yet
told Carrick what was going on. Surely there was really no
point until it actually happened.

'You know, I simply can't imagine Patrick as a policeman,'
Elspeth said, all at once, her mind obviously on the same
track as mine.

It was a pity that neither of us thought through what the
downside of this new venture might be.

At least I could now devote myself to the screenplay when
not helping Elspeth with chores. It transpired that she had
many friends in the area, who took her off to their homes
for coffee, bridge and supper parties, so I made myself at
home with a makeshift desk in a box room used for storage
and got to work. In between sessions I walked to get some
fresh air and exercise, exploring the village and the

surrounding maze of country lanes. At least the weather had improved, having turned cold, clear and breezy.

Patrick's nightly phone calls told of medicals, fitness tests – which rather surprised me – that had weeded out the candidates by about ten per cent, hours in classrooms, a written road-knowledge test and, in the latest call on the Thursday, that an hour or so in the morning had been spent square-bashing at Hendon Police College, which had caused another three people to walk out in disgust. This had been followed by a visit to a shooting range where, after throwing down a gentle challenge, he had out-scored the instructor.

'Didn't you mind the square-bashing?' I asked.

'Lord, no. It was only to get rid of those who thought they were too grand to have to do things like that. Besides which, you have to know how to carry yourself if you're attending passing-out parades. Oh, I'll be home for the weekend.'

'Have you been accepted?'

'No one's saying anything yet. Probably to keep everyone on a knife-edge. Some of the guys, ladies included, are all of a twitch about it, but what's the point? I got annoyed when the sprouts were overcooked two nights running, though.'

John, in his own wry words, was 'delivered unto the bosom of his family' on the following Wednesday, arriving with written instructions concerning gentle exercises, especially walking, and a diet sheet that Elspeth took one look at and then tore to confetti.

'It's for idiots who can't cook,' she snorted. 'Canned soup rather than takeaways! Not too many chips and burgers! Easy on the fizzy drinks and Coke!' Eyes flashing, she regarded her husband, who was somewhat frailly inhabiting an armchair. 'This evening you'll have fresh salmon with parsley sauce, new potatoes and broccoli – which is exactly the sort of thing all invalids should be eating.'

'I'm allowed to have a small tot of whisky before dinner,' he told her, chin jutting.

'I don't remember reading that,' she countered.

He wagged a finger at her. 'You've just condemned the

11

instructions utterly. And, my dear, I'm supposed to avoid all contentiousness.'

'Whoever wrote that wouldn't even know what the word meant,' Elspeth said triumphantly but she was smiling as she left the room.

Patrick and I had spent the weekend generally making ourselves useful, and early on the Monday he had set off for Portishead, just as I had guessed he might, but still with no confirmation that he had been accepted into the scheme. As far as my work was concerned I was galloping through the screenplay, which actually involved rewriting my own work of several years previously, bringing it up to date and making improvements as I went along. Recent involvement in the making of a film was proving to be a huge help.

Then, on the Thursday, Patrick came home shortly before dinner with an indiscernible look on his face.

'I'm in,' he said simply. 'And start Monday morning.'

Everyone offered him their congratulations.

To me, Patrick said, 'You were right, John Brinkley's involved, he rang me and broke the good news before I heard officially.'

'You don't seem to be as pleased as you might be,' I said.

'I'm to report to Manvers Street police station, Bath. I have to say I wasn't expecting it.'

'But that's wonderful!' Elspeth cried. 'You'll be right on the doorstep.'

'Does James know?' I asked.

'Yes, he does. And I should imagine he's not too happy about it.'

'But why not?' Elspeth wanted to know. 'The pair of you are good friends.'

'He'll assume those in charge don't think he's up to the job yet,' Patrick told her. 'But it's worse than that. Because of my previous army rank I'm classed as acting detective superintendent.'

'That's disastrous!' I said. 'It'll be bad enough to have you parachuted in like that but as his superior . . .' Words failed me.

'It really is only a pay scale,' Patrick explained. 'I have to take orders from everyone above the rank of sergeant. James won't see it like that.' He went off to find a couple of whisky tumblers, one of which he waggled interrogatively in his father's direction before pouring them both a tot from the new bottle of single malt he had brought in with him.

'This could be another test,' said John reflectively from his armchair, after taking an appreciative sip. 'This is wonderful – you're spoiling me. To see how you handle such a potentially difficult situation, I mean. They can't be that stupid at HQ as not to realize the state of affairs they're creating.'

'But most of the difficulty could well be James's,' Elspeth said. 'Patrick, be so good as to fetch the ladies a sherry – or whatever Ingrid wants.'

'Sorry,' he said and hastened away to amend the omission.

'Use those nice large schooner glasses,' she called after him.

'Well, I think it's really crass,' I said, nevertheless amused at the way she always keeps Patrick on his best behaviour even when he is really put out about something.

'Or a test for Carrick?' Patrick said when he returned. 'Or the powers-that-be are a bunch of insensitive thickos?'

'Ring James,' I suggested.

'I'll grovel,' Patrick said gloomily and went away again.

We could tell by his face when he came back into the room that the call had not gone well. He told us that Carrick had already complained about the arrangement, which he felt to be untenable, and although he recognized their friendship he felt they could not work together under those circumstances. Patrick, therefore, would kindly stay away until something else could be sorted out. Despite every assurance that Patrick had given him he was of the opinion that the Bath posting stemmed from an unverified supposition by everyone that he was no longer, or not yet, fit for the job.

'Scottish stubbornness and pride,' Patrick said, taking a fierce swig of his drink. 'Where do I go from here?'

13

'It'll blow over,' Elspeth said soothingly. 'He'll soon come round.'

Patrick shook his head. 'I've a nasty suspicion he won't.' He did not burden his mother with the news that Carrick had once taken a broadsword to him following another misunderstanding and there had been a brief but electrifying duel that the inhabitants of a certain Scottish castle are still talking about.

Two

Carrick's objections were overruled. I was made aware of this before the man in my life heard of it by the rather surprising development of a phone call to my mobile number from Carrick himself on the Sunday morning.

'Are you free to talk?' he asked anxiously.

I told him that I was, having stayed behind to watch over John as Patrick had accompanied his mother to church.

'I've been ordered to get on with it and stop arguing, so there's no choice,' he muttered. 'But I don't need help, I can do my job. I can't face having someone shadowing me around either, learning the job or not and him with a senior rank, whoever it is. Another thing; as you well know, we're not two of a kind, Patrick and I, and we'll be at one another's throats in no time at all. He's always worked to a different set of rules, ways that I simply can't adopt. So he and I will have to keep a distance, work on different jobs, if that's possible. Not that I won't be there to advise him if he wants it.' Carrick paused awkwardly and then continued, 'I just want you to know there's no ill-feeling, Ingrid, nothing personal, especially as far as you're concerned.'

'Patrick only asked to be in the West Country because of his father's illness,' I told him.

'Aye, that's as maybe. And I know that Patrick once saved my life – which makes it worse. I feel a right bastard being the way I am.'

'How can I help?' I asked when he stopped speaking.

'You can't. There's nothing anyone can do. We'll have to get by as best we can but I just wish everyone would understand that this isn't helping me at all. But who knows? Patrick might soon decide the job's not for him.'

We rang off and I hoped I had been mistaken about the hint of hope in his voice when he had uttered those final words.

Monday morning arrived and Patrick set off in dark suit and sober tie, the crooked smile he gave me as he went out of the door an indication of his apprehension. Everyone at the rectory was on tenterhooks all day and when he returned, quite early at just before six, and headed straight for the whisky we all imagined the worst.

I left it to Elspeth to ask the question. 'Well?' she said quietly.

Patrick swirled the golden liquid around in his glass reflectively for a few moments, chuckled humourlessly and then said, 'It was interesting in many ways. I didn't get to see James, just his sergeant, Lynn Outhwaite, who appears to have been delegated as messenger between us. And despite what I was told it would appear that I take orders from her. That doesn't actually bother me much as she's a nice girl and too busy to make things awkward. Anyway, I spent the first part of the morning touring the station with Sergeant Woods, who, by the way, has been told he can give me orders too but doesn't like to. The pair of us are old enough stagers to get around that. So, yes, we toured the nick, finding out what everyone does, then I was allowed out to do a little checking on a couple of cases; a shoplifting lady who obviously genuinely forgot to pay as her mother had died the previous day and a yobbo, all of fourteen, who'd been arrested for being drunk and disorderly and then made a complaint that the police had roughed him up at the nick making him fall over and hurt his head.'

'I trust you were very careful,' I said apprehensively, mulling over this potential nest of vipers.

Patrick seemed to have recovered his sense of humour but I doubt it was anything to do with the single malt. 'Oh yes,' he replied. 'There was no question of leaning on sonny boy to make him retract. Gone are the days of carte blanche. I just requested politely that he come to the nick, with his mother, who was present at this interview – Daddy's in Parkhurst – to identify the people who had done him over. He said he couldn't remember who they were. I then said that was very likely as a police surgeon who was present in connection with another case had remarked that as the arrested boy was out cold care must be taken to place him so he did not choke in the event of vomiting. Our man then kicked the wall a couple of times. After indulging in what went for thinking in his case, he admitted that he'd made it all up and had hurt his head falling into the gutter *before* he passed out. Would he get into trouble for wasting police time? his mother asked. I said we'd think about it but there was a slim chance he wouldn't.'

'What about the shoplifting lady?' Elspeth asked. I happen to know that this is one of her horrors; that she will leave a shop, her mind on other things, and completely forget to pay.

'I managed to persuade the manager not to prosecute.'

'Oh, well done!' she cried.

'And the police surgeon?' John ventured.

'Would you care for another dram?' Patrick asked him solemnly.

'But as far as James goes . . .?' I said to Patrick later when we were alone.

'Never the twain shall meet.'

'It's really as bad as that?'

'This was only day one, mind.'

'But you actually get on very well with one another.'

'Socially and for most of the time, yes. I just wish the guy would give me a trial run. He ought to realize that I'm not the sort to start throwing my weight about.'

'What James actually said to me might not be quite the whole truth of it,' I said. I had told Patrick about the phone call.

'How so?'

'James is probably worried about the kind of man you *can*

be. When you're cornered. When you're *in extremis*. When a man has threatened or hurt me. You've killed and maimed, Patrick. With your bare hands, with your knife, with firearms. When you found James where he'd been left to die inside that old boiler and the men who had done it had followed you ... James told me he'd never, ever, seen such filthy fighting tactics.'

'It was three against one.'

'Cheerfully,' I said. 'Cheerfully and with relish, according to James, you dealt out potentially crippling injuries.'

His eyes never leaving my face Patrick said, 'You've witnessed me—' He broke off.

'I still have the odd nightmare,' I disclosed. This was probably unfair of me as on that particular, different, occasion he had been fighting for his life following a period of ghastly maltreatment. And another time when he had broken a man's neck. The sound had been akin to that made by snapping a stick of seaside rock between gloved hands. Orders then, though, orders.

'You're too scary by half,' I said. 'For Bath, that is. And for someone like James who hasn't quite got over almost dying.'

'This will fail, then, you think?'

'Not necessarily. I suggest you stay right out of his way. If your paths do cross, pretend he's Elspeth. Treat him as you would her.'

'Buy him flowers, you mean?'

'Don't be pig-stubborn!' I bawled. 'No, GENTLY!'

Matters did not improve and as the week progressed Patrick's lips became tighter and the look in his eyes more strained. Tactful enquiry elicited the information that extra awkwardness and difficulty was being created by Lynn Outhwaite having to act as go-between. For, obviously, as Carrick's sergeant there was a need for her to be at his side when he left the station to deal with things directly. When this happened and she was required to break off from what she was doing in order to forward instructions and possibly information to someone working on another case it was Carrick himself who began to run out of patience.

On the Friday morning the inevitable happened and the two men met face to face in a corridor. There was no shouting match, the resulting exchange of views being conducted in the privacy of Carrick's office. Patrick assured me that he did not lose his temper, which I believed for I know him well enough to be aware of what it takes to make him lose control.

'So did you resolve *anything*?' I asked.

'No, we were interrupted. Lynn called him out and they shot off all bells and whistles. I went back to doing a Health and Safety risk-assessment of the nick.'

We discovered the reason for Carrick's hasty departure later that evening from the local TV news. Three bodies had been discovered by walkers in a disused farm building about two miles from Hinton Littlemoor. Such were the circumstances of the find that two elderly women had been taken to hospital suffering from shock. It would appear, yelled the over-excited young reporter, that the murder victims had been strung up by their feet and their throats had then been cut. The crime was already being dubbed the Ritual Killings.

James Carrick appeared on camera, with Lynn Outhwaite, mobbed by the media and looking a little driven. Questioned, he said merely that the murder victims had not yet been identified and that scene-of-crime officers would be working at the barn throughout the night.

'No one's said so but it's Hagtop Farm,' Elspeth said when the TV had been turned off. 'I'd recognize that building anywhere. There was such a fuss when it was erected. The farm's been an unhappy place for as long as anyone in the village can remember. And when foot and mouth struck a few years ago and all the cattle and sheep had to be destroyed it finished off poor old Barney Stonelake, the farmer, as well. They said he died of a broken heart. His son restocked and carried on for a while but when his mother had a stroke and had to go into a nursing home recently he had everything auctioned off and put the place on the market.'

I glanced at Patrick, the acute misery at his rejection tangible. Our eyes met and he put it into words.

'I should be there,' he said.

'Then go,' I said.

'James made his feelings perfectly plain this morning. I'd be accused of making trouble.'

Up until now I had vowed that I would not interfere. For, after all, everything was now different and there was no need for me to become involved in Patrick's new venture. I was discounting the words of a particularly poisonous civil servant, Nicholas Haldane, now in prison, who had once told me that without me Patrick would be nothing. It was untrue. But the female mindset does have its uses.

'Where are you going?' Patrick enquired as I headed for the door. He sounded a trifle alarmed, as if thinking that I was furious with him and raging off.

I blew him a kiss.

Two police vehicles were parked among others that possibly contained hopeful newshounds at the end of the lane that led to the crime scene, blue-and-white incident tape fluttering everywhere. I spoke to the constable who had flagged me down.

'Is Detective Chief Inspector Carrick still here?' I asked.

'Are you from the press?' he wanted to know.

'No. Would you please ask him if I may approach? My name's Ingrid Langley.'

'I'm afraid that no one's permitted to—'

'Please ask him,' I interrupted. 'It's very important.'

'To the case?'

'Yes.'

Of course it was, silly.

I sat, for some reason with heart hammering, while he got on his radio. The answer came quickly and one of the vehicles was moved so I could manoeuvre past it. The lane was very rutted and longer than I had imagined, the brightly lit scene ahead of me looking at first glance grotesquely like the venue for a rave.

The open area around the barn, which was of brutal, modern construction, covered what must have been at least six acres and consisted of sections of concrete with coarse tufts of grass and weeds growing in the cracks between them. There were various police vehicles parked there and other, unmarked, cars but they were reduced almost to toys by the size of the building itself. I could discern no trees or anything that might give a clue that here we were in deepest Somerset: this had been agribusiness, pure and simple.

Carrick and a young woman who must be Lynn Outhwaite – I had not met her before – left the building and came across as I got out of the car. By the illumination of the rigged-up lights I could see that Carrick's sergeant was dark-haired and petite. She was dressed in a very well-cut trouser suit and sensible flat shoes.

'What can I do for you, Ingrid?' Carrick said.

'May I speak with you in private?' I requested.

'This isn't a good time,' he replied.

'Two minutes,' I promised.

Carrick turned to Lynn. 'Please excuse me for a moment.'

He and I walked away for a short distance.

'I'm only here because you rang me,' I began. 'If you hadn't I would have minded my own business. But I can't, not now. Patrick is at the rectory when he should be here. And frankly, James, I didn't think you'd allow this to go as far as it has. You've never seemed to me to be the sort of person to kick a man when he's down.'

'I'm not,' said Carrick tautly.

'Well, that's where Patrick is. Down. Bet you never thought you'd see tears in his eyes, eh? You're so in awe of the very rare occasions when he goes over the top, usually when in imminent danger of losing his life, you seem to have completely forgotten that he's also hardworking, loyal, brave, sensitive to the feelings of others, unselfish and an extremely useful sort of bloke to have around.'

'Ingrid—'

I carved him up. 'To hell with your stubborn pride. I'll do you a deal. *I'll* act as go between. That'll free Sergeant Outhwaite to get on with her job.'

He just stared at me.

'Two for the price of one,' I went on. 'It's hardly such a drastic step. I've worked with you both before.'

'But I usually ended up by reading the riot act.'

'So everyone will have to grow up, won't they?'

Carrick is not stupid. He knew as well as I that I would not be spending my time relaying messages or little notes from one to the other. What I would actually be doing was acting as a fender.

'This isn't the first time I've done something like this,' I told him. 'When someone called Steve joined D12 and he and Patrick got off on the wrong foot. My presence helps – and then the problem goes away and people get on famously.'

It had worked for most of the time. I had no intention of mentioning the occasion I had been operating undercover with the pair of them and had not been able to prevent them fighting like Kilkenny tomcats outside a pub near Petworth.

There was a short, tense silence and then Carrick said, 'I'll think about it.'

'No,' I said. 'I want to know now.'

He turned on his heel. 'There's work to do.'

I tagged along – he had not actually told me to go away – and the three of us went through the wide entrance into the barn. Wisely perhaps, Lynn was keeping any opinions she had to herself.

More lights had been rigged inside, like the others connected to a portable generator. In the harsh glare a dozen or more people, most wearing protective clothing, went to and fro and there were flashes as photographs were taken. This was taking place on the left-hand side of the interior, all of which was empty but for rubbish, a couple of stacks of old pallets and what appeared to be an overhead gantry of some kind. I discovered later that it had originally been used with a hoist to lift and move heavy round bales of hay, straw and silage, a dusty layer of which, mixed with manure, covered most of the floor. From this gantry three still figures were hanging and even from where I was standing I could see that the ground beneath them was a lake of blood.

As we approached, one of those who were white-suited detached from the tableau and ducked under another cordon of tape to speak to Carrick. I recognized the pathologist, a professor of forensic science at Bristol University, Sir Hugh Rapton, from a book of his I had read. This was interesting: I thought he had retired from active service, as it were.

'Can you tell us anything yet, Sir Hugh?' Carrick said quietly.

'I can tell you more once they've been cut down.'

Carrick consulted the scene-of-crime officer, who confirmed that the preliminary stages had been completed, and preparations were made to lower the murder victims. Deliberately, I had not looked too closely up until now but saw with horror that one of the bodies was that of a woman. Illogical of me, I suppose, to assume that women are not disposed of in such ghastly fashion. The throats had been severed with such force that two of the heads were only attached by the spine and surrounding tissues. Blood still sluggishly dripped.

'Well?' said Carrick to me all at once, perhaps wondering if I had now changed my mind. It was as if we were strangers, his manner glacier-bleak.

I held the look, taking my mobile phone from my pocket. Several seconds ticked by and then I said, 'It was you who had to make up your mind.'

'He's not a man to come running,' Carrick said roughly.

'If I ask him to come on your behalf he'll come. James, Patrick is trying to make a new career for himself. But it won't be furthered on *your* patch. Can't you look at it from the point of view of helping him?'

Whether the DCI suddenly realized that he had been guilty of selfishness I do not know – I was making every excuse for him, bless his gorgeous blond hair and blue eyes, not least that when you have recently been at death's door it can affect all judgement for a while – but after a few moments of agonizing hesitation he made a gesture of defeat and walked away. I found myself looking into Lynn's bright, discerning gaze. 'Good,' she said quietly. I rang Patrick's number.

'According to Elspeth, Hagtop Farm was mentioned in the Domesday Book,' Patrick said. He had borrowed his father's car for the short journey. 'And before that it appears there might have been Viking connections. Vera Stonelake, who's now in a nursing home in this area, did quite a lot of research into the place some years ago and her findings were published in the parish magazine. The farm has a colourful history, not that it prevented her husband from demolishing some of it in the name of progress.'

James Carrick, who also has Viking connections as his mother came from Orkney, glanced up at the speaker from the notes he was making on the preliminary observations Rapton had made before he left. 'Can you get hold of the article?'

'No problem. My father always keeps the back numbers as a record. It isn't the first time bodies have been found here either – only that was in the original stone barn that was on the site. Do we yet know who these people were?'

'No, not yet. There was no identification on them at all.'

'I didn't think you could just demolish rural buildings like that,' I said. 'They're usually protected in some way.'

'You can't,' Carrick said. 'He probably just went ahead and hoped no one would notice.'

'Neither father nor son are pleasant characters, according to local opinion and my own personal knowledge,' Patrick went on. 'It might pay you to speak to Elspeth. Parsons' wives tend to have all the dark deeds kind of local info.'

'I'll do that,' the DCI promised.

'She asked me to tell you there'll be coffee brewing tomorrow morning at ten thirty should you be passing.'

Carrick looked at his watch. 'This morning as it happens, it's a quarter past midnight. I'll do my best to get there.' He reflected for a moment. 'This dreadful incident has to be big-time crime. But nothing much more can be achieved tonight. I suggest you both get some rest.'

I took a deep breath. So far everything had gone pretty well.

'Anything you particularly want me to do first thing tomorrow?' Patrick asked.

'How are you with post-mortems?'

'That wasn't something I ever got involved with in the army.'

'Now's the time to start, then. Rapton's kicking off at eight thirty if you'd care to attend.'

'At the Royal United?'

'That's right.'

'You're an old hand at PMs,' Patrick said to me encouragingly when we were outside. 'You attended one not so long ago when you were researching your last novel.'

'Do you really want me to come along?'

For an answer he gave me a big, brave, hopeful smile.

'But you're not remotely squeamish,' I protested. 'You've seen all kinds of ghastly sights, people blown up with their innards all over the place and things like that.'

'It's not quite the same as watching someone slice the top off a corpse's head with a bandsaw.'

I was not feeling particularly cheerful at the prospect either but gave him a big smile back and said, 'At least these'll be fresh. The last one had been dead for the best part of two years.'

They were fresh *and* bloodless, of course. This, together with the starkly lit and antiseptic environment of the mortuary and Sir Hugh Rapton's deft efficiency, helped to alleviate the grisliness of what was taking place. It was possible to become quite interested in a diseased liver, a heart showing signs of enlargement, the missing gall bladder and appendix.

'I would say this man had quite a few sessions in hospital,' Rapton commented as he completed the work of removing internal organs for analysis, on this, his first post-mortem on the list. 'Do we know their identities?'

'No,' Patrick replied. 'And I've never seen them before – my parents live in Hinton Littlemoor so I'm around the village quite a bit. For obvious reasons my father mostly knows the people who set foot in church.'

'In a nutshell then we have two white males and one white woman. They had been dead for less than twenty-four hours. One would assume that they'd been killed some time the previous night.'

I was making notes.

'The first,' Rapton resumed, 'this man here, as you can see, was around fifty-five years of age, and slightly over-weight, flabby really, five feet eight inches tall, weighing thirteen stone eleven pounds. And, as we've just observed, he wasn't very healthy. Also, there are streaks of what looks like white emulsion paint in his hair and under his finger-nails but obviously it'll be sent for testing. I'd say from his physique he was normally a couch potato so perhaps he'd just moved to the area and forced to do some decorating. That's just a guess, of course. I like to try to see beyond the obvious.

'The second male, whom we'll take a look at in a minute, was younger. He's twenty-five to thirty, six feet one inch tall and weighs twelve stone three. Fit-looking. There's a scar on his chin and his top front teeth have been crowned so he might have been a bad boy and got into fights.'

'Any private thoughts about that one?' Patrick prompted when the pathologist paused.

'He died with the kind of scowl on his face that suggested it was there for most of the time when he was alive.'

'He might have had a criminal record, then?'

'Just gut feelings,' was all Rapton said. 'If you'll excuse the pun.'

'And the woman?'

'Well, she's wearing a wedding ring but whether she's the wife of this man here . . .' He shrugged. 'We'll have to wait for the identification. Otherwise she's about the same age, around fifty, thin, malnourished-looking. Five foot six, eight stone dead. Sorry about another pun. She was wearing

26

quite a bit of jewellery – good stuff – some quite a lot older than the rest so that might have been her mother's. Robbery can't have been the name of the game, then. Nor had she been sexually interfered with. All these people were killed with what appears to be one slash of a very sharp knife. I would guess the blade would need to be at least ten inches long.'

'A machete?' Patrick asked.

'Could be.'

Almost two hours later, the PMs completed, Rapton said, 'Well, they were all finished off in the way I mentioned. There's no sign of other injury prior to the one that killed them; attempted strangulation or anything like that. But whether they were doped or poisoned first will emerge after tests. Somehow, I think not but don't quote me on that. Perhaps you'd be so good as to tell Carrick I'll try to get the results to him tomorrow. But I can't promise anything. Toxology tests are complicated and time-consuming – as he well knows.'

A few minutes later we were outside in the fresh air and gratefully took deep breaths. Even newly dead bodies smell dreadful when they are cut open.

'I honestly don't know whether I need a cup of strong black coffee right now or to throw up,' Patrick muttered.

'Perhaps you'll give me fair warning if it's the latter,' I requested.

We returned to the rectory, hoping to find Carrick there. He was not but arrived, on his own, a few minutes later.

'Learn anything?' he said to Patrick.

'Yes, human beings have much longer guts than one would have ever thought possible.'

'*Useful*, I meant,' Carrick responded heavily.

Patrick turned on him a wide innocent gaze. 'That's a hellishly useful thing to know, cheering too if you happen to lose a couple of yards somehow.' After I'd given him a look he continued, 'The younger of the two men might have had form.'

27

'He had,' the DCI acknowledged briskly. 'He did time for GBH and firearms offences. Plus attempted murder, which they couldn't make stick.' He took the tray of crockery from Elspeth as she entered the room, set it down on a small table and went on, 'Name of Keith Davies. He had a flat in a mill conversion in the village here. As did the other two, Christopher and Janet Manley.'

'*Really?*' Elspeth exclaimed. 'The three people who were murdered? How extraordinary!'

'Did you know them?' Carrick asked her.

'No, I didn't even know their names. I don't think they were particularly friendly with anyone locally. Frankly, though, they were the sort of people whom you thought might come to a sticky end.' She went away to get the coffee pot, leaving the DCI to marshal his thoughts and Patrick to hide a smile behind his hand.

'So, if you don't mind my asking,' Carrick said carefully on her return, 'what constitutes a person who might come to a sticky end?'

The pot poised for pouring, Elspeth said, 'Well, the older man threatened Helen Fuller when her dog ran into the communal garden in front of the mill, and soon after they moved in the woman picked some of the daffodils along the wall in front of the Jeffersons' house.'

'That isn't *really* serious,' Carrick pointed out.

'James, you're not with me at all on this,' Elspeth scolded. 'Foul language, aggressive behaviour and thieving came easily to them. Second nature. That kind of people.'

'And the other man?' he enquired humbly.

'Worse. Sullen, always looking over his shoulder, something to hide. Helen said he reminded her of the actors who play crooks in *The Bill*.'

'So she had a run-in with him too?' Patrick said.

'Well, you know Helen. A bit like her dog – often where she shouldn't be. Only this time he'd parked his car across her drive. He swore at her too. Frightened her a bit.'

'How did you discover their identities?' I asked Carrick.

'One of my constables is a local, he thought he recognized

28

the woman and had seen her driving into the mill. It was then a matter of asking him to knock on a few doors.'

'Young Tim Collins, no doubt,' Elspeth said under her breath.

Just then John entered and gave Carrick a sheet of paper. 'That article you wanted.'

'Many thanks,' Carrick said. 'How are you doing, sir?'

'Progressing well I'm told, thank you.' The rector seated himself. 'In the article Vera Stonelake mentions sinister happenings in the past with regard to the old barn but either she didn't research those fully or didn't regard them as suitable fare for a parish magazine as she didn't go into any more details. I can tell you though that I seem to remember that when I did a bit of reading up about this village the building had been the scene of a couple of suicides, one death from natural causes, plus the finding of another body where there were suspicious circumstances.'

'Was this all recently?' Carrick asked in amazement.

'No, by no means. I can't recollect the exact dates but all this happened over a two- to three-hundred-year period, the last occurrence, the suspicious death, I *think*, in 1966.'

'I doubt there's any connection but it'll have to be looked into,' Carrick said.

Elspeth moved to rise. 'Do you need me any more, James?'

'I was just about to ask you what you know, if anything, about Brian Stonelake, the son of the old lady who owns the farm. It's up for sale, I understand.'

Elspeth sat back in her chair again. 'You're going to think me a horrible woman who hasn't a good word to say about anyone, but I'd be surprised if Vera's will hasn't been altered from what she originally intended.'

'Gossip?' he enquired, tempering the question with a smile.

'No, by no means. Vera's a little confused now, you see. And when I visited her last week she said that Brian had been to see her with another man, and she had signed some papers. He had told her not to worry and that everything would be all right but she's sufficiently switched on to be concerned as she didn't know what the papers were.

Obviously, it's none of my business but the couple told John years ago that they intended to leave the farm in equal shares to their three children, Brian, who incidentally isn't the eldest, Jennifer and Susan.'

'So if he'd somehow worked a fast one and tricked his mother into signing a new will to disinherit his sisters, would that fit in with local thinking about him?'

'Oh, yes, he's a nasty piece of work. Always has been.'

Three

'The signatures could have been required for setting up a power of attorney so her son could manage her affairs now she's in a home,' I suggested.

'Yes, we mustn't jump to conclusions,' Carrick said. 'And of course we must now concentrate on the murders. I'll undertake an extensive search of the entire farm premises.'

'I wonder if there's any buried loot there,' I said.

Carrick got to his feet. 'I knew it wouldn't be long before your imagination leapt into action, Ingrid. Patrick, I'd like you to go and talk to everyone who lives in the converted mill and find out what they know about these characters and their movements. Ask whether they've seen any strangers hanging around or vehicles they didn't recognize. But there's no need for you to involve yourself with the first-floor apartments where the victims lived – Kevin and his scene-of-crime team will go over them later.'

'What about the victims' cars?' I asked quickly, before Patrick could say anything along the lines of 'Aye, aye, sir.'

'They haven't been found yet. Which, as I'm sure you'll agree, is strange.'

'Does Brian Stonelake actually live at the farm?'

'No. I think the place is completely empty now,' said Carrick, heading for the door. 'Thank you for the coffee, Mrs Gillard. No, please, I'll see myself out.'

A little silence fell after the sound of the front door closing and then Elspeth said, 'It's really wicked to strip out your mother's home before she's dead, isn't it? I knew that some of the larger pieces of furniture had gone to auction in Bristol but people were talking about skips up at the house.' She gave herself a little shake and began to gather up the cups and saucers. 'He's living in a rented place down where the station used to be if you want to go and smack his ears for me. In a bungalow called the Firs.' Over her shoulder she called, 'You're not going to get your own back and make James really beg you to help him when the going gets rough, are you, Patrick?'

'No,' he promised gravely.

Hinton Mill, like so many others in Somerset, had once been used for the production of paper. It was a handsome stone building on three floors, the window apertures edged with cream-coloured Bath limestone. We drove into an expensively paved parking area screened off from the gardens by horn-beam hedges, the gardens almost surrounding the property except for where the river formed the north boundary, where there was a wall. The drive curved round to a row of garages, also partially concealed by hedging.

We were fairly familiar with the layout as, out of curiosity, we had looked over the place when it had first come on the market, before the conversion, some eighteen months previously. The overall impression had been one of overwhelming dampness, a problem one assumed had now been addressed, and we had decided that the restoration, even if we had decided to move then, would be far too expensive for us.

'Well, whoever undertook the work didn't do it on the cheap,' Patrick said, getting out of the car. 'I seem to remember that this area was a mass of weeds concealing chunks of stone that had fallen off the building.' He gazed at me pensively. 'Are you taking notes or am I?'

'You're the copper,' I reminded him, taking my pad and pen from my bag and placing them in his hands.

'So it would appear that none of these vehicles belong to the victims,' he said, quickly listing the two saloons, one four-by-four and a BMW sports car.

'According to James, no.'

'James is still being a bit awkward.'

'He might be deliberately trying to make you lose your

rag. He might also be under orders to do just that. I can't believe that the army wasn't required to forward a reference.'

Patrick made a kind of snorting sound. 'The army was never around when I lost my rag.'

I did not comment on this and there was a short silence as we walked towards the entrance and then I said, 'One thing's for certain, though; it's proving to be a distraction.'

'What do you mean?'

'When you were working for D12 what would you have done with regard to the cars?'

'The cars?'

'Patrick!' I yelled at him furiously.

He started. 'There's no need to shout.'

'What would you have done?' I repeated.

At last, everything got switched on. 'I'd have immediately contacted base to get a check done on them.' He sort of sagged. 'Yes, you're right. I'm allowing this thing with Carrick to get in the way.'

'Tell yourself that he isn't a friend of yours. You don't know him. He's the boss. Solve the crime.'

'He'd really hate me if I solved the crime.'

'Bugger Carrick!' I hollered. 'This is *your* new career!'

Patrick gazed around somewhat apprehensively but no one flung open windows to throw anything or remonstrate with us. 'OK,' he said quietly and walked away for a few paces to make the call.

I went to the entrance door, expecting to have to contact those within over a security system as there was a row of bell-pushes alongside grilles and small brass plaques listing the residents but it was open. I was pleased to see that Patrick made a note of all the names as he came in and we went to the door of Flat 1, to the right in the spacious marble-floored hallway that was home to several large and exotic potted plants.

There was no reply.

Flat 2 was accessed off to the left and after ringing the bell twice we heard slow footfalls within.

'Yes?' said a lugubrious elderly man, opening the door about twelve inches.

'Police,' Patrick said briskly, showing his warrant card. 'I'm acting Detective Superintendent Gillard and this lady is my training adviser. I would like to ask you a few questions about the people who lived on the first floor. I take it you've heard about the deaths?'

'Yes, we but never saw 'em,' said the man sourly.

'May we come in?'

'S'pose you'd better or you'll only keep pestering me. Someone rang the doorbell early this morning, too early, but I didn't answer it. That could have been your lot.' A tall, heavy man, he led the way down the hall and into a large sunny room at the end of it. 'Keep it short, though, the wife's in bed with shingles and I've enough to do.'

We made suitable sympathetic noises and then sat down without being asked to do so. Patrick immediately got to his feet again and went over to the window to look out, glancing quickly at his notes as he did so. 'Mr William Brandon?'

'That's right.'

'Do any of your windows overlook the car park?'

'Not likely. That's why we bought this flat and not the other one on the ground floor – it's for sale by the way and they're in South Africa so it's no use knocking there. There's a hedge but they must get all the slamming doors and engines starting up.'

'Thank you,' Patrick murmured. 'But you do live right beneath one of the flats where the murder victims lived.' He smiled like a death's head, one of his tricks of the trade, and even though I should be used to it by now my skin always crawls.

'What about it?' Brandon asked sharply, duly rattled.

'Did you hear anything odd the day before yesterday?'

'No, nothing.'

'Not even in the hallway outside? No sounds of extra people going to and fro, no raised voices, nothing out of the ordinary?'

'Nothing that I noticed. It's pretty quiet here but for the people on the top floor in the studio flats when they have parties. I complained last summer when all the windows were open so you could hear their damned music even louder. Not music, an infernal racket. Loads of drink too judging by the din they made. And drugs, if the truth was known.'

'The residents of *both* flats on the top floor have parties? What, as combined efforts?'

'No, at different times. But they tell one another when they're going to have them so the others can go out for the evening. Or invite them. The rest of us can go to hell.'

'Who told you this?'

'Mrs Dewitte. She's the one in South Africa. She got invited.' Brandon guffawed. 'She's the kind of woman who would have been called fast when I was a lad.'

'Were there any parties last Thursday night?'

'No, thank God.'

'Do you know if the people upstairs, Christopher and Janet Manley and Keith Davies, were invited to the parties?'

'Couldn't tell you. Didn't even know what they were called.'

'The residents' names are all listed outside the main door by the intercoms.'

'Never looked at 'em.' Brandon, who had remained standing, now sat down lumpishly in an armchair. 'Is that all your questions?'

'Would you mind telling me what you did before you retired?'

'I do mind as it's none of your damned business but I'll tell you anyway. I was fortunate in being left a fairly large sum of money as a young man and having a good head for money matters I was able to put it to use. Stocks, shares, financing various projects for other people. That kind of thing.'

'I see. Have you noticed any strangers hanging around lately?'

'No.'

'Where were you on Thursday night?'

'Why here, of course. I've told you, the wife's ill. I can't bloody well go anywhere right now.'

'Are you quite sure you didn't hear anyone living above you leave the building on Thursday night?'

'I've just said so, haven't I?'

'Would it be all right for Ingrid to have a quick word with your wife?'

A pair of bloodshot, somewhat piggy eyes appraised me. 'Two minutes, then. First door on the left.'

The door was actually slightly ajar. I knocked.

'Do close it, my dear,' said a quiet voice when she had bidden me enter. Then, as I approached the bed, 'I did hear most of it, the acoustics of this place are rather weird. There, take a seat.'

I sat on the pink upholstered chair indicated, the hand that had pointed to it be-ringed and elegant.

'Marjorie Brandon,' said the lady. 'I'm sure you're not really his training adviser.'

'His wife, actually,' I said. 'But brought in to help because of previous experience.'

'Don't say another word,' she whispered in conspiratorial fashion. 'I like your husband's voice. I was on the stage, you know. He's a man used to giving orders and he uses his voice like a weapon if he has to, like all the best actors.'

She was a perceptive person.

'I'm not feeling all that bad,' Mrs Brandon went on. 'I came for a lie down as shingles makes you feel weak and tired. Do you think you could be really kind and get me some orange juice from the fridge? William's never had to look after me even the smallest bit before and forgets to ask when he makes himself a drink. Poor William, he's gone to seed terribly. You'd never guess in a million years how handsome he used to be.'

I found myself wondering if he had been a selfish pig in those days too.

'You want to know about those people upstairs,' said Mrs Brandon when I returned with the juice. 'Thank you, you're an angel. I'm afraid I can't really be helpful. I did speak to Janet a few times and said good morning to begin with to the men but they always ignored me so I stopped. The younger one looked a bit of a thug. I'm not really a snob but I wondered what he was doing here – it didn't seem to be his kind of place. I felt sorry for Janet though as even though they were living in this lovely part of the world and so must have been reasonably well off – I don't think either she or her husband went out to work – she never looked happy.'

'Did you hear anything strange going on upstairs on Thursday night?'

'No, you don't here. It's all quite well insulated. You don't even hear people going up and down the stairs. Just voices sometimes if they're laughing and joking a bit loudly. Oh, and the parties on the top floor when they have the windows open. It doesn't really bother me as it doesn't happen very often and people must have a little fun sometimes, mustn't they? But William rants and raves. I've told him he'll give himself ulcers but he never listens.'

'But you've heard no arguments and shouting in the flat above you recently?'

'No. Nothing like that. I think you ought to go and talk to the people who live on the top floor. They go out and about far more than we do and might have been friendly with the Manleys. I don't know about the other man, though, as I've just said, he was off-putting.'

'Have you met the people who live in the top-floor flats?'

'No, not really. They're a lot younger than us and all go out to work quite early. I think there's a couple in number five and a girl living on her own at number six. A boyfriend stays sometimes. I have said hello to people in the hallway as I've been coming in with shopping sometimes at the weekends but whether they were the actual residents or not I don't know.'

'So if any strangers were in or around the building you wouldn't necessarily have noticed.'

'No, I suppose not. But the outside door is locked at night.'

'Is there anything at all that you thought odd about anyone's movements here over the past few days?'

'No, nothing,' said Mrs Brandon after due thought. 'Sorry to be so useless.'

'Your husband told us he was left some money and was able to invest it to live on. So he's never had an actual career?'

'Well, he never went out with a briefcase and bowler hat to catch a train to the City in the mornings, but until he retired and we came here he was always going here and there on business and there were never any problems with money – not so far as I know. I didn't ask as I simply don't understand finance. I left everything to him. Silly, I suppose, but that's the way it was.'

'Is there anything else I can get for you?' I asked, having thanked her but thinking it a bit strange for a woman not to know more about where their money came from.

'No, thank you, my dear. I'll get up soon and make some lunch.'

'Can't he even put a sandwich together for the pair of you?' I was driven to say.

'Wouldn't know where to start – hopelessly impractical,' Mrs Brandon replied, laughing at my indignation.

It did not seem that we had a red-hot suspect in our hunt for a knife-wielding killer.

'I *think* Janet's husband had been a policeman at one time,' Mrs Brandon said thoughtfully as I rose to leave. 'I can't quite remember how I know – perhaps something she said.'

I thanked her again, wished her a speedy recovery and went back into the living room.

'He's gone,' Brandon said. 'Asked me to tell you he's having a look round outside.'

I surveyed him slumped in his chair doing a fair impression of a couple of hundredweight of gone-off lard and said, 'It's lunchtime and your sick wife is hungry. There's bread, ham, butter and salad in the fridge. Fix!'

And walked out, slamming the door hard.

Patrick was rooting around in the hedge. 'I was wondering about the murder weapon,' he said when he saw me. 'You never know where things are going to end up but I expect Carrick's lot did a full sweep along here this morning. Shall we talk to the people upstairs?'

Both flats on the first floor had been sealed off by Carrick's team. We carried on up the stairs to a wide landing with more plants and paused to look out of the large floor-to-ceiling window. There was a good view over the car park below and beyond, on rising ground, stretched the southern side of the village crowned by the church spire.

There was no response to either doorbell being rung.

'These people are not yet suspects,' Patrick said, partly to himself, stepping back from the door of number six. 'Therefore I won't use my skeleton keys to gain entry and have a look around as I might have done in the good, bad old days. And for all we know everyone's still in bed and has no intention of answering the door.'

'It might not be any kind of lead but Mrs Brandon had an idea Janet Manley told her that her husband had been in the police.'

'I'll check up on that before we do anything else,' Patrick said, but before he could reach for his mobile the door across the landing opened, revealing a man wearing a bathrobe.

'Sorry, I was in the shower,' he said. 'Are you the police?'

Patrick introduced us.

'I thought you'd be back.' He spoke with just a hint of a French accent. 'I am Pascal Lapointe,' he went on. 'This is my partner, Lorna Church.' Here he gestured in the direction of an attractive woman, also attired in a bathrobe, who was making coffee in the adjoining open-plan kitchen. 'Do sit down. Is it too late in the morning for coffee for you?'

We accepted even though by this time it was actually early afternoon.

'We didn't know these unfortunate people well, you under-stand,' Lapointe began by saying when he had seated himself. Lorna had gone away to get dressed. 'The truth is that we felt sorry for Chris and Janet. They did not say a lot but we got the impression they felt themselves exiled here, not really suited to country living, after a life in the city – London, I think it was.'

'Their choice, surely,' Patrick said.

A Gallic shrug. 'Ah, but there is a difference between retire-ment and exile, yes?'

'Do you think they were running away from something?' I enquired.

'Perhaps. But you must understand, this is just my own thoughts. Lorna says I have an overactive imagination.'

I was not alone there, then.

'We asked them up here on a couple of occasions. We have gatherings of friends, mostly from Bristol where we both work. You can love the rural life but it can be *too* quiet. Sometimes there has to be good conversation and plenty of good food, music and wine.'

'They didn't really fit in to that either,' said Lorna, re-appearing all at once wearing a black velour tracksuit and big fluffy pink slippers. They made an attractive couple; he slim and tanned, she a Nigella Lawson lookalike.

'You are just a little bit snobby,' Lapointe told her.

She pouted. 'It's true, though. Neither of them had any conversation and if you're honest you'd admit they didn't really enjoy themselves. They didn't like the food, didn't know what they were drinking and didn't even come properly dressed. Even you said that the English live in jeans and T-shirts whatever the occasion.'

'And the other man?' Patrick said. 'Keith Davies? Did you invite him up here too?'

Lapointe shook his head emphatically. 'No. At least – and I think you will find this strange – I sometimes got the impression that he was not far away. I once opened the front door when we had a crowd here as it was a very warm summer's evening and the flat was stuffy even though we had all the windows open, and he was out on the landing, smoking.'

'He wasn't our sort at all,' Lorna drawled.

'But there must have been a connection between the three of them,' Patrick said. 'Perhaps he felt left out and that was his way of letting you know.'

'He did not appear to be a sociable person,' said Lapointe. 'He—'

'You *said*,' Lorna interrupted, 'that he was as rough as rats and you wouldn't want him here.'

'Perhaps I was a little annoyed at the time and hasty in my judgement,' he told her, giving her a reproving look.

'Did the Manleys mention him at all?' I asked.

'I can't remember them doing so.'

'Did they all go around together?'

'I saw him driving them in their car on several occasions.'

At which point my overactive imagination kicked in and produced a quite bizarre theory. But this was not the time to air it.

'Did you go out on Thursday night?' Patrick asked.

'Yes,' Lorna said. 'We went to the pub for a meal.'

'The Ring O'Bells in the village?'

'That's right.'

'What time did you get back?'

'It was quite early – I think at about a quarter to ten.'

'No, it was much later than that,' Lapointe interposed. 'Around ten thirty.'

'Are you sure, darling? I thought—'

'You've forgotten. I wanted to see a TV programme,' he said with an air of finality.

The rest of the questioning was routine. Neither of them had seen any strange people during the past few days, or even weeks, the only visitor to the mill, to their knowledge, having been the boyfriend of the occupant of the other top-floor flat, Tamsin Roper. He apparently was a naval officer by the name of Owen, whom they thought had been on leave and staying with her.

'I think you will find they've gone to see Tamsin's mother in Bath today,' said Lapointe. 'They're taking her out to lunch as it's her birthday.'

'And Tamsin herself told you all this?' Lorna asked with another pout.

'Last week,' Lapointe answered evenly but speaking quite loudly. 'She's our neighbour. I talk to her.'

We left before war was declared.

'Miss Roper will have to wait,' Patrick said as we descended the stairs.

'To whom did the cars belong?'

He consulted the notebook. 'The BMW belongs to the Dewittes, the Discovery to Lapointe, the Audi to the Brandons and the Ford to Tamsin Roper. They must have gone to Bath in the boyfriend's car. So either the victims' vehicles were stolen by whoever killed them or someone on this side of the law had them removed and forgot to mention it to Carrick.'

'Lorna doesn't appear to have a car of her own, then?'

'Perhaps he drives her to work. It might be off the road. Who knows? We can ask her if it becomes important. Do we now go and batter Brian Stonelake for Elspeth?'

'Can I share an idea with you first?'

'Fire away.'

'The murder victims are a couple where the bloke might have been in the police, plus Keith Davies, who's done time. Do we have a bent copper, his wife and their minder burying themselves in Somerset as things got too hot on the home patch?'

'That's a passable theory. But why were they killed?'

'Revenge? Was Davies part of a gang? Were they all lying low because someone was out for their blood or until they could access some hidden ill-gotten gains?'

'You said something along those lines earlier but I thought you were trying to wind James up.'

'That's the last thing I'm going to do! No, I was sort of joking in an effort to lighten the atmosphere a bit, but, on reflection, it ought to be borne in mind.'

'The bodies didn't show any signs of violence that would suggest they had been tortured for the whereabouts of anything like that before they were killed.'

'There's every chance they could have volunteered the information. In exchange for their lives, perhaps. Only—' I stopped speaking, the mental images I was creating unbearable.

'We could ask Brian Stonelake if anyone's been digging holes on his farm recently.'

'Digging holes?' Stonelake said, giving every indication of puzzlement. 'No, I don't think so. Why should they? I used to get folk looking for mushrooms in the autumn and the odd metal-detector nutter, but that's all. I sent them on their way, don't you worry.'

Within roughly five seconds of meeting the farmer I had decided, rightly or wrongly, that here was no true son of the soil. I was probably biased by the truly hideous barn he and his father had built and in so doing swept away hundreds of years of rural history, but he did himself no favours. A shambling, unshaven beanpole of a man, he looked so shifty that if someone had informed me he was involved with running rackets on East End greyhound tracks I would have believed them. I told myself sternly that this was my first lesson in not pre-judging people and prepared to give him the benefit of every smallest doubt.

'But you haven't lived there for a while,' Patrick said.

'No, but I still take a walk round the place most days, especially up by the house. Can't think why you lot want to search there – it's quite a way from the yard where the bodies were found.'

'Did you know the murder victims?' Patrick asked.

The interior of the bungalow, as so often happens when the place is rented, had an unhomely feel to it, boxes stacked everywhere, some open and with the contents spilling out as though Stonelake had rummaged in them, looking for things. The beer opener? No, *no*, I berated myself.

The living room was comparatively tidy and contained some good pieces of furniture, antiques, but these had been pushed to the walls in haphazard fashion and were covered in dust. With difficulty I refrained from removing a half-drunk mug of tea, cold-looking, that had been placed on the top of a rather fine mahogany chest of drawers.

'No,' Stonelake said in response to the question, 'I only know that they lived in the village. How long are you lot going to be in the barn? There's a bloke coming to look over the place in a couple of days' time.'

'I couldn't tell you,' Patrick replied. 'And it'll take quite a while to search the whole farm.'

'You didn't answer my question – what the hell d'you have to do that for?'

'Mr Stonelake, three people have been butchered on your property. One item we will be searching for is the murder weapon.'

Stonelake threw himself sulkily into a chair.

'Have any dodgy people shown an interest in buying the farm?' Patrick went on. We remained standing, mostly because the rest of the seating was occupied by clothing, newspapers and a large and smelly dog that was either asleep or moribund.

'No, no one like that. I haven't had much interest at all. Farming's in a dreadful way. That's why I'm selling up now my mother's gone into a home. With a bit of luck I'll be able to flog off most of the land for housing but knowing my luck that would go against green-belt rules or some other crap like that.' He hurled a nearby phone book at the dog, which lunged to its feet and half fell off the sofa, sending things in all directions.

Once upon a time Patrick would have probably hefted Stonelake out of his chair and shaken him until his worn dentures rattled. Sadly, as far as this instance was concerned, he could no longer do so.

'Bloody thing,' Stonelake muttered. 'It's Mother's and if she didn't keep asking how it is I'd take it out and shoot it. Turned up one night, starving, and they took it in. Still, when the old lady goes a bit more ga-ga—' He broke off and eyed the animal meaningfully, and as if knowing what was being said it slunk nervously off into a corner.

Patrick brushed some of the hairs and dried mud from the seat vacated by the dog and sat down on the edge of it, staring hard at the other man. 'Your farm has a bit of a history, hasn't it?' he said. 'Bodies have been found there before – in the old barn that was demolished to make way for the new one. Suicides, a tramp, a suspicious death. Rather more than co-incidences, in the light of what's happened, wouldn't you say?'

Stonelake shrugged dismissively, not meeting Patrick's gaze. 'I heard about those but they were bloody years ago. Mum used to talk about it after she'd done some research in Bath library for something she wrote in the parish rag. Dad told her she musn't have enough to do at home if she was bothering with it, and I certainly wasn't interested.'

Patrick said, 'The murder victims were hanging by their heels and had been butchered like animals. Their throats were cut and two of them had had their heads almost severed. Have you ever employed anyone who had worked in a slaughterhouse? Anyone like that who might have a grudge against you and would try to implicate you in a violent crime?'

This was more like it, I thought, the questioner giving the impression that if no useful response was forthcoming then the man he was talking to might suddenly find himself dangling upside down from the ceiling.

'There was Shaun Brown,' Stonelake said, 'but that was a while back now. He helped me a couple of winters ago, with the cattle. He'd worked at one time for a meat-packing plant at Warminster, killing pigs, but I had no problems with the bloke. He wasn't strange in the head or anything like that. Not knife-happy or likely to go off and kill folk. Why should he be? It's an honest living.'

'You parted on good terms, then?'

'Well, no, not really. I had an idea he'd helped himself to some diesel – you know the red diesel farmers use? – for his van and we had words. He went off in a paddy and I never saw him again. Heard he was back at the meat plant.'

Patrick glanced at me and I wondered if he was thinking the same, that we had probably heard only an edited version of what had happened. Had Stonelake withheld wages to pay for the alleged theft?

'Oh, come to think about it I do know about the body that was found back in the sixties,' Stonelake went on, almost eagerly. 'I'd left school by then and was helping the old man. He found it, a bloke who was missing from home in Bristol. He'd been a real no-gooder by all accounts and had got into dealing drugs. Done time for it. There wasn't a mark on him and I seem to remember they ended up not knowing how he'd died. It was freezing that weekend and he was a scraggy little git so perhaps the cold got him.'

'Did you see the body?' I asked.

'Yes, I ran in the barn when I heard Dad shout. He was lying there all stiff like one of those things in shop windows.'

'And you?' Patrick said. 'You have a criminal record as well?'

I had an idea he was ready in case the other vented any fury on the hapless dog but Stonelake remained where he was, staring at the window behind Patrick's head.

'A driving ban for a year when I was a lot younger,' he finally admitted. 'You know . . . young and hot-headed.'

'Anything else?' Patrick enquired.

'No. You lot once tried to pin thieving fence posts on me but you couldn't make it stick.'

'I see. So you didn't once blast someone you thought might be a poacher with a shotgun.'

At this Stonelake did see red. 'That was gossip! Hearsay! The police never became involved with that. How did you hear about it?'

'Well, seeing as you've asked I'll tell you. It was me you took the shot at.'

'You!' Stonelake's face assumed a rather ghastly pallor.

'Yes, I was taking a short cut one evening through the woods down by the river. Fortunately only half a dozen pellets actually landed and I didn't get much sympathy at home as I'd been warned that both you and your father were trigger-happy.'

'We were always having people breaking down the fences after rabbits and pheasants in those days.'

'Oh, I didn't expect you to apologize,' Patrick said and rose to his feet. 'Chief Inspector Carrick should be searching the farmhouse and other outbuildings right now and if he finds anything that incriminates you I assure you I'll be back.'

On the way out the dog gazed up at him and, fleetingly, Patrick's long fingers gently stroked its head.

Four

'Is that true?' I asked when we were in the car.
'Of course.'

'Why didn't your father call the police?'

'Because he had an idea Barney Stonelake knocked his wife around, Vera often coming to church with bruises that she explained away by saying how clumsy she was getting. I seem to remember I was given the usual anaesthetic, a tot of whisky, and sent along to the doctor's. The pellets had only just penetrated my skin and GPs did that kind of first aid in those days.'

'It must have been when your parents first moved to the village and you were sort of between the police and the army.'

'Yes, I was living at home for a few weeks. I suppose there was a wish on their part, being quite newly arrived, not to make too many unpleasant waves.'

'I'm still surprised you didn't go and sort him out yourself.'

'I do as my mum and dad tell me even now, don't I?'

I had to smile. 'Prejudice apart, what d'you make of him?'

'I think I have to agree with Elspeth's view – he's a nasty piece of work.'

'He could be involved in the killings.'

'Easily – my only reservations being whether he'd be stupid enough to agree to have something like that happen right on his own doorstep.'

Well, perhaps not so close to home after all. We were surprised to discover that the old farmhouse was situated at least a quarter of a mile from the scene of the killings, later explained when we found out that the old barn that had been demolished to make way for the new one had originally belonged to an ancient steading not part of Hagtop Farm, the amalgamation having occurred in the eighteenth century.

We were using our own vehicle, a Range Rover, Patrick having not been issued with official transport, something he would not have wanted as his cars – except those he might use for a very short journey – have to be adapted due to the lower part of his right leg being man-made following the serious injuries he sustained during the Falklands War. This meant that we did not have to pick our way on foot through all the deeply rutted mud in the lane or get stuck in it, as Carrick's car appeared to have done, instead driving between all the other parked vehicles, through the gateway and right up to the front door. Through the uncurtained windows the now familiar figures of forensic personnel wearing white protective clothing could be seen moving about.

'What the hell's happened out there – have they been making a film about the Great War?' Patrick demanded to know of the constable on duty by the front door, jerking his head in the direction of the mired lane.

'Apparently an oil-delivery lorry going to the cottage farther up got stuck there a couple of days ago, sir, and so did the recovery vehicle for a while.'

'Have you seen the DCI?'

'He's in the yard somewhere, sir.' He pointed around the side of the house.

Carrick and Lynn Outhwaite were examining the interior of what appeared to have been an open-fronted cart shed, latterly used for tractors judging by the oily patches on the earthen floor. Hay was stacked up against the rear wall. Lynn spotted our approach and waved a discreet greeting.

'Any luck at the mill?' Carrick said to Patrick.

'No, insofar as no one seems to have heard or seen anything suspicious on Thursday night, but not everyone was at home. We'll have to go back. I'm not hopeful, the place was re-developed in such a way as to keep neighbours' noise to a minimum. There were a few insights into the murder victims, though. I'll write it all up for you.'

Carrick made no reply, going down on his haunches to have a closer look at the floor. 'This looks as though it's been disturbed.' He shook his head. 'Oh, I don't know, it could have been done by an animal.' Rising, he said to Lynn, 'I know this place is on the market but why has Brian Stonelake moved out already? Most people would live here to keep an eye on it.'

'Unhappy memories?' she hazarded.

'Perhaps he needed the money from the sale of the furniture,' Patrick offered. 'We went to talk to him, by the way. He told us that he was keeping a weather eye on the place.'

Clearly, Carrick tried to find a reason for objecting to the visit and I began to see the real depth of his resentment at Patrick's presence. There was more to it than that; perhaps weakened by his injury and haunted that he might never be able to indulge in the first love of his life, playing rugby, he somehow felt emasculated. Then being required to work alongside another high-octane male was probably just about the worst thing that could have happened to him.

'Any theories on Stonelake?' he asked grudgingly.

'He could have had a hand in the murders. He's shifty. But in all fairness that might only be because he's seen his sisters off for the proceeds of the sale. Anything interesting indoors?'

'Not yet, but we'll see what forensics turn up. I've told SOCO to take up a few floorboards.'

'Fancy a pint tonight?'

Carrick hesitated. 'Er – no thanks. I think I'll have to work late.'

'I could give you a hand, if you like.'

'Thanks. I'll give you a ring if I need you.'

We split up and Patrick and I spent the rest of the afternoon, wearing wellies, walking over practically every inch of the farm. We found nothing of interest to a criminal investigation even though the exercise did us good. No one appeared to have been digging holes either.

49

It seemed that Patrick was required to work no longer than a nine-to-five day, and having heard nothing from Carrick – after towing his car out of the mud – we returned to the rectory at a little before six.

'You know, I can't work like this,' Patrick said, slamming the driver's door on our arrival and speaking for the first time on the journey home.

'No, well, in recent years you've always been in charge so any awkwardness could be sorted out, pronto,' I said.

'Awkwardness apart, in D12 days you and I would have simply put our heads together, worked out what we would do next and gone ahead and done it.'

Well, sort of and some of the time, I thought. I said, 'And tonight we would have probably broken into Brian Stonelake's bungalow when, no doubt, he goes out for a pint or two, and looked for evidence. We can't do things like that now, the cops don't work like that.'

Patrick simmered all the way indoors.

'Things still difficult?' Elspeth said, after a glance in his direction as we entered the kitchen. 'Well, it was never going to be easy, was it?'

'It's like being back at school,' Patrick complained. 'I'm not used to being sent home for the night. He didn't even want to go out for a drink!'

'I should imagine James was relieved to be left to get on with the case.'

Patrick turned to her and I did not imagine the flare of anger in his eyes.

'You know perfectly well he didn't want you,' Elspeth went on. 'But I don't think you really realized what it would mean.'

'This man is a *friend* of mine,' Patrick whispered.

'It makes no difference,' she pointed out equally softly. 'Besides which—'

'What?' he asked when she stopped speaking.

'I'm not too sure you know what real friendship means.'

There was a silence and then Elspeth said, 'How many friends do you have, Patrick?'

Even I was shocked at this. It went right to the heart of something of which I have always been aware; Patrick has many comrades, brothers-in-arms and loyal subordinates who have served under him and would probably gladly die for him tomorrow. But genuine friends outside that specialist world?

Elspeth said, 'Forgive me for saying this, but if you had real regard for James you wouldn't have agreed to the posting.'

'But I thought I could help him!' he protested.

'It's not as simple as that and well you know it! Two men like you two together at work are like two stags circling one another, all horns and balls, frankly.'

Patrick's jaw dropped, not surprising really as Elspeth does not normally express herself thus. Then he gave her a look that I can only describe as agonized and left the room.

'Perhaps that was a bit unfair,' Elspeth said. 'After all, he had a terribly worrying time when James was shot.'

'Something along those lines was going through my mind earlier,' I told her. I did not add that only mothers are allowed to be that blunt.

'And if John hadn't been ill it wouldn't have happened because Patrick would have done his stint somewhere else. Oh dear, but at least I've made a steak-and-kidney pie for dinner. Do please see if there's a decent bottle of red wine in the rack, or even two, Ingrid. What do they call it in the navy? Damage control?'

She need not have worried, for there was no ill-humour on anyone's part following her remarks. We had just finished eating and I was making a brew of coffee when Patrick's mobile rang where he had left it on the hall table.

'I've got to go out,' he said round the door a couple of minutes later.

'I'll drive,' I said. 'You're well and truly over the limit. What's happened?'

'They've found the victims' cars and Carrick wants me to fill in for him until he gets there.' Patrick was grabbing jacket and outdoor shoes as he spoke. 'I've just been given an OS reference but no one quite remembered to issue me with any maps when I started this lark so I hope to God it's on one of those we have in the car.'

Luckily we did have the right one and I headed in the direction of Frome.

'How were they spotted?' I asked. 'I mean, we're going out into the sticks and it's pitch dark now.'

'There was a search underway for a missing child – who was eventually found safe and well at a friend's house,' Patrick replied. 'Police and others were looking around some waste ground, an old industrial site, just as it was getting dark and came upon two cars in a small disused quarry. They've been torched but one number plate is still readable.'

'Is James hoping to recover them tonight?'

'I wouldn't have thought so. It's obviously very important but would be much better undertaken during daylight. There can't be much, if any, forensic evidence if they've been set on fire.'

'So why are we going there?'

'I expect he's just being careful. Who knows, we might find other bodies inside them when we take a closer look.'

I got lost on all the wasteland, but eventually, after bouncing over acres of boulder-strewn terrain and broken-down fences, spotted the lights of another car. I was aware that Patrick was enjoying himself hugely and he alighted before the Range Rover had come to a complete standstill, like a sheriff in a Western dismounting from a still-moving horse. He went over to the crew of the area car, at a guess from Frome. I followed.

'Gillard,' he said. 'Are the vehicles easy to access?'

'Yes, sir,' he was told. 'The quarry's virtually a walk-in job.'

'Perhaps you'd be so good as to lend me a good light.'

A bright beam came to rest on me. 'And the lady, sir?'

Well, I was wearing a long woollen skirt with sparkly bits on it, mostly on account of the cold draughts in parts of the rectory.

'Miss Langley's under training and was called out without having had time to change. Come on man, the torch!'

It was handed over and he plunged off into the quarry, the trainee having to hurry over the rough ground in order to keep up and suddenly remembering that there was a track-suit that fitted me in the car.

'If I hold your arm will we be reported for inappropriate behaviour?' I said.

Patrick snorted derisively but slowed down a bit.

Trees and rocky outcrops loomed on either side. Very soon we had to take things very carefully and pick our way over and around increasing amounts of rubbish; old fridges and washing machines, chunks of concrete, bricks and split plastic bags containing rubble, some of it looking like broken asbestos tiles.

'I'll get the Environment Agency in to have a look at this lot,' Patrick said under his breath. He flashed the torch around, the beam illuminating a cliff face ahead of us. Among piles of scrap wood were the remains of the two cars.

I said, 'They couldn't have been driven in here so they must have been pushed in from up top.'

'It might pay to come back in the morning and see what's up there. A set of tyre tracks or some other traces would go down a real treat right now in this case.'

The vehicles were severely damaged where they had crashed down, one upon the other, the top one seemingly having then slid off into some bushes, which had subsequently been consumed by the flames. Amongst the blackened stems and twisted metal was a blob of melted plastic, perhaps the container in which petrol had been carried to start the fire.

There was nothing recognizable inside the cars. Patrick gave me the torch and endeavoured to lever open the boots of both with a length of angle iron he had come across lying in the grass but the heat had buckled the metal and they were jammed. He then re-acquired the light and spent several minutes searching the floor of the quarry, moving in increasingly wide circles.

'Nothing,' he said. 'I suppose it's too much to expect that one of the killers would drop his wallet . . .'

The twin beams of car headlights swung across the cliff, revealing for an instant a lot more dumped rubbish, so presumably James Carrick had arrived. We waited for him.

'There's not a lot to see,' Patrick called to the approaching light from a flash lamp. 'Watch out for that glass.'

'Thanks,' said Lynn Outhwaite's voice. She joined us. 'I told Chief Inspector Carrick I'd check to see what would be required to recover the vehicles.'

'You might need a crane from up there,' Patrick said, pointing skywards. 'Or a tow truck to winch them out through here. I take it Carrick's not with you. There's no real need for his presence.'

'He was coming but wasn't feeling too good – worn out, really – and went home. You may as well do the same – we can't do anything until morning.'

When we had taken our leave of Lynn and were on the outskirts of Hinton Littlemoor, Patrick said, 'Go past the rectory and drive by Stonelake's place slowly, would you? You never know . . .'

By this time it was just before midnight. The night was fine and cold, the roads almost empty of traffic. We went past the church and downhill to the old railway station and goods-yard site, actually quite close to Hinton Mill. It had not been fully redeveloped as the builder of the bungalows, which were rightly regarded as 'cheap and nasty', had gone bankrupt.

Stonelake's rented home was on the right-hand corner as one turned into the small estate and I drove by, turned in the cul-de-sac at the end and then approached it again, slowing right down, switching off the headlights. But for the sickly glow from one of the orange street lamps that had so exercised some of the residents in this heritage area the bungalow was in darkness.

'Stop, would you?' Patrick requested.

I pulled up and turned everything off, opened my window and there was silence but for a breeze rustling the leaves in the adjacent beech hedge. We sat there for a while – in this game you have to possess the patience of a cat – and then heard the distinct sound of a nearby dustbin lid clattering, a thump and, a couple of seconds later, the slam of a door.

'Down!' Patrick hissed.

On his side of the car footsteps approached and went by. As soon as they had gone past we sat up again and cautiously looked round. It was Stonelake, his dog with him on a lead, a shotgun crooked over his arm, walking quickly in the direction of where we had just turned the car.

Then, man and dog some thirty yards from us, Patrick quietly got out and disappeared down the sideway from where the man had just emerged. Almost immediately he was back.

'I had an idea it was something like a whisky bottle that just went in the bin and I was right,' he reported. 'Shall we break all the rules and have a look round this place?'

'No, I think we should follow him,' I said.

There was a short silence and then he said, 'It's a real opportunity to see if he's got anything illegal in there. We might even find the murder weapon!'

'Patrick, you *can't* poke around in this man's house without a search warrant,' I said through my teeth.

'Ingrid—'

'You've had rather a lot to drink this evening and you've stopped *thinking*!' I was really angry now.

I could tell, even in the dark, that he was offended by this for, in truth, he had not overindulged. But it seemed better to use that as an excuse than to throw in his face the real reason for his bad judgement, which was that he had not yet adjusted to what I shall call the new rules of engagement.

'It's been a long day,' was all he muttered before shutting the car door and setting off in the direction Stonelake had gone. I went to follow, remembered the tracksuit again, changed into it in the street and caught up with him.

When we reached the cul-de-sac we saw there was a wide gap between the bungalows where, presumably, it had been planned that the road would continue for the second phase of the development. A couple of yards of concrete petered out into churned-up mud and last year's dead weeds. There was no moon and after leaving the street lights behind we were walking in almost total darkness. Neither of us was suitably shod, or dressed, for silent tracking, our only aid Patrick's tiny 'burglar's' torch, which he now switched on briefly to examine the ground.

'He has the dog with him,' he whispered. 'It'll hear us and keep looking round.'

'He might be too drunk to notice unless it barks,' I whispered back.

We maintained silence after this and kept going almost blindly but seeming to be following a meandering path of sorts. I was expecting at every second to be challenged by Stonelake or even fired on by him.

Then, up ahead, some hundred and fifty yards away, Stonelake switched on a torch. We instinctively crouched down but the beam was not being shone in our direction: he was merely using it to light his own way. Which, of course, was exceedingly useful to us. We watched the light jump around as man and dog negotiated a stile and then the illumination became obscured by trees.

Patrick walked a little faster and went on slightly ahead as now there was not sufficient room on the path for us to go side by side. I preferred it like this: he has had a lot more practice at this kind of thing than I.

We went on, gently upwards, and quickly came to the stile. It was a rickety affair with a barbed-wire fence on either side but we succeeded in getting over it without damaging either skin or clothing. Then I saw the notice: HAGTOP FARM. NO TRESPASSING.

A couple of hundred yards farther on we came to a gate, climbed over it in case the hinges squeaked and then entered woodland. Still the light from Stonelake's torch wavered in front of us, sometimes disappearing momentarily as he wended his way between the trees.

In order not to stumble over tree roots or brain ourselves on low branches it was necessary for Patrick to use his torch, fleetingly, every few yards, and then all we had to do was memorize what we had seen. I proved to be less than perfect at this and tripped, going headlong into a small thicket. By the time I had extracted myself and pulled out a thorn from my hand, by feel, Patrick had gone. Then, somewhere up ahead, I saw the momentary tiny flicker of his torch.

One could only advance with extreme caution. This went on for rather a long time, too long, and having lost all sight of Patrick I was thinking that I ought to give up and wait for him, or for something to happen, when something did.

The roar of the shotgun, sounding only a matter of yards from where I stood, was followed by incoherent and furious shouting. Taking advantage of the fact that the trees seemed to be thinning out, I risked all and hurried. Then I saw a light.

Patrick had Stonelake's torch, a large flash lamp with a handle, and was keeping the beam fully on him, shining it in his face as he stood with his back against a tree. He also held the shotgun; he had broken it and had it across his arm. He must have heard my arrival for without turning round he said, 'Unload the other cartridge, would you? My torch is in my left-hand jacket pocket.'

'This is my property!' Stonelake bellowed. 'You're trespassing, you bastard! You've assaulted me and I shall make you pay for it!'

I removed the cartridge from the shotgun.

'Shut up,' Patrick said placidly. 'I'm impounding this weapon and taking it to the nick. You can make a case for retaining your licence when you go to collect it.'

'You know damned well I was only going to shoot the bloody dog!'

'There are laws about killing animals in ways likely to cause suffering.' To me, Patrick went on, 'Give him twenty quid from my wallet.'

'Bribery to keep quiet?' Stonelake sneered.

'No, for the dog. We'll find a home for it. Then you can tell your mother the truth, can't you?'

The man snatched the money, and his torch, and slouched off back in the direction we had come.

'Where is it?' I asked, casting around with the tiny light with which we had been left, hoping to see eyes reflected in the beam.

'It bolted. Probably the last anyone'll see of it.' Patrick actually sounded quite upset, not difficult to understand given recent events at home. /

'It might have run home,' I said. 'To the farm, I mean.'

Patrick gazed up to where a group of trees could just be discerned on the skyline, a new moon rising just above them.

'It's quite a long way from here, if my memory of the local topography's correct. That stile was on the western boundary of the farm. It might be worth going back and driving round by road.'

But we did not, walking instead across three fields, the last steep and rutted with sheep walks that followed the contours of the ground. At the top of it, by a gateway that led into a lane, we made out a graveyard of old and rusting farm machinery, piles of bricks, coils of wire and rubbish and a vast pile of manure surrounded by a moat of stinking effluent that the now weak light from the torch failed to show up. We arrived in the lane filthy of foot and reeking.

'Which way?' I wondered aloud.

'To the left,' Patrick said.

'Could it be that the Manleys and Davies blundered into some kind of criminal set-up that Stonelake's got up here and paid the price?'

'I'm beginning to believe that something like that is perfectly possible. Some price, though.'

Ten minutes later we walked, nay squelched, into the farm entrance. There was no sign of the dog.

'Whistle it,' I suggested. 'Do we know its name?'

'No.'

Patrick whistled, one of those thumb-and-finger ones that few women have ever mastered.

No dog.

'It might not be used to being whistled,' I said lamely.

The torch was almost dead and we switched it off to save what was left of the battery, walking round the side of the house and towards the tractor shed where we had come upon Carrick and Lynn. Then, a dark shape detached itself from the deeper shadow within and crept towards us, tail waving hopefully. Arriving at Patrick's feet it cringed there, tail still brushing the ground, and he bent down to stroke it. As his hand went down its back it drew away, whimpering.

'A couple of pellets must have hit it,' he said. 'I did wonder. I only managed to knock up the gun at the last second. That makes two of us, mate. The vet, then, straight away.'

'The car's in the village,' I reminded him.

'Shit. So it is.'

The dog left us and went back into the cart shed, sniffing at the bales of hay. Then, judging by the noise, it began to scratch and dig at the base of them.

'God, don't say it's found another corpse,' Patrick said.

We hefted away some of the top bales, still could not see into a space between them and a wall, and moved some more.

'No, it's just sacks of animal feed,' Patrick said, having clambered up to look by the last glimmerings of the torch. 'He must be hungry. No, hang on . . .' And with a scramble he had disappeared. Moments later, 'There's a whole pile of horse tack under a tarpaulin here. Saddles, bridles and driving harness, which is super black patent-leather stuff. Worth hundreds, if not thousands of pounds. I reckon this is stolen property.' His head appeared above the bales. 'You know what this means, don't you?'

'Stonelake is a crook after all and not just a horrible man.'

'Yes, and I can arrest him. But only when we've got ourselves some transport.'

The torch finally went out.

Lynn Outhwaite arrived, doggedly, together with an area car, a different one, and with typical Lancastrian decisiveness as well as enormous loyalty to her boss, suggested politely that she dealt with Stonelake and that the dog ought to go to the RSPCA as there could well be a prosecution there too. She pointed out that the business of the twenty pounds ought not to have happened although she realized that it had occurred before we found the tack, which she thought might fit descriptions of items stolen from an equestrian centre in Chipping Sodbury several weeks previously.

Packed off to bed for the second time that night we handed over the shotgun and ammunition, accepted a lift back to the village, drove into Bath and gave the dog into the care of the duty RSPCA inspector. I tried to erase a lingering memory of sad brown eyes and drooping tail as it was lifted into a cage in the van, and failed.

Five

At eight thirty the following morning Patrick rang Tamsin Roper, who lived in the other studio flat at the mill, and asked when it would be convenient for him to ask her a few questions. He was lucky, as undoubtedly had been the case with the timing of our arrival at Stonelake's bungalow the previous night, because she had the day off. She told him that as long as he arrived during the next half-hour – she was going out – she could see him that morning.

I did not deem it necessary to accompany Patrick, for after all I was not actually supposed to be holding the man's hand. His departure had postponed my planning on having a chat with him about how much longer I would be needed and then, on second thoughts, I decided that this might be far easier resolved by talking privately to James. I left for Bath, borrowing Elspeth's car, having left a message on Patrick's mobile, which, unaccountably, was switched off.

Manvers Street police station was in a state of what appeared to be organized turmoil and I found Carrick in his office.

'There's good news,' he said. 'We found what gives every indication of being the murder weapon not half an hour ago – a large knife encrusted with blood.'

'Oh, brilliant! Where?'

'In amongst that heap of stolen horse tack at the farm. And as Lynn had already arrested Stonelake and charged him with handling stolen property, with a bit of luck we can prove he was an accessory to murder as well. Hopefully he'll soon be singing his heart out.'

'But are the two crimes connected?'

'I'm keeping an open mind on that but they probably aren't. Is Patrick here? He can sit in and get a few pointers when I question Stonelake shortly.'

I did not mention that Patrick had once been one of Her Majesty's prime interrogators of what used to be referred to as traitors, telling him instead where Patrick was. In fairness, though, it might be something of which Carrick was not aware.

'Oh, it doesn't really matter, there'll be other opportunities.'

'James . . .'

In the middle of sorting files that had been placed on his desk and tossing them into various wire trays he paused and looked up. 'Yes?'

'We need to talk.'

'I know. I've been thinking about it. There's no need for you to stay any longer. Everything seems to be running smoothly.'

I sat down and made myself comfortable. 'You must be quite relieved that Patrick hasn't blown his top by now. And no, James, nothing's running smoothly.'

He frowned.

I said, 'There's absolutely no excuse for your continuing treatment of Patrick. I can't go home. Not until there's a working relationship between the pair of you that approaches what it used to be when Patrick worked for MI5 and you handled a couple of cases together that happened on your patch. But you're virtually ignoring him.'

The DCI steepled his fingers and rested his chin on them. 'I know. But it's not going to work and I'm not very good at handling things that I'm sure are going to fail.'

'You mean you don't think Patrick will make a good policeman?'

'No, I genuinely think he will. But in London, perhaps working undercover for an outfit that isn't quite so accountable as us ordinary plods. Here is where it's going to fail.'

'You think of yourself as an *ordinary plod* when you're

only in your mid-thirties and already Detective Chief Inspector? Hasn't it occurred to you that there could be mutual benefits in having this somewhat high-flown rookie with a background of national security dropped in your lap? Aren't you ambitious? Wouldn't you like a much better job in a special undercover outfit? In one of the new serious crime units being set up? Or in counter-terrorism? It doesn't seem to have occurred to you that you can *use* this situation.'

I had not meant to say most of this: it was just my being offended by proxy, so to speak.

Carrick was saved from making any immediate response as there was a knock on the door and someone brought him yet another file. When they had gone he gave it a cursory glance and then hurled it in the direction of one of the trays, missing.

'I'm going to get myself some coffee,' he muttered, getting to his feet. And left the room. Moments later he returned to put his head round the door. 'Sorry. Please come with me.'

'I'm only trying to help,' I said when we were seated in the canteen and I had bought us a couple of slices of cake to go with our coffee, having an idea he had left home without bothering about breakfast.

'I know, I appreciate it, and I've just come to a decision. If you really want to help then back me up when, later today, I ask Patrick to revert to working on other cases. It's the only solution to a difficult situation and it frees you up to go home. I have no problem with his consulting with me on anything and in that respect we will have a working relationship. How about that?'

All I saw, gazing at him, was utter wretchedness. This man was deeply, deeply depressed. For some reason he simply could not apply himself to the situation.

'James,' I ventured gently, 'everything *is* all right between you and Joanna, isn't it?'

He looked surprised. 'Yes, of course. She's been really fantastic. No one could have wished for better support. Why do you ask?'

'Just worried about you a little,' I replied. 'Yes, I'll do whatever you think best.'

Under the circumstances there was nothing else I could say.

I returned to Hinton Littlemoor as I could hardly keep Elspeth's car for much longer. She did not like driving John's, an old Volvo estate very useful for collecting jumble-sale goods, as it was now difficult to get into reverse gear. There was no one in and I did not have to be a great detective to know that the couple had gone to the charity coffee morning advertised on posters throughout the village.

Telling myself that I might as well pack my belongings, I went upstairs. It was important to remain positive for, despite what Carrick had said, nothing had actually failed, not yet. Patrick and James were working under the same roof, it would not be for all that long, about two and a half months, and unless something unforeseen happened Patrick was well on the road to a new career.

Everything was so hunky-dory I just wanted to burst into tears.

My mobile rang and it was Patrick, his voice coming and going as the reception is very poor in the village, to tell me that he had just arrived at the nick. Tamsin Roper had not had anything really interesting to say, having not personally known the murder victims, and had not seen or heard anything strange over the previous Thursday night or early Friday morning. She had suggested that Patrick speak to her boyfriend Owen Hurst. He had suffered from toothache and been unable to sleep, spending his nights in the living room, which overlooked the parking area, to avoid disturbing her.

'I think we shall have to accept that it's probable the killer, or killers, did not actually visit the murder victims at their own homes – in other words didn't go in and grab them – and they went out voluntarily to meet their fate. It must have been someone they knew and, or, trusted.'

'Is Stonelake talking? I know James was going to question him.'

'No idea. I'll find out.'

'Patrick—'

But he had faded away completely and could not be reached. I had been about to break it to him that James was taking him off the case.

By the end of the afternoon I had worked myself up into a real state of nerves, picturing a showdown at that unlovely concrete construction a stone's throw from Bath railway station; Patrick really losing his temper, James having him ejected from the building, and worse. Sometimes a writer's imagination can be complete hell. My tension headache had reached a peak by the time Patrick was expected home and when I heard tyres crunching on the gravel drive it took all my willpower not to go rushing outside.

John, who was improving daily and had had a good report from his consultant, caught my eye and rattled a couple of whisky glasses together with pretend nervousness, making me laugh. He had sensed my mood although I had said nothing about an expected crisis.

I forced myself to sit down. Out of our view Patrick let himself in through the front door and there was the usual light clatter as keys, phone and jacket were spread around the hall. I performed a swift appraisal when he entered the room and could detect no immediate desire to strangle perfect strangers with bare hands.

'A winter warmer?' his father suggested.

'Seems madness not to,' was the reply. Mostly to me, Patrick added, 'Carrick's taken me off the murder case.'

'He said as much this morning and I tried to warn you earlier but we were cut off,' I told him.

'So I'm in charge of investigating horse-tack theft – which is apparently big business and until just an hour ago was the responsibility of Sergeant Outhwaite.'

'That's good,' John commented diplomatically, handing over a tot.

'Trailers too. Apparently folk in rural locations are having to clamp them or they disappear overnight.' Patrick flopped into a chair. 'Here's to crime.'

'It would appear that I'm superfluous,' I said, feeling weak with relief that there had not been a bust-up.

I was given a big grin. 'You're never superfluous but I know you want to go home, see the children and get on with the film script.'

Later, when we were on our own, I said, 'Has anything really been solved by this move?'

'No. Despite what I said just now I've no intention of completely dropping the murder inquiry and want to find out more about the victims. I hate going behind James's back but I don't think the man's at all well. He's had a nasty bit of news in the past few days too; been told by the docs he shouldn't play rugger again, or not for a pretty long time. By then, of course, he'll be too old. He'd started training again in a quiet way too.'

'How awful for him. Did James tell you so himself?'

'No. Sergeant Woods beckoned me aside just before I came home this evening. Carrick had mentioned it to him but not gone into any more details. Life's cruel sometimes. Anyway, I'm going to delve into the rural-crime side of things as well, as Stonelake's no doubt into all kinds of scams. So first of all I intend to interview the bloke who used to work for him, Shaun Brown. He may be involved with Stonelake – or know a few people who are.'

'I might stick around for a couple more days,' I said in off-hand fashion.

'Good.' One eyebrow quirked, Patrick then whispered, 'Fancy an early night?'

'Expecting a famine in that direction soon, then?' I teased, having detected a certain gleam in his eye.

'Emails do have their limitations.'

Our lovemaking that night brought to my mind that first time under a hot summer sun on Dartmoor. He had been eighteen, I fifteen and until that moment we had been as children, quite innocent of one other, holding hands as we walked home with the dogs, Patrick with the bag that had contained our picnic lunch. His main attraction to me was his ability to make me laugh, that is until that afternoon when we had laughed until we cried, hugging one another and I had felt the warm wiriness of his body flowing beneath my fingers through the thin material of his shirt. Children then one moment and as close as it is possible for two people to get the next.

Perhaps it was to be expected that when we finally rolled away from one another, replete, we slept deeply and dreamlessly, the window closed against a cold northerly gale roaring through the treetops, hearing nothing of the destruction that was going on not very far away outside.

The shock of seeing what had taken place during the night could very well have killed John Gillard. As was his habit he arose early, made himself and Elspeth a pot of tea and then, while it brewed, slipped on a jacket and went outside, the gale having eased, for a short stroll down the drive, which had a newly refurbished border on either side.

I felt Patrick jerk awake at his father's shout and then there were hurrying feet on the landing and, moments later, Elspeth urgently called Patrick's name. We both shot out of bed, threw on dressing gowns and went downstairs.

John was seated on a kitchen chair, gasping for breath, hands shaking. Elspeth had her arms around him.

'What is it?' Patrick said.

John waved speechlessly in the direction of the door to the outside and then had the unusual experience of having his son go down on his knees before him.

'Dad,' Patrick said softly, enveloping John's hands in his own, 'calm down. You'll do your new ticker arrangements no end of harm. What's happened?'

John panted, 'It looks as though someone's driven a tractor into the drive . . . and then through the hedge into the churchyard. The new shrubs . . . the fence . . . all your mother's work planting bulbs. A lot of it . . . utterly ruined. Who could . . . do such a thing to us? I think there's . . . damage to the graves too . . .'

Still kneeling, Patrick said, 'I'll have the garden fixed. Today. Please don't upset yourself.'

Then proceed to track down the perpetrator before hanging, drawing and quartering them at the nearest crossroads, I thought grimly.

Patrick went out to have a look, came back directly and hurried upstairs to get dressed. Donning boots he then returned to the garden to fully assess the damage and was gone for such a long time that I threw away his tea as it had gone cold.

Elspeth, fearful for John as he was shivering uncontrollably, had persuaded him to get back into bed and phoned the doctor. All I could do was have a quick shower and get dressed then make myself useful by staying around in case Elspeth needed me and lay the pine kitchen table for breakfast.

Then I heard a police siren, realized Patrick had called out the cavalry and went outside.

The devastation about three-quarters of the way down the rectory drive was appalling, a huge swathe of damage cut through turf, border, new hedging and post-and-rail fence. Whatever had done it – the gap was wider than the small tractors that the local farmers used to negotiate the neighbourhood's narrow lanes and gateways – had carried on into the churchyard, knocking over gravestones, breaking a branch off a tree, even scattering the flowers covering a new grave, ploughing them into the torn ground. There was a large pile of earth over on the far side and that was where several people were clustered.

I noted in passing as I walked round and entered the churchyard by the lychgate, which was roofed and totally impassable to vehicles, that the tracks of the digger, or whatever it had been, which had caused the damage suggested it had also exited through the rectory garden.

'The headstone's over there,' I heard Patrick say, pointing, as I approached the group.

The damage was even worse than it had appeared when viewed from the adjacent driveway. Everything impeding whatever had gone on here had been ruthlessly smashed out of the way. Even a little row of what I knew to be babies' graves had been bulldozed flat.

There was also a large hole in the ground.

'It's an exhumation,' Patrick said to me.

'What, you mean someone's actually dug up and stolen a coffin?' I exclaimed.

'Barney Stonelake's, no less,' Carrick murmured. 'That's not to say we won't find it dumped just down the road somewhere.'

I said, 'So whoever it was gained entry through the rectory drive because they failed to knock down the churchyard wall?'

'You're probably right, Ingrid,' Carrick said. 'Yes, that would explain it. Why would anyone want to desecrate the grave of that poor old man? A grudge against his son?'

'There was the chap whom he sacked because he thought he was stealing diesel,' Patrick pointed out. 'Shaun Brown.'

Frowning into the hole, the DCI said, 'There's a list, I assure you, of folk Brian Stonelake's upset, assaulted, sacked, short-changed and almost certainly stolen from over the years. It's disgusting, though. The people who do things like this are filth.'

'I called you because I think there might be a connection with our current investigations, including the murders. There *has* to be: everything going on round here has Stonelake written all over it.' Patrick gestured angrily in the direction of the upended headstone.

'There could well be a connection,' Carrick agreed. 'Or is it vandalism, pure and simple?'

Normally, I knew, we would not have so closely approached what was, of course, a crime scene for fear of destroying valuable evidence, footprints and so forth. But the despoiler had done his work well, seemingly obliterating any possible incriminating traces by scraping up the turf surrounding the excavation into a small pile and then driving over it.

'Is there much damage at your parents' place?' Carrick asked Patrick.

'It's quite bad,' Patrick answered. 'The new borders were only finished last week. If you'd be good enough to have SOCO take pictures I'd like to arrange to have it put right, today if possible. My father's pretty cut up about it.'

'There's nothing to stop you having it put right today even if I don't think it serious enough to call in SOCO – but you might invalidate any insurance claim.'

'Bugger insurance,' Patrick said quietly.

Shortly afterwards Patrick and Carrick departed in the latter's car and the house went quiet. I had thought I would work on the screenplay but found myself unable to concentrate on it. All I could see in my mind's eye were those three ghastly still figures hanging in the barn. Later again, the doctor having come and gone, I made sandwiches for everyone's lunch. John was all right but had orders to rest for the remainder of the day: apparently he had run full tilt down the drive with the bad news, not yet recommended. Then, at just after three, I asked Elspeth if I could use the phone and rang Patrick. I had had an idea.

'Gillard,' said that well-remembered voice.

'What's happening?'

'James and I are just outside Shepton Mallet at a roadside cafe having a well-earned mug of tea and a bun. Someone's found the coffin.'

'Really? Where?'

'In a ditch. It's empty, though – there's no body.'

'That's ghastly!'

'We're on our way back to the nick now. D'you want to drive into Bath?'

You bet I did.

We arrived almost together, the men mounting the steps at the rear entrance as I was cruising around looking for a parking space. Carrick waved me to a slot nearby with someone's initials painted on it, explaining afterwards that whoever it was was on leave.

'A woman walking her dog on the outskirts of Oakhill found the coffin,' he said to me when we were seated in his office. 'She immediately rang the police as it obviously wasn't a new one that had fallen off a lorry delivering stuff to an undertaker.'

'Surely someone didn't drive a JCB all the way from Hinton Littlemoor to Oakhill in the middle of the night with a coffin in the bucket!' I said, or rather, hooted.

Patrick said, 'No, a van or pickup must have been involved as well. Plus a couple more blokes, of course.'

I was finding this all too fantastic. 'But that must have made the whole exercise even more expensive. Just to get even with Brian Stonelake? It doesn't make sense.'

'And where is poor old Barney?' Carrick said.

'Perhaps something valuable had been hidden in with the corpse,' I suggested.

'Your loot theory,' Carrick said dubiously. 'Well, it has to be borne in mind for, as you say, digging up the churchyard wasn't cheap. Unless someone *really* hates Stonelake.'

'Have you had any unidentified human remains found in the area?' I asked. 'I mean, there's always the thought that Barney was never buried at all.'

'Ingrid, that would mean that undertakers were in on the scam and Uncle Tom Cobley and all,' the DCI retorted, his Scottish accent more pronounced than usual.

To Patrick, I said, 'I've been thinking and have a proposal to make. You and I have worked together for several years now and I think we make a good team. I think I've something to contribute now and if you'll have me I intend to apply to join the scheme. They may not want me and of course I'll have to go through the selection process but—' I broke off because Patrick was smiling at me.

'Brinkley asked me if you'd be interested,' he said. 'Even if it was only on a consultancy basis. In other words if I ran out of ideas I'd get on the blower to the oracle.'

I found myself under Carrick's frosty blue gaze.

'Before we discuss this further I have to tell you that I had a complaint,' he said. 'From a Mr William Brandon, who lives at the mill. Remember him?'

'Of course,' I replied.

'He told me that a woman who had been described to him as Patrick's training adviser made offensive remarks to him during an interview at his home. Is that correct?'

'No, what I said to him wasn't offensive and it wasn't during the interview. I told him to fix his sick wife some lunch.'

'Is that all?'

'Yes.'

'You took a dislike to this man?'

'He's like something you haul out of a long-blocked drain.'

'Ingrid, you can't behave like that, however you feel. I had to apologize and I think you ought to go round there and do the same. If you're going to be involved with law enforcement you must learn that there are rules of behaviour.'

'I understand,' I said.

Carrick turned his attention to Patrick. 'And you're still behaving as though you're working for MI5. Ingrid isn't your training adviser. You simply can't lie and con your way through this job. If I've said it once I've said it a hundred times – it's more *accountable* than what you're used to.'

Quietly, Patrick said, 'Ingrid *is* my training adviser and since we got back together again after being divorced for a while some years ago – she slung me out because I was turning, no, had turned, into a supercilious prig – she's the only reason I've recovered and become a half-decent person after being blown up in the Falklands. One of her bad faults though is that she gets very shirty if she thinks anyone or anything is being neglected, in this case, Mrs Brandon. I wasn't present when the remarks were made but I'll try to keep her under control in future.' Into the silence which followed this he said, 'Does this mean you're against what Ingrid is suggesting?'

Predictably, Carrick now looked embarrassed. 'No, not at all,' he said. 'OK. It's actually a good idea and I'm happy to have her along on condition that you both bear in mind what I've just said. But I insist that she doesn't get involved in any potentially nasty situations.'

So he still needed me as a buffer but it would be difficult to explain to higher authority if I got the smallest bit dented.

Patrick said, 'I shall have to clear it with Brinkley. If it's all right with you I'll endeavour to do it now.'

This he did and permission came with the same proviso;
I was to learn, assist and advise where appropriate – something Brinkley assumed, wrongly, had been my only role with
MI5 – and not on any account get mixed up in anything
dangerous or in which firearms were involved.

Patrick obviously had not told anyone that I was a real
whizz with a sub-machine gun.

'You didn't ask *me* if I was interested in helping you,' I
said to Patrick when we were alone.

He feigned shock. 'I thought you went and beat James to
a pulp because he hadn't called me out.'

'Thank you for the lovely things you said just now.'

'It's true, though, isn't it?'

It looked as though I was in. Ye gods, what had I done?

Patrick got out of the car and stretched luxuriously. We had
left James at the nick and driven back to Hinton Littlemoor
ostensibly on the case of thefts of horse tack and trailers but
actually to talk to the residents about the Manleys and Keith
Davies. I was quite surprised that Carrick himself had not
suggested it, Patrick supposed to be off the case notwith-
standing, as someone with family connections in the village
was likely to get better results than an outsider.

'We know none of them were churchgoers so that rules
out quite a few possible sources,' I said. 'They must have
gone in the pub though surely.'

'Almost certainly. I suggest we leave that until later,
concentrate on the village shop before it closes and then talk
to people who don't tend to go in pubs.'

I already knew that the members of the walking group
who had found the bodies were not from the immediate
locality but from Bath U3A and had already been questioned.
Nothing they had said had provided any leads. The shop cum
post office might be more fruitful. It was run as a cooperative by volunteers, the result of a 'buy-out' by local people
when it had looked as though the village would be left
without a shop at all when the previous owners retired.

It was to be expected though that recent events would have

left everyone subdued and this was the impression I received after we had entered, the conversation among the three or four people present muted and strictly to do with the business in hand. There was a good range of health and organic foods but I have a notion that folk who have suffered personal trauma do not necessarily feel better for munching on pumpkin seeds. I chose some chocolate ginger for John and a box of crystallized fruit for Elspeth.

There was no one being served at the post-office counter, behind which stood Norman, an employee of that organization and not part of the cooperative. He was one of the church wardens and although only in his early fifties possessed the gravitas of a much older man. It amuses Patrick that Norman and his wife Brenda always treat him as though he is still in short trousers.

'How is your father?' Norman asked him. 'Such a dreadful thing to happen.'

'Fine, thank you,' Patrick answered. 'No damage done at all.'

'I hear you're a policeman now. No doubt you're investigating the vandalism.'

Perhaps it was not general knowledge yet that a coffin had been stolen.

'No, not really,' Patrick told him. 'I'm after information about the Manleys and Keith Davies – the murder victims.'

I approached the shop counter to pay for the sweets but it was close to where the men were talking so I could hear what was being said.

'Outsiders,' Norman said dismissively. 'Brought their own nemesis with them from the city, no doubt. Folk round here are more interested in catching those who ruined our lovely churchyard.'

'Well, the dead might have been disturbed a bit but these people you so lightly dismiss as being of no account were living and breathing when someone slashed their throats for them,' Patrick said, not bothering to lower his voice. 'Did they come in here? Buy stamps? Post parcels? If so, where to? Did you bother to pass the time of day with any of them?

Ask them how they were? Whether they'd settled in all right and were enjoying living in the country?'

There was rather a heavy silence and the young woman who was handing me my change gave me a thumbs-up sign, eyeing Norman with distaste.

'I never meant they were of no account!' the man exclaimed resentfully.

'Think,' Patrick went on inexorably. 'Did they use this post office?'

'Yes – well – yes, I seem to remember the woman did,' Norman blustered. 'But I didn't know their names. I was never given a credit card or anything like that. Just stamps I think she bought. No parcels. I never saw her husband or whoever he was.'

'And the younger man?'

'He might have been the one who asked if he could renew his tax disc here. Yes, I'm fairly sure it was him from the pictures in the paper – horrible pictures that you know were taken of the bodies. But I said no, he'd have to go to Bath. He looked at me in the most unpleasant way and then shouldered his way out.'

The woman serving behind the shop counter spoke, but not to Patrick, to another woman searching through a rack of birthday cards. 'Didn't your Tina go out with that chap, Doris?'

The woman bridled. 'She did *not*! She met him for a drink in the Ring O'Bells on a couple of occasions, that's all. Not her sort at all, I assure you. She soon broke *that* off.'

Patrick regarded her with gentle gaze. 'Where might I find Tina?'

'My daughter had nothing to do with that man!' shrilled her mother.

'No, but he might have mentioned the names of a few of his friends.' When there was a continuing silence Patrick added, 'A little chat with me now might be preferable to one at the police station later.'

'She's at home,' Doris said grudgingly. 'Between jobs at the moment.'

She plonked the money down for the card she had chosen and stalked out.

Another woman peered around a revolving stand holding postcards of local views. 'Has Tina ever worked?' she ventured cautiously to no one in particular.

'Left school with a GCSE in bullying and bunking off,' said a younger voice and a girl came into view, carrying a pile of small boxes from a side room.

'My daughter Sarah,' Norman announced proudly. 'She helps in here for an hour after she gets home from college. There's nothing like encouraging a community spirit.'

Sarah had rather too close-together eyes to be attractive and a mouth that tended to purse disapprovingly like her father's.

Patrick said, 'Sarah, can you tell me anything about the Manleys or Keith Davies? Did you ever serve any of them? Did you ever see them with anyone else in the village?'

'No,' said Sarah with a shake of her head. 'I think I once sold the woman some bread and a couple of other things. Not a chatty sort of person. Besides, I wouldn't have anything in common with a woman like that.'

'A woman like what?' Patrick asked, clearly puzzled.

'Well, you know . . . from the city. Living shut away from everyone in a posh flat.'

'D'you know where Tina lives?'

'In Rose Street – on the council estate. It's the one with the plant things made out of old car tyres in the front garden.'

There was no mistaking the sneer on her face.

'Remind me to write a novel set in a rural idyll,' I said when we were back in the street.

Tina did not appear to have been warned of our imminent arrival so I could only assume that her mother had taken herself elsewhere.

'Keith?' she said, glancing at Patrick's warrant card. 'He was a just a bloke I chatted to in the pub.'

'May we come in?' Patrick asked.

The girl shrugged. 'S'pose.'

Tina led the way into the living room and turned off the TV. She was thin, anorexic-looking even, and unless I have lost my skill in evaluating people's state of mind, very unhappy.

'You're the vicar's son, aren't you?' she said when everyone had sat down.

'That's right,' Patrick answered, not about to explain the difference between vicars and rectors.

'I thought you were. You look like him. He came round when Dad died. I was surprised really as we never go to church. What do you want to know about Keith?'

'Anything you can tell us that might lead to his killer.'

Tina was sitting bolt upright on the edge of her chair. 'Look, I only sat and talked with him in the pub a couple of times. We never actually went out together. I wouldn't have done. He wasn't very nice really. I suppose I felt sorry for him.'

'Did you actually meet him in the pub?'

'No, outside when I was walking past to go to the postbox. I wouldn't have the nerve to go in the pub on my own anyway.'

'Not many people your age in the village?' I queried.

'No, and the ones that do don't speak to me.'

'Why did you feel sorry for Keith Davies?' I went on to ask.

'All three were like fish out of water. They—'

'You met all three?' Patrick interrupted.

'Just the other two once. We talked for a little while – the couple were quite pleasant really – and then they moved to another table as they were having a meal.'

'Do you mind telling me what you talked about?'

'Just ordinary things. The weather, how quiet the village was in the winter – things like that.'

'When was this?'

'Last month. Keith really started to chat me up after that but I backed off. Although he could be quite fun to talk to he was rough – started rows with people when he'd had a couple of pints. I had an idea he'd been in trouble with the law.'

'Some girls might find that glamorous in a dangerous sort of way,' Patrick commented with a disarming smile.

'Not me. I went a bit off the rails with stupid boys at school, got in with the wrong crowd. It seemed a real hoot at the time but where has it got me? Nowhere. No qualifications. I'm stuck in this snobby dump and can't even get a job in the Co-op in Radstock.'

'You're very young, plenty of time yet,' Patrick told her, probably feeling that it was not his place to give her any more advice on the matter.

'I can't get over it,' Tina whispered, staring at nothing. 'Those people, those poor people that I spoke to, sat with at that table for a few minutes, are all dead. The other bloke even bought me a drink. They were miserable, you could tell that. Hated living here. Keith had already said to me that he hated the countryside. Cow muck all over the roads, he said. Idiots on horses with no regard for motorists. No proper street lights. I didn't agree with him but I could see his point. And now they're all dead and—'

Astoundingly, Tina then burst into tears.

Even more astoundingly, after we had done our best to comfort her, I found myself asking her if she would like to visit us in Devon and help Carrie look after the children to see if she would be interested in training as a nanny.

In the middle of all this Carrick rang asking us to be present when he questioned Brian Stonelake shortly.

Six

Stonelake had been told about the desecration of his father's grave. It was impossible to gauge any reaction, his face giving nothing away, with its usual dour expression as he sat next to his solicitor, who had grey hair, suit, tie, face and teeth and who, after new tapes had been put into the recorder and it had been switched on, objected to the fact that there were three of us about to tackle his client during this second interview.

'Miss Langley is a trainee,' Carrick explained, introducing us to him. 'She won't ask questions, or if she does, it will only be in order to clarify matters in her own mind.'

This seemed to satisfy the man, whose name Carrick had just told us was Mr O'Malley.

'Would you mind if she took notes?' Carrick went on to enquire of him.

I was given an all-over glance. 'As long as they roughly match what is recorded on tape,' he drawled sarcastically. 'And I would like to point out that it is normal for notes to be made at the first interview, any salient points being clarified at the second.'

'That is standard procedure,' Carrick agreed urbanely. 'And if you remember, another of my colleagues sat in and endeavoured to do just that. Perhaps this time though you might encourage your client to reply in more helpful fashion to some of the questions than by saying, "No comment," and then something worthwhile can be achieved. If Mr Stonelake still refuses to cooperate I shall apply to a magistrate for a warrant for further detention.' Then to Stonelake, 'But hear this: you're not going to be bailed even if you agree to answer

79

our questions about the finding of a knife on your premises which we now know was a murder weapon. I shall have you remanded in custody.'

Whereupon acting Superintendent Gillard looked upon the detained person with malicious cheerfulness. Carrick, still perhaps nursing a few grievances, then bounced him into cautioning Stonelake and he calmly did so, without having to resort to any scraps of paper upon which he had written it down. Sometimes I love Patrick to *bits*.

'So,' Carrick said, making himself as comfortable as the bolted-to-the-floor chairs permitted, 'after three people were murdered on your farm we found a bloodstained knife among a pile of stolen horse tack in the old cart shed by the house. It's a large knife, the sort of thing used by chefs for cutting up meat, and the blood on it is human. Can you explain how the knife might have got there?'

I knew that DNA testing would take longer.

'No,' Stonelake said sullenly. 'I don't have cooking knives. I don't cook. The killer must have chucked it in there.'

'But it's hardly close to the scene of the crime.'

'No comment.'

'We've traced the owners of all the saddlery and harness, by the way,' Carrick continued. 'Except for a matching American saddle, bridle and—'

O'Malley butted in with, 'There's nothing to connect my client with the thefts of the horse tack except where it was discovered. The farm's not lived in now. Anyone could have hidden it there.'

'If you'll kindly allow me to finish,' Carrick said. He resumed, 'And all of these people, again with one exception, had bought logs, kindling or hay from you in the past twelve months. Now, I know we're not talking about that charge right now but it seems to me that if you've concealed your ill-gotten gains in the cart shed you might very well hide a weapon with which you'd murdered three people there as well.'

'No. It's nothing to do with me,' Stonelake said.

'None of it?'

'None of it. I just kept a few bags of animal feed in there. I'd forgotten about them and the bales must've been piled in front. Likely been there since Dad reared calves in the building.'

'Odd then that they should look so new, have sell-by dates of two years hence and be for ponies,' Patrick murmured. 'Tell the truth. Everything stashed away in there was stolen or dodgy, wasn't it?'

'No!' Stonelake bellowed.

'Why have a space behind the hay bales?'

'It was handy because of light-fingered locals, that's why!'

'Oh, so you did have a habit of hiding things there.'

After a short pause, looking a bit sick, Stonelake muttered, 'Sometimes.'

Patrick turned to Carrick. 'Chief Inspector, would you say that the crime rate in the Hinton Littlemoor area warranted such precautions?'

'No,' Carrick answered. 'Mr Stonelake, how well did you know the Manleys and Keith Davies?'

'I didn't.'

'Not at all?'

'No. Never clapped eyes on 'em – to know who they were, I mean.'

'It wouldn't appear that any of the people we've spoken to have a good word to say on your behalf. They seemed to think it was just the latest nasty occurrence at Hagtop.'

'The other things were all in the past, nothing to do with me or my family.'

'So you and your father didn't take pot-shots at those walking on your land; mushroom-pickers, bird-watchers and so forth, immediately deciding they were poachers and opened fire? Or perhaps you didn't want them there because of your criminal activities.'

Stonelake was shaking his head all through this last question. 'We might have been a bit hasty a couple of times but no one's going to the trouble of knocking off folk on my property just to get back at me for that, are they?'

'You're right. That's what convinces me that you're in this

up to your neck. There are quite a few valuable antiques in Mr and Mrs Manley's flat and also an open fireplace where they'd obviously had a wood fire. Are you sure you didn't supply them with logs before you left the farm?' When Stonelake did not respond he added, 'It's fairly easy to do a bit of forensic work on the unburned logs in the basket there, and find out if they came from your woods.'

I shot a sideways glance at Patrick, fairly convinced that this was the Scottish version of old baloney, but he was looking fixedly at Stonelake.

'I bought in some wood as well.'

'Who from?'

'Just a jobbing gardener bloke who'd sometimes be asked to take down trees, or lop them. People expect the wood to be taken away if they've no stove of their own.'

'What's his name?'

'I just know him as Frankie. Surnames don't matter.'

'What about Keith Davies?'

'What about him?'

'Did you *know* him?'

'No. I said as much just now, didn't I?'

Patrick said, 'Come now, you spend some, if not most, evenings in the pub, don't you, when you're not drinking at home. Do you mean to tell us that you didn't bump into him down there, someone who had a reputation for being confrontational and in everyone's face even when he was sober?'

'He might have been there but I don't know what he looked like, do I?'

'The victims' photographs were in all the local papers.'

After, one assumed, considerable efforts on the part of mortuary attendants to produce something that could be presented to the general public.

'I don't read the papers.'

'There seemed to be a hell of a lot of newspapers scattered all over your living room.'

O'Malley interrupted with, 'This is pure conjecture and a waste of time.'

'Where were you on the day of the murders?' Patrick asked Stonelake, ignoring the solicitor.

'As you just said yourself, in the bloody pub.'

'The bodies were discovered late afternoon by a walking group. Were you in the pub at lunchtime?'

'Yes – no – I can't remember.'

'Were you at home, then? Think, you must be able to remember.'

'Well, I can't,' said the other after a pause.

Carrick said, 'I obtained a warrant and had your bungalow searched. There are some rather good pieces of furniture there.'

'It's mine! All of it. Belonged to my parents.'

'Not to mention a couple of bronze equestrian figures after the style of Stubbs and some silver dishes which were packed in a box in the loft.'

'They're mine too.'

'Well, I don't think they are, as both closely fit the descriptions of items stolen from a country house in Wiltshire last month. Rare items, worth a lot of money. Too hot to try to get rid of yet, eh?'

'I don't know what you're talking about.'

'And now there's the bad business of what happened in St Michael's churchyard,' Carrick continued.

Stonelake shrugged angrily. 'No comment.'

Rightly, this got under Carrick's skin. 'I think that if someone had removed my father's coffin from its place of rest I would have something to say on the subject. Mr Stonelake, this is a very serious matter and perhaps if I now tell you that I've just been told that no human remains had ever been interred in it you'll come up with one or two theories.'

Stonelake looked appalled. 'What? He was never in there? Where the hell *is* he, then?'

'You tell me. Was his coffin a good place to hide stolen property?'

Stonelake lunged out of his chair at Carrick but was fielded neatly by Patrick before he could do the DCI any damage, and reseated, gently.

'My client would like a short break,' O'Malley said quickly.

'Certainly. Ten minutes,' Carrick said, magnanimously adding, 'I'll arrange for some tea to be brought in.' He stopped the tape, gathered up his papers and at a sign from him Patrick and I followed him out.

'You'll have lost the momentum,' Patrick observed as we sat in the canteen, absorbing sludge-coloured coffee.

'I know, but I'd rather lose it early on than later when I'm obliged to give him a break and might be on to something more useful. Sorry, I forgot to mention the stuff we found at the bungalow. It was confirmed earlier today that it came from Westbury House. They've photographs of the art collection there so there's no mistaking it.'

'Did forensics have any ideas when you spoke to the lab just now as to what had been in the coffin?' Patrick asked.

'There was just that black dusty stuff. No trace of anything else. Remember seeing it?'

'Of course.'

'Tea.'

'*Tea?*' Patrick and I exclaimed together.

Carrick rubbed his hands over his face. 'Yeah, loose tea. But not new tea, used and then dried-out tea. It's enough to give you the screaming habdabs, isn't it?'

Despite what Carrick had hoped nothing useful was achieved that night and Stonelake was remanded in custody. The DCI looked fit to drop.

'So let's go through what we have,' Patrick said. 'It almost goes without saying that Stonelake nicked the horse tack. Or nicked most of it and is a fence for the rest. The feed's stolen too. Plus he's certainly in all kinds of similar scams, including the things found in the loft at his home and other crimes that we don't yet know about yet. But I don't *think* he's involved in whatever's going on with regard to Barney's coffin. The look of shock on his face when Carrick told him was genuine and I'm not sure he's *that* much of a bastard. I'm keeping an open mind as to whether he's involved in the murders but we might learn a bit more at the mill. But when you think about it, if a serious crook wanted a nice quiet place to take people apart to gain info from them or just kill them what better venue than an empty barn out of earshot of everywhere that belongs to the local bad boy who will automatically become the police's number-one suspect?'

It was the following morning and we were walking down the rectory drive on our way to the mill, where we intended to have a look round the murder victims' flats having 'acquired' the keys and the case file. Neither of us felt comfortable at going behind Carrick's back.

I said, 'But that theory suggests that the crime's a local one and not organized by some city gang. It's not as though the building can be seen from any main roads. You'd have to live in the area and know about Stonelake and that the farm was, at present, uninhabited.'

'One explanation could be that a gang member lives in the vicinity and reports back to the big bossman.' Patrick paused, looking thoughtful. 'Or *lived*. It could have been Davies himself.'

'It would be a good idea to examine his criminal record in some detail, then. See who his connections were. But if he was a past member of a gang and the killings were some kind of score-settling where do the others fit in? Was Chris Manley really a policeman before he retired?'

Patrick patted the file that was beneath his arm. 'I was too weary last night to plough my way through every word of this – up until now Carrick's been sitting on it like a broody hen – but a quick flip through told me only that investigating the victims' pasts is still on-going.' He stopped to survey the damaged border. 'At least this is being fixed today.'

Plants had appeared as if by magic on the rectory doorstep, mostly young flowering shrubs, some of which John's parishioners had obviously dug up from their own gardens. And other gifts; pots of spring bulbs, a bouquet of viburnum and winter sweet that was filling the dining room with scent, even some new fence posts.

We sat on a seat on the village green to read through the reports again.

'No sign of a struggle in either property,' Patrick murmured, still reading. 'Fingerprints everywhere but only those of the inhabitants, plus Davies's in the Manleys' but not theirs in his. So he came to see them but they stayed out of his place. That would tie in with what Pascal Lapointe said; that he was working for them as a driver. And as you suggested, as their minder. We must be careful here; it did not make Christopher Manley a bent copper just because he employed an ex-con.'

'It's strange that they all lived in the same building. The Manleys could have got caught up in something iffy that Davies was up to.'

The doors of both flats had police seals but we had the means to reseal them. We decided to have a look at Keith Davies's home first perhaps, on reflection, subconsciously thinking it might be the most rewarding. Patrick immediately voiced the thought that went through my head and I wondered, not for the first time, if there was such a thing as telepathy.

'Are we being superior and clever-clogsy imagining we'll spot something that about a dozen experts have missed?'

'Professionals with experience in another branch of investigation will always have a fresh slant on any case,' I said.

Hand on the doorknob he said, 'Ingrid, that's so bloody good I'm going to write it down and use it in the ten-thousand-word essay I'll no doubt have to write at some stage.'

The place smelt stale, understandable, I suppose, as it had been shut up for several days. The way a home smells though can immediately tell you a lot about the people who live there. It was clear that Davies had smoked, liked fry-ups and, in either kitchen or bathroom, a drain was blocked.

'I take it we can touch things,' I said.

'Carrick didn't say anything about SOCO not having completely finished. Nor does their report and although I remembered to pick up a couple of pairs of gloves I shouldn't imagine we can take the place apart.'

'Why can't we if they haven't?'

'I like your reasoning. How can we if they haven't?'

Exasperated, I said, 'What did they tell you on the training course?'

'We didn't cover it.'

'They always seem to yank everything out of cupboards on the telly.'

'Yes, but this isn't *Frost* or *Morse*, is it? This is me getting the old heave-ho if I screw up.'

I was beginning to yearn for our MI5 days. I said, 'I suggest we have a good look at everything but leave it exactly as we find it. And stop worrying – it's probably my fault for suggesting you tread lightly.'

It was too much to expect that we would find anything that would be a further insight into Davies's criminal past. The information in the case file was basic but sufficient; he had served two years for GBH – the sentence possibly a light one because he had vented his wrath on a mobster wanted by the police, who had promptly arrested him in hospital – and six months for being in possession of a firearm, a sawn-off shotgun. He had been implicated in several other crimes, including attempted murder, but there had never been sufficient evidence to bring a strong case against him. There was a note in Carrick's handwriting to the effect that Davies had worked as a 'casual' for various underworld outfits, as a driver, wielder of baseball bat for intimidation purposes, thug in attendance, whatever was required.

We split up and I had a quick look in the kitchen, the source of the smell, I immediately discovered. There was a pile of dirty crockery in the sink standing in a puddle of putrid water, a dishcloth steeping in this resembling a decomposing sea-slug. I pulled the plug out but the water stayed exactly where it was. The rest of the room was not much better but I searched everywhere. I even looked in the fridge-freezer and cooker. In one of the wall cupboards hidden behind cans of baked beans I found some cash, two hundred pounds in fifty-pound notes. I was convinced that the spaces beneath the units had already been searched but got down on my knees, unclipped the boarding and looked anyway. There was a lot of dust and fluff but nothing else.

'Just some money,' I reported to Patrick on my way past

the bathroom door. He appeared to be dismantling the front of the bath.

'Genuine or counterfeit?' he queried.

I went back in the kitchen, cursing myself for not having checked more closely. 'It looks all right to me,' I called. 'No, it's not. The notes all have the same serial number. Do you have any plastic evidence bags with you too?'

He had remembered those as well and the notes were carefully placed in one. We then went over the bedroom and living room, grubby but tidy, even shaking out magazines and old newspapers to see if anything had been concealed between the pages. It seemed to take a very long time. Luckily for us Davies had had few possessions other than his clothes, most of which would have been quite expensive, some weight-training equipment kept in the spare bedroom, and a top-of-the-range home-entertainment system with extensive CD and DVD collections, mostly of the head-banging variety.

I had volunteered Patrick to go through the contents of the chest of drawers as rummaging through strange men's underwear has never been quite my thing. He found a few porn magazines and some more money, legal tender this time. Then he turned his attention to the apartment's walls, looking behind the two mirrors and three pictures on a quest for a safe, but found nothing. All the carpets were well fixed down so it was unlikely that any floorboards had been taken up in order to hide things in the space beneath.

'An anonymous kind of life,' Patrick commented. 'No photos, letters or records of any kind, just a few paid bills. Not even a birth certificate. You know, there's no mention of any search of a garage in the file with regard to Davies, only to the Manleys'. Theirs just held empty boxes and a couple of old bikes.'

'We'll have to follow that up – I thought everyone here had a garage.'

'So did I. There must be a cache of his personal stuff somewhere. In London, perhaps – in a suitcase on top of a wardrobe at a crony's place.'

We locked up, resealed the door and went across the landing to the Manley's home.

It quickly became apparent that here we were faced with something very different; the Manleys had lived surrounded by a glorious muddle. Their possessions seemed to be fighting to escape from every confinement, some succeeding and spilling out on to the floors. The police search had not helped matters and as we entered the living room the vibration of our footfalls caused a tottering pile of books to avalanche from a shelf and crash on to a sofa.

'It'll take all day to go through this lot,' I said in despair.

'You wanted to join the cops,' was the uncompromising reply.

We repeated the previous procedure; I started in the kitchen, which smelt faintly of fresh paint, Patrick the bathroom, doing the smaller rooms first. The job was more pleasant than the previous one in that the place was fairly clean but the amount of stuff meant it took a lot longer. I learned to exercise caution as every opening of a cupboard or unit was likely to precipitate a mass breakout by the contents. Finally, after three-quarters of an hour, I had made huge improvements in the stowage arrangements but found absolutely nothing of interest.

'There's a picture of them on their wedding day over there,' Patrick said when we met up again in the living room. 'He didn't appear to be in the police then – unless he didn't want to get married in uniform.'

All the clutter – beneath and around which, as Carrick had said, there were some fine old pieces of furniture – yielded very little of interest. Like the other residents of the converted mill, the Manleys were the first owners of the flat, solicitors' letters and other documents confirming that they had moved in during March the previous year. They had come from Hammersmith, West London. There was no record of Christopher Manley ever having been in the police, something I think the pair of us had taken for granted. Had Carrick actually checked?

'There are pay chits here,' Patrick said suddenly, delving

to the bottom of the box file we were going through. 'Well, well, he worked as a guard for one of the security companies connected with Heathrow Airport.' He ruffled through the slips of paper. 'For three years at least.'

'Policeman sounds better than security guard if you're moving to a slightly select village,' I observed.

'Yes, but where did these folk get the money from, eh? These flats must have cost between two hundred and fifty and three hundred thousand pounds.'

'Perhaps they won the lottery.'

'What, all of them?'

'They might have been in a syndicate.'

'I agree, but how do you explain the fact that Davies appears to have been keeping an eye on the other two – even working for them?'

'You get targeted by quite strange people if you've come into money.'

'They could have chosen to remain anonymous. And, by all accounts none of them enjoyed living here.'

'Patrick, people do move to the countryside and then realize it's not for them.'

He gave me a sideways look. 'You're playing devil's advocate.'

'No, I'm just trying to look at things from all angles. We don't *know* that the Manleys were criminals.'

'But the circumstances do point to people removing themselves from circulation and keeping their heads well down. It's worth checking if there were any significant thefts from warehouses at Heathrow while Manley was working there.'

I remembered something. 'Christopher Manley's body had what Rapton thought was white emulsion paint in the hair and beneath the fingernails. Someone's been painting in the kitchen – the ceiling looks freshly done.'

'I would have thought the place was a bit new to require painting.'

'Perhaps there was some kind of culinary disaster.' All too vividly I could recollect leaving the lid off the blender and having home-made soup dripping from the ceiling.

I left Patrick to it and went into the master bedroom. There were no surprises in either of the fitted wardrobes; everyday, dreary even, clothing all smelling a little fusty, shoes in heaps, a few travel brochures, umbrellas and an old walking stick. The chests of drawers followed the same pattern; no jewellery to speak of, greyish undergarments (I left Manley's to Patrick), washed-out sweaters, a couple of cardigans, a whole drawerful of gloves, scarves and hats. This woman had not spent any money she might have had on her appearance.

We had not found anything much that related to Janet Manley herself and I did not feel that I was violating her privacy, or memory, as I opened an Edwardian writing box I noticed on a bedside table. Perhaps it had belonged to her grandmother.

The box was not in very good condition. When opened it formed a sloping writing surface covered with red leather, the gold tooling on it almost worn away in places. Both halves of the box had compartments beneath them and at some time a repair to the broken hinges of these had been attempted with sticky tape, now disintegrating. In the front section, nearest the lock, was a tray for pens and it had a tiny 'secret' drawer beneath it in which was a very old and broken pearl necklace.

The shallowest compartment contained birth, marriage and death certificates, mostly referring to Janet Manley's parents and grandparents. I paused, beguiled by her maternal grandfather's occupation; tram driver. The Manleys' own marriage lines were there: they had wed in London, his occupation noted as central-heating engineer. It did not look as though he had ever been a policeman.

The other, deeper, side of the box held very little, a couple of Victorian postcards, a few letters from an aunt in the States dated over twenty years previously, a few old buttons, a St Christopher medal and a little notebook containing pressed flowers.

Did these people have a family? I wondered. Nothing had been said about next of kin and there were no birth certificates in the box to confirm the existence of any. No photographs of babies or children anywhere in the flat, come to think of it.

There was what looked like black dust in the bottom of this section of the box. But it was not ordinary household dust as it was far too dark in colour with a few larger particles. Carefully, I pushed some into a little heap, took a pinch of it and dropped it into a sample bag.

It looked a bit like tea.

Seven

'So what the hell's the significance of tea?' James Carrick said. 'It would appear to be similar to the stuff in Barney's coffin, old and dried out. We might have a link but I'm damned if I can see how. The lab's getting quite excited about it and has sent it off to a boffin at Kew but I don't see how knowing whether it's PG Tips or Earl Grey is going to help us at all. However, I'm willing to try anything if it solves a case.'

It was later that same day and we had just met Carrick, who had forgiven us, Patrick having convinced him that there had to be some kind of connection between the murders and the other cases and written up a report of our findings, such as they were, to give to him. The sample of dust had been taken to the lab.

Handing over the case file Patrick said, 'There's no mention in that of a search of Davies's garage.'

'No, he'd rented it out to another of the flat owners. It should have been mentioned.'

'D'you want us to go and talk to Shaun Brown?'

Carrick hesitated, then said, 'He ought to be eliminated from enquiries, if nothing else.'

'Does he have a record?'

'It's not a name that springs to mind. You'll have to check.'

Lynn Outhwaite appeared, obviously looking for someone. 'Superintendent Gillard, there's a Mr Hurst at the desk asking for you.'

'Tamsin Roper's boyfriend.' Patrick reminded Carrick. 'Other than the Dewittes, who are abroad and have been for some time and are therefore out of the investigation altogether, he's the only one who was at the mill last week I haven't spoken to.'

'Good of him to come and find you,' the DCI commented, gave us a tight smile and departed.

'That man's going to start drinking soon he looks so wretched,' I hissed in Patrick's ear as we retraced our steps to the front of the building. 'We shouldn't have counter-manded his orders.'

'If he hasn't already.' Patrick stopped in his tracks. 'Shall I chuck it in?'

'I don't know what to say.'

'I'll talk to Hurst, as he's waiting, before I make any deci-sions.'

Owen Hurst was not at all as I had expected, being short, dark and bearded, reminding me irresistibly of Toulouse Lautrec.

'I thought I'd pop by, seeing as you'd expressed an interest in talking to me,' he began in a deep, pleasant voice after Patrick had thanked him for coming. 'Must confess to being curious, having never been inside a nick before.' His brown eyes twinkled.

'You should have joined the army instead,' Patrick said, straight-faced. 'Then you'd know exactly what they're like.'

Hurst laughed and continued, 'The ship's alongside at Pompey in refit but I've had no end of trouble with a tooth lately and having been on leave for a few days had to have the bloody thing out the day before yesterday so was sent back on leave for the rest of the week. General anaesthetic,' he went on to explain in case we thought him a wimp. 'Jaw op, stitches, that kind of job. Tamsin's looking after me.' He touched one side of his face, which did look a bit swollen.

We were talking in one corner of the general office as Patrick had not been allocated a room of his own. He said, 'I wanted to ask you if you'd seen or heard any unusual activities last week at the mill, on the Thursday night or very early Friday morning.'

'Well, I might have done, actually. As Tamsin probably told you we went out for something to eat – after I'd dosed myself up to the eyeballs with painkillers and some antibiotics an emergency dentist had given me. We got back around eleven. The tooth gremlins were hard at work again by then so I took some more painkillers and prepared to doss down on the sofa. Couldn't sleep. It was stuffy so I opened a window for some fresh air. At one thirty – I looked at my watch – I heard a couple of cars start up. Thought it a bit odd because the place is normally like a tomb at night. Then I heard voices, they were talking over the sound of the engines. Just a few words and then they drove off.'

'Could you recognize the voices?' Patrick enquired.

'No, but I reasoned that it wasn't Tamsin's neighbours across the hall as from what she's told me about them they don't behave like that. Besides, I think Pascal told Tamsin that Lorna's car was being repaired as she'd had a minor bump. It must have been the people below us. Not the retired couple on the ground floor obviously and the other people, Dewitte I think their name is, have been abroad for yonks. But the really odd thing is that about ten or fifteen minutes later I heard another car start up and drive away, so who that was is anyone's guess.'

'You didn't get up and look out?' I said.

'No, you don't bother unless it gets to be a real nuisance, do you?'

'Did you hear anyone returning?'

'No, must have dropped off after a while. And of course I didn't check in the morning. I mean, it didn't seem to matter at the time.'

Patrick said, 'Can you remember whether the vehicle that left after the others was a petrol or diesel model?'

'Petrol, I *think*.'

'Anything else about it? An old banger or a more expensive-sounding car? Or the kind of thing a young man might own with twin exhausts and spoilers that gets driven into the ground?'

'Oh, fairly smooth. A saloon car of some kind.'

To Patrick I said, 'The Brandons can't have had visitors because Mrs Brandon is recovering from shingles. That can be contagious and she wouldn't have felt like socializing anyway.'

'It's not impossible that someone who wasn't supposed to park there did, for a short while. We shall have to talk to some more people,' Patrick replied, and then asked Hurst, 'I suppose you didn't hear any movement, or people shouting, in the flats below yours, before the cars started up?'

'No, everywhere's very well soundproofed.'

'Had you ever spoken to the Manleys, or to Davies?'

'I don't think so. I'm not at the mill very often and I've only known Tamsin for four months or so.'

'Would you mind making a short statement along the lines of what we've discussed and signing it before you go?'

'Not at all. Glad to be of help.'

'I've rung every meat-packing plant, sausage and pork-pie manufacturer in the Warminster area listed in the Yellow Pages trying to track down Shaun Brown and drawn a blank,' Patrick reported a little later. 'He doesn't have a criminal record. He's probably back doing casual farmwork as he did during past winters for Stonelake.' He thrust back his chair and stood up. 'This is like throwing stones in a pond and not even getting ripples.'

'You're probably stirring up the bottom, though,' I said. 'I suggest we go out into the big blue yonder and ask at a couple of farms in the Hinton Littlemoor area. Farmers know everything that's going on in the rural community.'

'Then talk about chucking it all in?' he queried with a rueful smile.

'If you want to.'

He pecked my cheek and we went out.

It was sobering to discover how many farms that Patrick could remember from his younger days were no longer in existence; the land sold off, the houses now private residences, holiday homes or, in one case, an exclusive restaurant. Finally, we struck lucky, driving down a lane having seen a sign on the main road with WITHINGTON JERSEYS painted on it.

I took a slow stroll as Patrick went off to knock at the farm-house door, there being no one about. He returned quite quickly.

'He doesn't work here now but has done in the past. They still had his mobile number.'

Shaun Brown, it transpired, was mending fences on Landsdown and the directions of how we might find him, if we wished to speak with him immediately, were complicated.

'Well, if we hadn't had this bus we'd have had to borrow a Land Rover,' Patrick said. 'Shall I drive? For some odd reason I can remember the way better then.'

As a result of all that military training and service in various middles of nowhere, I thought.

We were greeted by a somewhat surprised smile when we arrived on a windy ridge with wide-ranging views over Somerset, having climbed steeply, crossed two streams and had to stop and open and close three gates.

'Mornin',' said our quarry, laying aside his tools.

Patrick produced his warrant card. 'We're here in connection with the murders at Hagtop Farm and a couple of other cases. When were you last at the farm?'

Brown's brow furrowed and he squinted into the bright distance as he sought to remember. He was a personable man, in his late twenties or early thirties, definitely a hewer of wood or drawer of water but nevertheless appearing, even at first glance and despite his comparative youth, to be imbued with that quality that I can only call country wisdom.

'Must have been about this time last year,' he said. 'When Stonelake threw me out, sayin' I'd helped myself to diesel. He'd decided he didn't need me no more and used it as an excuse not to pay my final week's wages.'

'Were you aware that stolen property was hidden on the premises?'

The other guffawed. 'It was no secret that the man was on all kinds of fiddles but I needed the money real bad so who'd go searchin' around looking for trouble?' After a pause he said, 'Stonelake's a chip off the old block – his dad was worse in a way. I used to like the old lady, though, she was a real rose in a patch of thorns.'

'You weren't involved in any scams of his?' The question was asked lightly but the intense stare was as good as nailing Brown to his own handiwork.

'No, I wasn't,' he replied. 'I've never done anythin' illegal. Not in my whole life.'

'Did he get many visitors to the farm when you were there?'

'Dodgy ones, you mean?'

'Yes, if you like.'

'Sometimes. Some of them were reps, I s'pose. God knows who the others were. I kept right out of it.'

'Are you aware of ever having met the murder victims?'

'No, I haven't been near Hinton Littlemoor since I left Hagtop last winter. In case I bumped into him and lost my temper. It's daft but some local people think the place is cursed, seeing there've been deaths there in the past and then all the animals being killed in the foot-and-mouth outbreak. Tainted ground, one lady I spoke to called it.'

'Have you ever heard any gossip, anywhere, linking Keith Davies, one of the victims, with Brian Stonelake?'

'No, I haven't.'

'Did Stonelake ask you to take stuff anywhere – things that weren't really connected to your everyday work?'

'No. Oh, logs. I delivered those with a tractor and trailer.'

'And unloaded them yourself?'

'Mostly. Sometimes if it was fairly local, but at big houses, nobs' places, I'd leave the trailer overnight and their gardener or handyman would unload them. Stonelake used to go himself to collect it, and the money, the next day. He always went for the money – didn't trust no one.'

'Can you drive a JCB?'

'Yes, of course. You have to be able to handle a digger in my job.'

'Do you own one?'

'Wish I did.'

'Where were you last Sunday night into Monday morning?'

'At home, with the wife.'

'Are there any other witnesses to your having been at home?'

Brown was getting annoyed. 'Only the baby. What's this all about, then?'

'Haven't you heard? Someone dug up Barney Stonelake's coffin.'

This latest development had not had time to reach the presses.

Brown was horrified. 'You think that was me? I'm a churchgoing man, I am. Ask our priest, Father Nairn.'

Patrick was unrepentant. 'Do you know anyone who would? For cash? Plus someone else with a van?'

There was a silence.

'Think,' Patrick prompted. 'Two or three reprobates as thick as thieves with access to earth-moving equipment and vehicles. From Southdown St Peter, perhaps? That's where quite a few villains live.'

After another long pause Brown said, 'But if I give you any names and they've done nothing wrong . . .'

Patrick was all charm now. 'You're on a complete winner. I take all the responsibility and if they get leaned on but have done nothing wrong they won't know who mentioned their names. If they're guilty you're vindicated.'

'You could try the Tanner brothers. But they don't live at Southdown, they're from Hinton Littlemoor, or at least, they live in one of those old miners' cottages that are away from the village up towards the plantation. Take care, though, don't take the lady here with you. They're real rough. Always in trouble, pickin' on people smaller than themselves.'

'Thank you,' Patrick said. 'Sorry to have taken up your time.'

The trainee then took Brown's address in case we wanted to talk to him again. On an afterthought I asked him, 'What's the name of Stonelake's dog?'

'Whisky. It's a bearded collie under all the muck.'

For some reason the name filled me with gloom.

On the way back to Bath, Patrick pulled off the road into a pub car park.

'Lunch?' he enquired.

'And decision time,' I told him. 'No beer.'

'You're right on both counts,' he groaned, getting out. 'Just plenty of clear-headedness.'

'OK, this has *got* to be resolved,' Patrick said, when we had taken the edge off our hunger with excellent roast-beef sandwiches. 'I propose – and this is just something I'm putting on the table, so to speak, as you're involved as well – that when we next see Carrick face to face I offer to throw in the towel. We'll watch his reaction. If he jumps on the nearest table and dances a hornpipe we'll jack it in. If not, we stay. If he swithers, politely, we go anyway. How's that?'

'Well, I don't want to go solo,' I said. 'I haven't actually finally decided to be your Watson, not in a hands-on capacity. Yes, I'll go for that suggestion.'

'Fine, so that's on hold until the big moment arrives. Until then, what have we got? Not a lot other than the Tanner brothers. I like the sound of them, just the sort of hairy bullies I could do with giving my knuckles a workout on.'

'Tell James what you're doing this time,' I urged. 'Keep everything on the line so he doesn't feel left out.'

'I intend to.' He went outside to phone. When he returned he looked worried. 'James knows of them quite well,' he disclosed. 'They work, when they feel like it, at a small quarry south of Bath, and he also happens to know that they're there now as they've very recently been questioned in connection with another case involving violent assault. He's dead keen, said he'd handle it himself and is on his way there – pronto.'

'With backup?'

'I made a point of asking. No, Lynn's doing something else and no one else is spare.' Patrick stuffed the last piece of his sandwich into his mouth and stood up, jerking a thumb in the direction of the exit in lieu of speaking. I quickly wrapped the remains of mine in a napkin, drank the rest of my orange juice and followed him out.

We would ride shotgun, as invisibly as possible.

'What's the name of the quarry?' was my first question when we were under way.

'Fine Stone Ltd. I already knew a bit about it as it's one

of the last private firms around here, family owned, and produces, as the name suggests, best-quality Bath stone that's used in restoration work.'

It became obvious that we were approaching our goal when the road, verges, bare hedges and trees became etiolated with a thin covering of fine white dust. We progressed as though a cloud of smoke was billowing behind us. Then, up a steep slope off to the right, was the entrance.

'Is Chief Inspector Carrick here yet?' Patrick asked the man on the gate, having shown him his warrant card.

'He is, but we don't allow *anyone* unauthorized in the workings while we're operational, so you understand, so we've put out a call for the men he wants to see,' said the security guard. 'You can park by the office.'

Patrick lowered his voice. 'Look, I don't want him to know we're here. Can we leave the car on that rough ground over there and walk in?'

The man thought about it. 'I suppose so,' he said at last.

'Is there any way we can reach the office without him seeing us?'

'You spying on him or something?'

'Of course not. We're both in training for anti-terrorist work and it's part of an exercise.'

We were subjected to a searching gaze. 'OK, if you go in the gate and keep close to the left-hand side of the road you'll be out of sight from the windows but if he's hanging around outside I can't help you. When you get closer you'll have to risk it. But stay on the road. On no account take any of the smaller access routes to the quarry. They're strictly off-limits to you. Understand?'

'Absolutely,' Patrick said. 'Thanks.'

We were issued with hard hats, signed a visitors' book and were finally allowed through.

'Kind of him to tell us about the other access routes,' Patrick said. 'Most helpful.'

'But they probably won't go anywhere near the office,' I pointed out. 'Just lead to some Godforsaken hole in the ground.'

After walking about fifty yards along the road, which penetrated thick woodland, we could see one corner of what looked like a Portakabin, presumably the office in question. We proceeded in single file and after travelling the same distance again with more of the portable building coming into view came to a track that led off to the left. Patrick threw a glance over his shoulder to see if anyone was watching us and hurried down it for a short distance, stopping just before the path curved sharply round to the left.

'It's bearing off in the wrong direction,' I said.

'I know. We'll go through the trees. I just want to observe, that's all.'

It was very difficult to progress silently as the ground was thick with dead twigs and leaves. We went extremely slowly, placing each foot with care. Then, after a while – accidentally or not the navigation had been spot-on – two dark rectangles loomed ahead of us. We headed towards the right hand one after the sound of a toilet being flushed emanated from the other. Patrick came to a halt.

Voices.

We crept closer until we were right beneath a row of three ventilator grilles in the rear wall, the branches of the trees over and around everything.

'I'm sorry about the delay but they won't be long now, Chief Inspector,' a woman said. 'Won't you take a seat for a moment?'

'No, thanks, I spend far too much time sitting at my desk or behind the wheel of a car,' Carrick's mannered Scottish voice replied.

I could imagine him standing, perhaps in the doorway or looking out of one of the windows, one hand in a trouser pocket jingling the loose change, a habit when he was impatient. One could hear the soft footfalls as he then paced up and down.

At least another five minutes went by. Carrick was offered, and refused, coffee, the phone rang several times and a lorry arrived to collect stone, covering everything in another layer of dust. I noticed that Patrick's hair and eyebrows were hoary with it. Then what sounded like a dumper truck chugged up and stopped close by. Moments later the Portakabin moved a little as more people entered.

'Shall we talk outside?' Carrick said. In all probability the lorry driver was still within, dealing with paperwork.

Patrick's lips moved as he silently swore, the voices going from hearing range, out into the open air, and gestured to me to reverse slightly so that he could squeeze past and edge, as far as he could, down the three-feet-wide gap between the cabins. This had sheets of boarding of some kind stored there and gas bottles, empty, I guessed, but at least we were still mostly hidden from view by it all.

Carrick's voice was carried on the light breeze blowing towards us through the gap.

'I understand you're responsible for the plant here,' he said.

There was an inaudible reply.

'Did that include last weekend?'

Another mumbled response.

'Where were the pair of you last Sunday night and early Monday morning?'

'In bed,' someone growled.

'You'll have to do better than that. Who's responsible for security here at weekends? Who has the keys?'

'Danny.'

'Always?'

'When he's not on holiday.'

'Was he away last weekend?'

Silence.

'I'm trying to trace someone who used a digger last weekend for illegal purposes. How many JCBs do you have here?'

'Two.'

'Are they in this vicinity?'

Another silence.

'We can carry on with this down at the nick if you like,' Carrick said silkily. 'I'm talking about serious criminal damage.'

'We haven't done nothing!' a man roared.

'Show me the JCBs.'

Then there was only the sound of the distant hum of machinery.

'They've moved off,' Patrick whispered, backing out of the small space. 'We must follow now, even if Carrick sees us.'

Still trying not to make too much noise we made our way towards the front of the cabin and Patrick, who was in front, paused to peer around the final corner. He then shot off and must have gone inside for I heard him say in a high-pitched cockney accent, 'Oppos of the guv out there, miss. Got a coupla sets of ovies we could borrow so as not to get our clobber mucked up?' And reappeared, a matter of seconds later, with some orange-coloured workmen's overalls. We scrambled into them and set off after the three figures already in the distance, walking in a kind of canyon cut in one side of a hill. Piles of stone were everywhere, spoil probably, but such was the huge scale of the place there was plenty of room for large vehicles to pass easily between them.

'There's one JCB parked in that gully over there,' Patrick said, quickening his pace. 'I'm worried that the pair of them will take him to a nice private place, thump him and then do a runner.'

'It would be an incredibly stupid thing to do.'

'These men are bound to be incredibly stupid and they'll be picked up in no time at all as they'll then probably head for home and switch on the telly. Carrick's the one I'm concerned about.'

The trio, who were heading away from where all the noise of activity seemed to be coming, disappeared from sight behind a rock pile as the canyon curved slightly and we jogged to catch up. When we saw them again they were much closer. Patrick scooped up a piece of equipment lying on the ground, it looked like part of a large drill, and slung it across one shoulder, I assumed to help disguise us. We pulled the safety helmets further down over our eyes to partly cover our faces and carried on.

Then the group stopped and one orange-clad figure pointed over to the right towards something we could not see. Both men with Carrick were big and burly, with awesome beer-bellies. They went in the direction indicated and as we resumed walking saw they were going into a dark cave-like entrance in the rock.

We ran, on tiptoe.

Near the entrance we stopped, Patrick breathing hard under his heavy load, and listened. Carrick was talking and he did not sound particularly pleased.

'I have an idea you've led me here on a wild-goose chase,' he said. 'No, you stay right where you are, the pair of you. Now listen!'

There was the sound of a scuffle.

Patrick marched in but I stayed where I was.

'Where's this go?' I heard him ask loudly, still with a cockney accent, the tone of his voice possessing tooth-jangling, chainsaw qualities.

'What?' someone bawled.

'This effin' thing.'

'Where did you get it from?'

'Back there.'

'It's bust!'

'I know it's effin' bust.' There followed a pithy description of the other's lack of intelligence, family history, sexual orientation, that kind of thing, at which point I decided that a little reinforcement might help things along a bit and walked in.

I had little time to assimilate my surroundings, only that it was an endless-looking cave, for although the move had the desired effect it caused the two suspects to endeavour to remove themselves from the scene and, side by side, they ran straight at us.

There was a loud 'Ooooff!' in unison as the metal drill thingy hit the pair midships, Patrick having thrown it, and they went over backwards in a cloud of dust and obsceni-ties. Both climbed to their feet and showed no sign of surrender.

'You're both under arrest!' Carrick bellowed.

The man nearest to Patrick took a swipe at him with a fist like a ham joint. Patrick ducked, side-stepped smartly and caught him with a real oblivion-maker to the side of the jaw. Out of the corner of my eye I saw the other man running out through the entrance, Carrick after him. Reckoning that my husband needed no support right now I set off in pursuit.

The big man could move amazingly quickly for his size. I saw it all: he was run down as though he was standing still and I found myself coming to a halt, beating my fists together in my agitation at the sight of Carrick launching himself in a tackle that had the pair of them crashing to the ground. He was up first and whether it was something that the other man said as he got to his feet or any move he suddenly made against the DCI I could not tell as Carrick was standing nearest to me, blocking my view, but suddenly his quarry was flat on his back, definitely not moving.

'Good,' Patrick said, still a bit breathless, appearing by my side and appraising the situation.

'What about the other one?' I asked.

'Handcuffed to a large chunk of scrap steel.'

Carrick finished using his mobile as we approached. 'Well, I don't know who you are but I'd like to thank—' he began.

We had removed our helmets halfway through this.

'But – but you didn't look like you!' he protested. 'You didn't even move like you. I actually glanced round and there was just a couple of blokes slouching along.' He surveyed his trophy, who was fully conscious but had thought it safer to stay put. 'So, it looks as though we've got the churchyard hit squad or even accessories to murder. In my view, if they run they're usually guilty.'

'Still want us on the job?' Patrick queried.

'Yes, I think I need you.'

He was in pain, holding his side.

Eight

Telltale clues were found on the JCB that was parked in the gully. The small mangled branch of a bay tree and large splinters of preserved new fencing timber of a type used at the rectory were jammed into the bucket mechanism, together with obvious damage to the machine where it had been used as a battering ram were not conclusive evidence that would stand up in a court of law but it was a start: enough anyway for Carrick to get to work on the Tanner brothers. I was still not sure if he was totally convinced there was a link with the Hagtop murders but as hardly anything of a horrible nature had happened in Hinton Littlemoor since two men were hanged in an orchard by Judge Jeffreys as punishment for joining the Duke of Monmouth's rebellion it was a safe enough bet.

Carrick asked Patrick to help with the questioning but I was barred, ostensibly on account of my trainee status in what would be a difficult situation. Carrick elaborated by saying he was worried that I might be targeted by the detainees with foul language or, as he put it, that of a sexual discriminatory nature. More to the point, I had an idea that if I was not present those doing the asking would feel more free to utilize similar turns of phrase if they so chose. As far as Patrick was concerned, the Tanner brothers might learn a few new words.

They were questioned separately and, memories of the circumstances of their arrest no doubt still as fresh as a daisy in their minds, soon started talking. Other than blaming each other for everything they were eager to give the name of the man who had hired them. He had not said who he was at the time: they had recognized him from a photograph in the *Bath Evening Chronicle*.

Keith Davies, who was now dead. We had our link.

'They were told to choose a night as soon as possible when there was little or no moon and when it was windy or raining hard so there would be less risk of them being heard,' Patrick told me, continuing with his account of what had transpired. 'When you think about it they could have waited months for the right conditions.'

We were at 'home' at the rectory that same evening.

'So this must have been set up, at the very latest, a couple of weeks ago,' I said. 'Obviously, before the murders. Did they reveal what was in the coffin?'

'They said they didn't get involved with that part of it. It needed two people to dig out the last of the soil and lift the coffin from the grave – Davies was adamant that it was not to be damaged so they couldn't use the digger for all the work – and then they both rode in the cab to a piece of spare ground half a mile away marked on a makeshift map they had been given where they met another bloke with a van. They helped load the coffin into the van and were then paid and told to bugger off and say nothing. They swear they didn't question that anything other than a body was inside the coffin as it was heavy and were not happy with what they had been asked to do. The promise of five hundred pounds each appears to have helped alleviate their consciences slightly but they admit they got semi-plastered before they did the job.'

'Davies was dead by then. Who was the one with the van?'

'They don't know. They hadn't seen him before. I think I believe them – their stories tally and they're too thick to make up anything elaborate. Needless to say they're also terrified someone's going to come after them next.'

'It goes without saying then that if Barney was never interred in his coffin something else was, something valuable. But as James said, that means undertakers were involved and Heaven knows who else besides. Who were the funeral directors?'

'I asked Dad to look in his records and it was an exceedingly respectable and long-established firm from Bristol, Littlejohn and Makepeace. Enquiries are progressing, as they say.'

'Perhaps someone packed whatever it was in tea to stop it moving around or rattling.'

'But according to forensics it's *used* tea, Ingrid. You're not telling me someone saved up old teabags in order to use them for that when all they had to do was go out and buy some bubble-wrap. And why would some be in that box at the Manley's flat?'

'It might not have come from the same source as that in the coffin.'

'No, and we won't know until we get more forensic findings and hear from the botanist at Kew. But it's a bit of a coincidence.'

'Are we baffled?'

'Baffled.'

One of the burned-out cars was confirmed to have belonged to the Manleys due to the just readable part of a number plate, so to assume that the other had been Keith Davies's did not appear unsafe. There was no evidence of any kind to be found in the hulks, not even when the boot lids had been forced open. The vehicles had been pushed into the quarry from the higher ground above it, the strands of wire of a flimsy fence having been cut. We were assuming that the same people, or others, had then made their way to the cars and set them ablaze. No useful tyre tracks of any vehicles that might have been involved, not even the ones about to be destroyed, were found above the cliff as the ground was very dry and stony. The softer terrain in the rubbish-choked quarry below might have yielded information but the search for the missing child by upwards of fifty people had obliterated everything. The only shred of good news to come out of all this was that the polluted mess was going to be cleared up.

The rectory garden had been repaired, the gifts of plants

incorporated therein and volunteers and the PCC had made good most of the damage to the churchyard. But there was still a gaping hole where Barney Stonelake's coffin had been, and according to John and Elspeth that evening, it was giving rise to some local unease.

'It's the old folk,' Elspeth explained. 'They don't like things like that. Restless spirits and so forth.'

'But the poor old man was never there and even if he had been he'd surely be haunting the Tanner brothers, not the village,' Patrick said with a grin.

His mother had entertained the WI to tea; some thirty ladies, all home baking, their sole topic of conversation the murders and the raid on the graveyard. 'It's not funny, Patrick,' she snapped.

John said, 'Jimmy Reeves told me that people have been looking in their sheds and old outhouses in case the undertakers stashed Barney somewhere like that.'

His wife surveyed him closely for signs of similar levity and seemed to find none. '*Surely* not!'

Whereupon Patrick could contain himself no longer and left the room, his rude laughter, however, regrettably still audible. Moments later the laughter ceased when his mobile rang.

'What is it?' I asked when he had called me out into the hall.

'That was Carrick from home. A man's body's in the process of being fished out of the Avon. There might be a connection – his throat's been slashed too. James is on his way but thinks we ought to attend as well.'

A crowd of gawpers clustered along the balustraded esplanade that overlooks the river had a good view of the weir by Pulteney Bridge, which is illuminated at night, hence the ease with which the body had been spotted. The fire brigade had been called out to assist and were utilizing hooks on long poles that they use to pull straw from burning thatched roofs to drag the corpse to dry land. This had still meant venturing out on to the top of the slippery weir but fortunately the river was low and the flow of water over it gentle.

By the time we arrived and Patrick had been apprised of

this information the body, wearing what looked like a dark T-shirt and jeans, had been placed face down on the concrete walkway at the bottom of the gated steps one had to descend in order to gain access to the weir. At least, it should have been face down for it was lying on its front but the open eyes were actually staring sightlessly straight ahead, the chin flat on the ground, the neck virtually severed.

'For God's sake get the whole thing back from the edge,' Patrick ordered. 'Or we might lose the head.' He turned to me. 'D'you want to wait up top?'

I rather felt that I did. Besides, there was not enough room for everyone on this narrow access path just above the water. I went back up the steps, got back in the car and switched on the radio to try to take my mind off what I had just seen.

Dead fishlike eyes.

It seemed that I sat there for a small eternity, not really listening to a symphony concert, while the blue lights on the nearby vehicles revolved mesmerically, radios yammered and, gradually, the bystanders began to drift away. Carrick arrived, going from sight down the steps. Soon afterwards an ambulance that had attended the scene was driven away: they are never used once death has officially been certified. A little later the body was collected by undertakers in a fibre-glass 'shell' coffin and loaded into a plain van. Then Patrick and Carrick came into view and approached the Range Rover. I switched off the radio.

'Another nasty one,' James said to me through the open window.

'How long had he been in the water?' I asked, really for something to say.

'The pathologist thought no longer than twenty-four hours but obviously won't know more until he does the PM.'

Patrick said, 'No ID on him, just like the others.'

'Pure delaying tactics,' Carrick commented. 'But it'll do the bastard no good at all – we'll get him.'

Someone called to him and he went off, his parting remark to us, 'That was the kind of lowlife face that might be in a mugshots file.'

'We might be looking at a copycat killing,' Patrick observed as he climbed aboard.

'Or he could have been the man who drove the van and helped push the cars into the quarry,' I said.

'We mustn't be in too much of a rush to make that link.'

Carrick's instincts were proved to be sound and the dead man was soon identified – initially from police records and then as a result of enquiries undertaken the following morning – as Peter Horsley, aged twenty-nine, from the district of Totterdown in Bristol. From truanting at school he had progressed to a life of petty crime and was known to Bristol CID for breach of the peace, assault and social-security fraud. In between short-lived jobs he had served a total of three years in prison, in bite-sized chunks, as Carrick put it when we met up with him just before noon. The local grapevine, in the shape of a snout referred to only as Taz, was insistent that Horsley had got above himself by becoming caught up in a turf war.

'I'm cautiously leaning towards it being a copycat crime,' Carrick went on. 'The method of killing does appear on the surface to be the only similarity to the Hagtop murders and, as far as I can ascertain, Horsley never drifted into the Bath area – from a criminal point of view, I mean.'

'Could he have been an old oppo of Keith Davies's?' Patrick said.

I said, 'But Davies came from London.'

'Horsley could easily have visited London. It's quite possible they met there.'

'Do you want to dig a little deeper?' Carrick asked him.

Patrick knew precisely what he was being asked to do. 'OK,' he replied.

Carrick waggled a finger. 'But Ingrid isn't in on this, and that's an order.'

'Ingrid's been on far more dangerous assignments than drifting around a few iffy pubs, whether it's near Bristol docks or in the East End of London.'

'I don't care. I wasn't responsible for her in those days. I am now and she's not going. Right?'

'James, she's supposed to be under training.'

'These were your Commander Brinkley's orders, one of the conditions. Didn't you have to take orders from him when you were with MI5?'

'Like hell I did! No, never.'

Right from the beginning of this new venture Patrick had been keeping his temper beautifully, if not heroically. I now ratted things up by completely boiling over.

'I'm bloody fed up with you discussing me as though I'm a loaf of bread!' I yelled. 'Just allowed to follow along, nanny your bloody pathetic fragile egos, drive the car when you're over the limit, take notes and do the washing up. Balls to the pair of you!'

I stormed out.

'Attagirl!' said Derek Woods from the desk with a big grin, presiding over a reception area awash with strangers all wearing funny looks that pointed in my direction.

It would be satisfying to report that I went away, performed stunning undercover detective work, solved the crime and then swanned back into the nick with a bulging, neatly typed file and tossed it, with enormous nonchalance, on Carrick's desk. Real life is not like that. What actually happened is that I consoled myself with a lunch consisting of hundreds of cal-ories in very upmarket surroundings and then went back to the rectory for a feverish afternoon's writing.

At some time during the afternoon Patrick returned – he was still, with Carrick's permission, taking time off to help John with parish matters – by taxi, for I had 'purloined' the car. This particular afternoon his task involved nothing more than taking his father to a meeting and then on to see an old friend, thus freeing Elspeth to have time for herself, who told me of the arrangement when I went down to make some tea.

'I'm sort of dreading seeing him and James again,' I confessed, filling the kettle. 'I sort of told them to go to hell this morning.'

'Good for you!' she declared stoutly.

'Worse, the entire police station heard me.'

She giggled. 'Perhaps that's why Patrick came in a bit

warily earlier on. I take it the case is a difficult one and everyone's tempers are getting a bit frayed – not that I want you to think I'm prying, of course,' she hastily added.

It was not giving away sensitive information if I revealed one aspect of the inquiry. 'Elspeth, what do you know about tea?'

'Tea?'

'Dried used tea was found in Barney Stonelake's coffin. And in a box containing documents in the Manleys' flat.'

She sat down at the kitchen table. 'How strange. What sort of tea is it?'

'We don't know yet. Some samples have been sent to a professor of botany at Kew.'

'But *used* tea.'

'Yes.'

'I suppose they know that because the leaves have unrolled – I mean, Earl Grey has huge leaves and we put them on the garden because they block the sink.'

'Yes, it had been in water.'

'That doesn't mean it'd been used to make tea to drink.'

'No, you're right. I'm just quoting what the initial forensic report said.'

'In Victorian times used tea was dried again by the big houses and given to the poor. Or even sold cheaply.' She brooded. 'And now you say some was in the coffin and a box at the Manleys'. Coffins, boxes . . . You know, this reminds me of something but I don't know what. Perhaps I'm just thinking about the old tea chests in the loft . . .'

I worked until just before dinner, feeling all bloody-minded about continuing with the police work. OK, I thought, I'll stick out the initial period and then go home to Devon to write and help Patrick out over the phone, but only if he asks me to. To swing between two careers was madness and I would not see the children anywhere near often enough.

I had heard him return with John but stayed where I was for a while and then went down. There was no question of our having words in front of anyone.

My husband gave me a winning smile, a glass of wine and

a kiss, in reverse order, and a little later after some general conversation we all sat down to dinner.

Elspeth was serving the dessert when she suddenly froze. 'China!' she exclaimed, staring at the bowl containing fresh fruit salad. 'That's it!'

'What is?' John asked blankly.

'Tea! China – only it was porcelain – was packed in crates of tea. And when divers went down it got into their air hoses and masks, even though it was hundreds of years later.'

'Sunken wrecks, you mean?' I said. 'The Nanking cargo and others like it?'

'Yes.'

'It's worth following up,' Patrick mused.

John said, 'There have been quite a few wrecks found since – one of the chaps involved with several of them was Michael Hatcher if I remember rightly – but surely the china that was found wouldn't be so valuable that people would stash it away and be prepared to commit murder for it.'

I said, 'Some of the larger pieces of porcelain might have been worth a lot of money. Were there any warehouse raids at Heathrow while Christopher Manley was a security guard there?'

'No,' Patrick replied. 'I checked. But I only had those wage statements we found to go on. He could have worked there a lot longer.'

We drove back into Bath after dinner as Patrick wanted to check on the post-mortem findings. He had announced his intention before we sat down to eat and had only consumed one glass of wine with his meal. Preparing to leave he had, however, glanced in my direction with a questioning look on his face.

'D'you want me to come with you?' I had asked.

'I always enjoy your company.'

'So what were the findings of the inevitable debriefing with James?' I persisted mulishly.

'If you get killed he's going to say that, as he put it, you were outwith his control.'

115

'Look, I'm quite prepared to forget it if my presence is throwing a spanner in the works.'

'No, it's not. And if it comes to the crunch, you're *my* responsibility.'

Men.

Carrick was having a well-overdue evening off and taking Joanna out for a meal as it was her birthday. The report was in his in-tray and Patrick switched on the desk lamp and sat in the DCI's revolving chair, swinging gently from side to side as he read.

'Horsley had been belted over the head with something like an iron bar before his neck was slashed,' he said. 'The former probably killed him outright as there was still suffi-cient blood in his body for testing that revealed he'd been drinking heavily up until the time of death. Hardly any water in the lungs so he was dead when he went in the river. We need to find where he was killed. Someone will have had to do some fairly meaningful clearing up.' He glanced up. 'Fancy a trawl round some dodgy Bristol nightlife?'

'It would mean getting changed into dodgy nightlife clothes or we'll stick out a mile. I assume you mean to work under-cover.'

'No, I was thinking of going in twenty-four-carat Bill and spreading unending terror.'

I was not so sure of the wisdom of this. 'Do we know if he was married or had a girlfriend?'

'Apparently the latter. Kylie Walker. We could go and see her first.'

It was the kind of housing estate where, in the words of my Scottish friend Linda, social workers wipe their feet on the way *oot*. No visiting car would escape being dismembered as soon as the owner was safely out of sight, alarm systems or no, so we parked in a slightly more salubrious area about a quarter of a mile away and walked back.

People skulked, I knew, just out of the brightest of the ghastly illumination provided by the orange-tinted street lights, by rows of lock-up garages and in doorways. A few youths slouched on a street corner. I had those back-of-the-neck prickles engendered by the certainty that one was being watched, taken stock of, evaluated. I jumped out of my skin when a dog suddenly threw itself at a gate we were passing, baying to get at us, its teeth bared, crazed with a hatred of strangers.

Patrick made for the youths who had started kicking around an empty beer can in desultory fashion. One, seeing our approach, sent it hurtling viciously in our direction at head height. Patrick caught it one-handed and carried on walking, an amiable smile on his face.

'Can you direct us to Brunel Court?' he asked the kicker, profferring the can, but not necessarily as a peace offering.

The can was ignored and a severe case of acne pondered on the advisability of replying before visibly deciding that his personal safety could well depend on it. 'Yeah, over there.' A jerk of the head. 'That block, wiv the white van outside.'

Patrick manoeuvred himself subtly so that he could note our destination while keeping a weather eye on the present company. 'Thanks. Did any of you know Peter Horsley?'

''E's dead.'

'I'm aware of that.'

'You the fuzz?'

'Yes.'

There was a general edging away.

'We need to catch his killer,' Patrick pointed out.

Another, younger, boy piped up. 'Well, it's no good comin' 'ere. The bloke wot topped 'im ain't one of us. Pete 'ad got 'isself caught up in big-time stuff.'

'Shuddup!' snarled the first youth.

'Well, 'e's got to know, 'asn't 'e?' protested the other. 'An' then 'e'll bugger off an' leave us alone. Someone told our mum an' our mum der go, "It'll be the end of 'im." Last month, that woz. Mum's always right,' he finished triumphantly.

'Who was the someone?' Patrick asked.

'Dunnow. Could've been Kylie, his girlfriend.'

'And you don't know any of Horsley's chums?' Patrick asked.

'"E didn't 'ave no chums 'ere,' said the first youth. 'Bragged of posh bods who called 'im on their mobiles.' He spat in the gutter. 'Pathetic git.'

'Thanks,' Patrick said again, tossed the can unerringly in a nearby bin and we left them.

'Our mum *der go*?' I echoed under my breath.

'Said. It's pure Bristol,' Patrick revealed. 'Interesting that Kylie's name was mentioned.'

Disenchanted youngsters of both sexes were hanging around in the entrance and stairwell of the block of flats, drinking, smoking and generally making a nuisance of themselves. They ignored us and we ascended the stairs to the fourth floor, the lift being out of order even if we had felt like braving its stinking environs.

It was late and we would possibly be getting Ms Walker out of bed, I thought as Patrick rang the doorbell. If she answered the door at all. But footsteps were heard within almost immediately and the door was flung open wide. The disappointed expression on the face of the young woman who had opened it made it no secret that she had been expecting someone else.

'Yes?'

'Miss Kylie Walker?'

'Yes.'

'Police,' Patrick said, producing his warrant card. 'Can we have a quick word with you?'

'I've given my statement.'

'Follow-up investigations,' came the impassive reply. 'May we come in?'

'Look, can't it wait until tomorrow? I've a friend coming round.'

'You'll have to come to Bath nick unless you want to be grilled by the Bristol heavies again.'

She wilted against the edge of the door. 'Oh, all right, then.'

'Ten minutes,' Patrick promised.

In the dim light of the hall I could see that she was very petite, very pretty and had her lower lip pierced with a stud. Leading the way into a living room she gestured resignedly to a settee covered by a leopard-print throw and sat down well away from us on an upright chair near the door.

'You want to know about Pete and me,' Kylie said.

'Not in the sense of being nosy about your relationship,' Patrick assured her, not seating himself.

'Oh good,' she said dully. '*They* did.'

'I'd like you to tell me as much as you can about his friends, contacts, where he worked when he had a job, things like that.'

'Well, he didn't have friends really.'

'He had you.'

'Yes, but we've known each other for always. His family used to live next door when we were in Seymour Road. I looked after him when he was little.'

'But surely you're younger than he was.'

'Too right. By five years. And I was bigger and taller. But he was always a big baby. He didn't have no brothers and sisters so I was sort of his sis. Bathed his grazed knees, wiped his bloody nose for him when he fell over.'

'Ah, so he lived with you because he didn't have anywhere else to go.'

'Sometimes. We were an item for a short while when he was younger. I'd left home and got this council flat here. I really thought he was going to make a go of himself then but he started drinking and messing with drugs so I threw him out. Sometimes he'd come back when he wasn't in prison: no money, nowhere to live, the usual with useless men.' She flared up. 'You know, like stinking drains. You think you've fixed it but the smell comes back again.'

We were getting the relationship angle after all.

'But you didn't really have to put up with him,' I pointed out.

'I felt sorry for him, I suppose.'

'Where did he live when he wasn't here?' Patrick asked.

'At his Mum's. His Dad's dead. She's partly disabled and

lives in sheltered accommodation that only has one bedroom so if he goes there he has to sleep on the living-room floor. She'd got wise to him and wouldn't give him any more money. Not that the poor soul can afford to, with only her pension to live on.'

'Did people call round here wanting to talk to him?'

'I can't remember anyone. He'd have probably climbed out of the window and shinned down the drainpipe if they had as the only folk likely to come looking for him were those he owed money to.'

'Did he ever mention a man by the name of Keith Davies?'

'No, but he was like an oyster was Pete – never told me anything.'

'Other unpleasant types, then. Did he ever work for a criminal gang?'

'I can't tell you about that. There were a few iffy ones he *said* he knew but I didn't know whether to believe him or not. He was the kind of fool who thought he could impress people by talking like that. I'm not naming names anyway. I don't want to end up in the river too. And there's probably nothing in it.'

'Someone murdered him,' I said. 'Have you any idea why they would? Murder's not just empty talk.'

'Well, he must've bitten off more than he could chew, mustn't he? Or really got up some big Godfather's nose.'

I thought Patrick might press her further on this but he said, 'He did have a few proper jobs, though. Do you know what they were?'

Kylie shrugged. 'One or two. He didn't talk about it in case I asked him for some of the money back he'd had off me. I think he worked in the Post Office sorting place one Christmas a year or so back, but don't take that as gospel.'

'Someone said something about him bragging about getting calls from people using mobiles. Any idea who they could have been?'

She shook her head. 'No. And they'd have had to have rung here. Pete didn't have one.'

'While you were out at work?' I said.

'It would figure.'

'Which is where, if you don't mind my asking?' Patrick said.

'At Littlejohn and Makepeace. I'm a secretary there.'

'The undertakers.'

Kylie smiled. 'They prefer to be called funeral directors, you know. I remember now. I got Pete a job there as a driver but it didn't last. He was rude to everyone, even the bereaved. He was a real toad when you think about it.'

Nine

We had made another connection: Littlejohn and Makepeace had arranged Barney Stonelake's funeral. I nevertheless found it hard to understand how someone who worked merely as a driver for a funeral director could somehow 'lose' a corpse and substitute valuable items in the coffin with a view to hiding them efficiently until they could be disposed of, for financial gain, without anyone else in the company knowing anything about it.

Patrick and I considered postponing the second phase of our night's work, wondering if it might prove to be more worthwhile first to interview Mr Littlejohn and his partner. We already had an appointment with them the following morning. (They were, we had learned, personal friends of John and Elspeth, which was unlikely to make it any easier.) But we were on site, so to speak, and, more to the point, my other half was gasping for a pint. We went to a pub near the old docks, which have been extensively redeveloped and improved, the old warehouses now boutiques and restaurants with apartments above. According to Carrick, the Barge hardly ever closed, a state of affairs that was only tolerated by the constabulary because the landlord was a mine of useful information concerning the local riff-raff. He was also prepared to arrange delectable bacon sandwiches to be made, gratis, for those officers of the law who happened to be passing in the wee small hours, a useful arrangement for all concerned. It seemed that Patrick would not need to practise his role of lean, mean, policing machine after all, not tonight anyway. He must have thought so too and, unwisely and uncharacteristically as it turned out, dropped his guard.

It was late by now, even by normal closing-time standards, but the pub, scruffy and old-fashioned in comparison with the newly transformed neighbourhood, was heaving with people. We plunged within and finished up when we had bought our drinks crammed together into a tiny niche at one end of the bar.

'Just as well we're married,' Patrick said, giving me a manic kind of grin and having to raise his voice over the racket. 'It's no good, we'll have to take it in turns to swig. You first.'

He was not entirely joking, it really was that snug, and I gratefully drank some of my iced orange juice and lemonade. It was the kind of place where the white wine would be out of a box stored lovingly on a radiator, and anyway, I would probably end up driving. By the time Patrick was on his second pint people were beginning to leave, probably to go clubbing, and we found ourselves with more space.

The bar having thinned out and any conversation less likely to be overheard Patrick caught the attention of the barman, an individual of generous proportions who slotted seamlessly into his surroundings as he had a black beard and eyepatch. I wondered if both were props but they looked genuine enough.

'DCI Carrick recommended this place,' Patrick said quietly by way of introduction when the man had berthed opposite us, 'on account of the excellent beer and communication. Would the latter be from your good self?'

'Would you be working for him?'

'In a manner of speaking, yes.'

'Do you have any ID? You can't be too careful these days.'

Patrick showed his warrant card, with discretion, and then said, 'We're wondering if the man whose body was found in the Avon at Bath was a customer of yours.'

'The Horsley bloke?' For such a big man he had a very soft voice.

'Yes, him.'

'I can't say that I ever saw him here. In fact I didn't

recognize him at all from the picture in the paper. But the name rang a bell when I saw the article. He was a bad lad, wasn't he?'

'A complete shit by all accounts,' Patrick replied crisply.

'Bad lads don't tend to show their faces in here because they know I run a tidy pub. But his name was possibly *mentioned*, if you get my meaning. Excuse me for a minute.' After attending to a another customer he returned to say, 'I have an idea it was in connection with someone stealing money from his old mum.'

'You mean, he did?'

There was a slow nod.

'Surely though feelings wouldn't have run so high among your normally law-abiding regulars that they'd beat him over head with an iron bar, almost slice it off and then chuck him in the river somewhere upstream of Bath.'

Breath was drawn in graphically through a fine set of teeth. 'That vicious, eh? No, perhaps not.'

'Who would, then? Had he got himself into some kind of trouble with the big boys?'

'Nah, he was probably too stupid to have worked for people like that. Yes, I know you're going to say they employ bruisers to do the dirty work but even bruisers have to be streetwise. Horsley was just a provincial thicko. That's just my opinion, of course.'

'Of course. We're also investigating three murders and the theft of a coffin from a village churchyard near Bath, crimes which would appear to be connected. You might well have heard about it all. A body had never been in the coffin and the funeral was arranged by the company Horsley worked for for a short while. We have yet to check whether the times coincide.'

'So where's the body?'

Patrick shrugged. 'I doubt whether anyone would do something as silly as bury it in their own back yard. Somewhere out in the sticks, no doubt. Is there anyone you're aware of who would be likely to know more about Horsley?'

After pondering the man said, 'No, sorry, I don't. I'm

really guessing but reckon he wasn't part of any particular scene around here, more of a loner.'

'How about a man called Keith Davies?'

'He's dead too, isn't he?'

'That's right – one of the murder victims.'

'Carrick came over to sound me out about him just after it happened. I didn't know the bloke. He didn't drink here – as far as I'm aware. But then again, he didn't live round here, did he? Someone said that he had his roots in London. You'd need to trawl round a few sewers there.'

'There's a big bossman in there somewhere,' Patrick continued. 'And something sufficiently valuable to make it worth while killing four people.'

'Well, there's nothing on the grapevine round here about it. I wish you luck.' And with that our informant went back to work.

'There was nothing really useful there,' I commented.

'No, but we must look at it from the point of view of raising the police profile. I intend to go into Davies's records and try to find out where his old haunts in London were with a view to paying a visit. But obviously it depends what turns up. That reminds me, we must polish up your self-defence skills, can't have you getting hurt if we do head for scumbag places.' I was feeling all warm and soppy about his concern for my safety when he absent-mindedly added, 'James'd skin me alive.'

We left, Patrick calling in at the gents on the way while I walked slowly to the car park, which was at the front. When he did not return after a suitable interval I wondered about tummy wobbles, gave him another couple of minutes and then went back to check.

From where we had been standing the gents' was approached through an archway into another bar and then out through a door that led to the exterior and rear of the building. I checked the entire interior of the pub to see if he had paused to speak to someone else but there was no sign of him. Heart thudding by now, I ran back to the door through which he had disappeared and followed my nose. It was incredibly dark outside: surely a lamp, or lamps, had failed. Then I heard unmistakable sounds coming from within a dimly lit entrance.

I assimilated the fact that every light bulb but one had been smashed in the stinking interior and that it was at least six against one, grabbed the man nearest to me, a comparative lightweight, swung him round and his head came into violent contact with a hand-drier. I was vaguely aware of him off balance, falling over his own feet and taking a header into one of the cubicles but had already got hold of someone else, by the hair: I can get really carried away by this sort of thing. He yelped, tried to twist round so I released him and chopped him across the throat. He subsided, choking.

Another two had Patrick by the arms while a third rammed punches into his body and there was yet another using his feet. I got in a much better kick, a real Jonny Wilkinson, to the front of this individual's jeans and he folded up with a piercing shriek. The others then noticed me for the first time and one made the mistake of letting go of Patrick to come in my direction. I ducked under a hand outstretched to grab me, got my fingers round his belt, heaved, twisted round, tripped him and he nosedived to join his friend, who had been struggling to his feet, in the cubicle. They both crash-landed highly satisfactorily on and into the lavatory pan.

Something caught me a glancing blow to the head and my world revolved. I curled down, ears ringing, into a protective ball and then a leg thumped backwards into me as someone in reverse gear sort of flew over, obviously trailing bits and pieces, to smash head first into a hand basin. I stayed where I was, no longer required, as the remainder were, as the saying goes, mopped up.

Patrick, gasping for breath, hauled me to my feet. He then staggered into a cubicle and threw up. All floor space seemed to be occupied by bodies, heaving and still, but I managed to step between them, grabbed a handful of paper towels, soaked them under a tap and when Patrick emerged, thrust them into his hands. But he retched and had to turn to continue helplessly vomiting.

In the end I cleaned him up and we both walked fairly tall to the car. There was an unspoken agreement between us that the incident would not be officially reported, the six left as a reminder that Carrick's troops were not to be trifled with, whether they were on home ground or not.

The questions remained, though: who, and why?

Unofficially the DCI's reaction the following morning was predictable. As Patrick had once put it in another similar situation, he 'hooted and skirled'. For quite a long time. It was only my repeated insistence that I was absolutely, quite, completely and *utterly* unscathed – besides, he was hardly likely to demand that I remove my top and bra to reveal my bruised ribs – that mitigated things a little.

Carrick fired at Patrick what was hopefully his final salvo. 'And here's me thinking you were invincible in the hand-to-hand stuff.'

Patrick, who was also bruised in the body, if not a little in the spirit, replied, 'Six against one when you're in the middle of a pee is some odds. But up to a point I agree with you – I am a bit rusty.'

'Who were they? Any idea?'

'Not the first clue. Rent-a-thugs. Someone smashed almost all the lights so I couldn't even see their faces.'

'You might at least have brought one in so we could have found out.'

'In the heat of the moment,' Patrick said grimly, 'I probably forgot that I was a copper.'

And I had wanted to get him out of there before any more of them rolled up. Patrick had been in no fit state to deal with anyone else.

Carrick looked shocked, perhaps not having realized how bad the situation had been. Then he said, 'I simply can't believe it has any bearing on the cases we're investigating. I trust Calvin too, he's the landlord, by the way. He wouldn't have been in any way responsible.'

'God, I thought his name was Blackbeard,' Patrick muttered.

'Did you recognize anyone in the pub?'

'Half of Bristol was in the pub.'

'I keep forgetting you've not been here long.' Carrick shot to his feet. 'I'll go over there. No one takes apart people who work for me and gets away with it.'

'They didn't and it's a distraction,' Patrick said, also getting up, only with a wince. 'Possibly a deliberate one. It might be more worthwhile to go and call on Horsley's mother.'

'*You* go and see the old lady. Who knows, she might know who he was working for. Then interview the funeral directors.' He made for the door.

'We have an appointment with Littlejohn and Makepeace at ten,' I reminded them both.

'OK, do it the other way about,' Carrick snapped.

The door slammed.

Patrick smiled serenely. 'Good. We're just part of the team now to be bawled out if necessary, bless his tartan reach-me-downs.'

'I do have one question for you, though.'

'What's that?'

'Has anyone shown the Tanner brothers a photograph of Peter Horsley with a view to them identifying him as the van driver on the night they dug up the coffin?'

'You know, I don't think we have.'

I blew a loud raspberry at him.

The partners were the grandsons of the original founders, both in their early forties. They were exceedingly sombre, the situation being a dreadful one for them.

We discovered that the first to greet us, Neil Makepeace, lived with his wife and two children in a hamlet two miles from Hinton Littlemoor; the other, David Littlejohn, was unmarried and had a flat in Bath. The headquarters of their business, where we had come to talk to them, was in the west of the city of Bristol, and as Neil himself observed with a very brief smile, neither of them had the inclination to live over the shop.

'My first question,' Patrick said, when the introductions

had been made, 'is how is it that you conducted Barney Stonelake's funeral when there are any number of funeral directors much nearer to home, in this case, Hagtop Farm?'

'Oh, that's easy,' said Neil. 'Mrs Stonelake's brother, George, and our fathers, set up the Hinton Littlemoor Clay Pigeon Shooting Club. Some time in the fifties, I think it was. Their people originated from round there and a couple of months ago I moved back into the area. Your father is one of the members. So, in a way, it was family. It would have been unthinkable for them to have asked anyone else to have done it.'

He looked a countryman; ruddy of complexion, bright blue of eye. David on the other hand was of slighter build, more quiet and thoughtful-looking.

'How is your father?' he now enquired.

'Well on the mend, thank you.'

'He's a fine shot. Do you shoot?'

'Sometimes,' Patrick replied. 'Just for the pot.'

Sometimes he's been known to poach pheasants with a Smith and Wesson too.

Neil then asked someone to make us coffee and the questioning resumed.

'I do understand that this is very embarrassing for you,' Patrick continued, 'but the situation is this. The coffin was removed from the grave, as you're aware, and was found empty near Oakhill. According to our forensic people no body had ever been in it, at least not for any length of time, hours perhaps but certainly not days. How could this happen?'

The partners exchanged glances. 'We simply can't explain it,' Neil said. 'The only possible explanation is that someone with access to keys got into our premises during the night on the day before the funeral. It had to be an insider, there were no signs of a break-in, which would obviously have alerted us to a problem.'

'There's no actual staff presence during the night, then?'

'No, our staff, or David or I, take it in turns to be on call. People would only be in the building if we had received a call-out.'

'Was a man called Peter Horsley working for you at that time?'

Again, there was an exchange of glances. 'I shall have to go and look that up,' Neil answered.

'Brian Stonelake intends to sue,' David said quietly when Neil had gone out of the room. 'It's a ghastly business – could ruin us when you think about it.'

Patrick got up and looked out of the rain-streaked window. The business was housed in what had been an early Victorian stables and carriage house which had belonged to a mansion long since demolished. It was a smart red-brick building that had had a sympathetically designed but modern office extension added quite recently. The original high wall to the front remained with spikes along the top to deter trespassers and access was gained through a handsome archway furnished with new, heavyweight oak doors that led into the paved yard.

'There's a fairly new and sophisticated security system,' David said into the silence, perhaps wondering if Patrick was checking the position of CCTV cameras.

'No, it had to be an insider job,' he said.

'I can assure you that neither Neil nor I were involved in this scandalous affair.'

Patrick turned to face the speaker. 'It never crossed my mind for a moment that you were.'

The other smiled nervously and said, 'Like your father, you're a slightly daunting man.'

'Oh, I can be a hell of a lot more daunting than this,' Patrick said and then mitigated the remark with a smile and soft chuckle.

'Yes,' Neil announced, returning with the coffee. 'Spot on. We were going to get rid of him anyway as he was so scruffy and downright unpleasant to everybody but he failed to turn up the following Monday.'

'And the funeral was on . . .?'

'The previous Thursday. At nine thirty. Both David and I officiated. It seemed the right thing to do.'

'I understand that coffins are transported on trolleys these days.'

'Sometimes but not always. We carried Barney.'

David said, 'But he wasn't in there, Neil.'

'God, no. I'd forgotten that for a moment.' He served the coffee.

Patrick said, 'But was it the right sort of weight? You didn't notice anything different one way or another?'

'I can't remember noticing. But you must understand it would have been the last thing we were expecting.'

'All that it contained when it was found was a small quantity of tea – used, dried-out tea leaves. A sample has been sent away for proper identification. Now, is there any way that this substance could have originated here?'

'Not a chance,' Neil said emphatically. 'No food or drink is permitted anywhere near the chapel of rest or where human remains are stored, for obvious reasons. Everything else apart, the health and safety people would go berserk.'

I said, 'People do sometimes request that items be placed in coffins, though. Did anything like that happen with the Stonelake burial, a keepsake, something Barney treasured? Anything that could have had tea leaves in its folds or pages?'

'No, there was no such request,' Neil said.

I opened my mouth to ask them about possible contamination from clothes the body had been dressed in but Patrick spoke first. 'Assuming, then, that Horsley – I'm not sure that you're aware of it but his body was fished out of the Avon a couple of days ago – somehow got hold of the keys. Would that have been easy for him to do? Could he have coped with the alarm system? What about the cameras?'

'Good heavens! No, I wasn't aware of that. We didn't have an alarm system then. Just lots of old-fashioned locks and bolts and I'm afraid bunches of keys were literally hung on nails in an office without much of a check being made on them. We'd held back until the new extension was finished so the whole place could be done, cameras and all, at the same time. There was no money kept overnight on the premises, you see.'

'And then? He would have had to arrive with transport of some kind, say a van, entered the building, surely with an accomplice, taken the body from the coffin where it been placed – what? – overnight?'

'That's right.'

'And then substituted something else of a similar weight, but we don't yet know what.'

'The funeral was early, the first that day, so we tended to get everything ready. But the casket wouldn't have been screwed down, just in case there were any last-minute instructions along the lines of what we were talking about just now – items to be placed in with the deceased and so forth.'

'They took a huge risk.'

'No, it *was* screwed down when we went to collect it,' David suddenly recollected. 'I raised hell and no one knew who had done it. But in the event it didn't matter.'

'Did you ever see Horsley with anyone else? Did he get a lift to work?'

Neil said, 'No, he just appeared. I never saw anyone drop him off. Did you, David?'

'No.'

'Did he ever mention his mother?'

Neil grimaced. 'We're talking about a man who for the most part remained sullenly silent. When he did speak it was to swear at someone or demand some kind of rights. Full of their rights, these yobs of today, aren't they? But you feel obliged to give them a chance.'

'Did you see any change in him just before the Stonelake funeral? Was he nervous? Jittery?'

But neither man had noticed anything different, Neil muttering that he might have seemed a bit more shifty-looking than normal but then again it could have been his imagination.

We had, at least, had our suspicions confirmed and established some kind of timetable.

Sitting in the passenger seat of the car Patrick looked up from making notes. 'Lunch. Loads of gravy and mashed spuds, bangers, liver, fried onions.'

'I'm glad you're feeling better.'

'Actually I hurt all over – but I'm still famished.'

132

'You're unlikely to get anything like that in a pub.'

'No, I've had my fill of pubs for a while. Whither to then, wench?'

'Home, I'll cook it for you.' ,

We had said nothing to Elspeth, or John, about the fracas of the night before but little escapes her. No questions were asked just then and, as I had half expected and shopped accordingly, both were glad on this dank and chilly day to exchange their lunch of cheese and fruit for a large plateful of hot comfort food.

'I didn't expect to see you until tonight,' Elspeth said afterwards. 'Is everything all right?' She fixed Patrick with unswerving gaze.

'Yes, but we were both hungry and cold and—' I began lamely.

'I got a bit roughed up last night,' Patrick interrupted. 'It was my fault. I'm not as fit as I used to be when I worked for D12. But Ingrid is, she rescued me and is now West Country champion of the noble sport of throwing grown men into lavatory pans.' He whooped with laughter, holding his ribs, and as he has a very infectious laugh we all ended up cackling until the tears ran down our faces.

Sometimes you have to get your laughs where you can.

'Mrs Horsley?' Patrick said to the elderly lady who anxiously peered at him around a door held on a security chain.

'Yes.'

'I'm Detective Superintendent Gillard and this lady is Ingrid, my wife and assistant. May we come in and talk to you about Peter?'

'That's a rather funny arrangement.'

'I agree, but I assure you, it's perfectly genuine.' He showed his warrant card and she took it and closed the door. When it seemed that she had decided to keep it and phone the police, fearing us to be bogus callers, the door was opened again with the chain removed.

'It looks all right,' Mrs Horsley said, giving it back. 'You'd better come in.'

The door of the tiny semidetached bungalow opened straight into the living room. It was all immaculately clean and tidy and we sat in armchairs that had hand-embroidered covers on the cushions. Fresh flowers were in a vase on a coffee table and there were others on the window ledge.

'We're very sorry about Peter,' I said. This was not a lie, everyone is sorry when a mother loses her son, whatever he had been in life.

'I failed him, really,' said Mrs Horsley sadly, seating herself. 'But it was always going to be difficult. Perhaps I'd better explain – I didn't say anything about it to the police who've been already. My husband and I fostered Peter. He was one of those abandoned babies – found in a bag in a shop doorway. We couldn't have children of our own so over the years we fostered quite a few. It seems terrible to say so but was something my Tom said from the beginning. Peter was a bad one. He had all the chances the others had but was bad right from the start. Heaven knows who his mother was, probably some poor ignorant little girl who'd had him literally thrust upon her by a nasty piece of work. I believe that, you know, horrible people often have horrible children. And now he's gone, the world got rid of him like trash as though the world knew what he was.' She wiped a stray tear away with the corner of her apron, realized she was still wearing one and, almost angrily, took it off and threw it aside.

'He'd got in with the wrong people,' Patrick said. 'Have you any idea who they were?'

'Not an inkling,' declared the lady. 'He kept everything under wraps, even with me. The only time I ever saw him in recent years was when he was broke and had nowhere to stay.'

'Did he ever mention a man called Keith Davies? Or Christopher Manley?'

Mrs Horsley's lips pursed. She was in her seventies, I thought, and although she walked with a bad limp could not be described as failing, bright darting brown eyes denoting a keen intelligence. She said, 'He once threatened me with someone he called Keith.'

'Threatened you!'

'Yes, it was when I told him I couldn't afford to keep giving him money. I knew he was spending it mostly on drink, he was staggering drunk when he came round that particular evening. He said he knew someone who'd make me change my mind; this Keith. Keith had been sent to prison for grievous bodily harm. I showed him the door and got all the locks changed the next morning so he couldn't get in – I'd always given a key to him until that day.'

'No surname was mentioned?'

'No.'

'Do you know if that was before or after he gave up his job at the undertakers'?'

'Oh, before. It was a while ago now and I only heard about the job thing from someone else. I wasn't even at home when that happened. A friend and I went to Torquay for a little bridge-playing holiday.'

'For a week?'

'Chance would be a fine thing. No, just for a long weekend. My neighbour went as well.' She smiled a little grimly in recollection. 'I think Peter must have tried to make it up to me because when I came back he'd worked on the garden. I'd been on to him for ages about the unevenness of the paving slabs, how dangerous they were, but he never did anything about it. Not until that weekend before he lost his job, or gave it up, you say. But he made a terrible mess of it and I ended up having to pay a man to put it all to rights.'

We asked if we could view the garden and duly gazed through the kitchen window over a neat rectangle of lawn, a tiny patio, a couple of shrubs and not much else. We went out there. Trees in larger and more mature gardens on the farthest boundary made the whole area very private, and high fences separated Mrs Horsley's home from those on either side. Anyone digging a makeshift grave would have gone unnoticed.

135

Ten

The body was found a matter of only six inches below the patio paving slabs and, as James Carrick observed, it could so easily have been discovered by the gardening contractor Mrs Horsley had hired to make good the botched job her son had done. Arrangements were made for her to be taken to a friend's house to stay overnight and for most of the next day, while the search and subsequent exhumation was carried out.

Although decomposed it was possible to see how the old farmer's body had been stamped on and battered, presumably with a spade, to make it fit into the shallow hole that had been dug. When I learned this I felt sick and was all for tossing the remains of the perpetrator down the nearest mine shaft, followed by several tons of cement.

Who was behind it all? Had the attack on Patrick in Bristol been connected with the case? If so, someone had seen us in the pub and acted on impulse, as surely no one had followed us there, something about which we are both very vigilant and careful. Was there any point now in going to London?

Before any decision could be made about this we received the report from Kew. It arrived by way of a phone call to Carrick, shortly to be followed by an email. The Professor of Botany admitted to becoming hugely enamoured of the task and had enlisted the help of colleagues involved in every pertinent branch of science, one of whom had access to an electron microscope. In short, and leaving aside all scientific language and Latin names, the samples of tea, one from the coffin, the other from the box at the Manleys' flat, were identical and were a very early variety not now commercially grown – we could see drawings of the plant in the Lindley Library if we so chose – which had originated in China. The sample had partially rotted before it had dried out and as microscopic salt crystals were present the conclusion had been drawn that the tea had been immersed in salt water, in an estuary or the open sea. Minute fragments of feldspar and grains of sand were also present, the former being one of the ingredients of Chinese porcelain, the other being kaolin, or china clay. None of the evidence confirmed that the sample had come from a shipwreck but that was the cautious conclusion of those involved in the investigation, as porcelain exported to Europe in the eighteenth century had been packed in tea, in itself worth a small fortune at the time, for the voyage.

I almost missed the postscript, a short paragraph to the effect that the writer apologized for getting even more carried away by the romance surrounding the find, but were the Avon and Somerset force aware that gold ingots were often loaded aboard such vessels as well? Further research would no doubt yield more information but the writer himself, very regretfully, could not spare any more time.

Elspeth had been right.

'It's coming together,' Carrick said, rubbing his hands, not in glee but because we had just come from the burial site and the weather had become bitterly cold. Blowing on his fingers, he went in the direction of the canteen, with us in tow, where we warmed ourselves on thin, salty soup of indeterminate ingredients and bread rolls that could, and probably had been, used as cannonballs. They had run out of butter.

The body had already been removed by the time Patrick and I had returned to Mrs Horsley's home but Carrick had been present since the find had been made, hence his chilled state. This apart, I thought he looked haggard, ill.

'Gold ingots,' he said thoughtfully, stirring his coffee. 'Where are they, if that is indeed what they are? Probably abroad by now.'

'That kind of thing must have a very limited market,' I

said. 'I realize that they're likely to be melted down but historical ones might be worth even more left as they are because of their provenance. If whoever has them is keeping them hidden until he can find the right buyer . . .'

'That development, having found the right buyer, might have prompted those involved to unearth them now,' Carrick said. 'Ingrid, would you go to the library this afternoon and see if you can find more info?'

It would be nice and warm in there and was only a short walk away.

'That's a good idea,' Patrick said with an 'I'll come with you' look on his face.

Carrick had other plans for him. 'I'd like you to accompany me to talk to Brian Stonelake again. I feel I ought to be the one to tell him we've found his father's body. And who knows, he might have remembered a bit more about his own criminal activities.'

I needed to pause for a short while in order to mull over the various aspects of the case before I sought out even more information. Pared right down to basics the situation so far was thus: three people, who knew one another, had been brutally and horribly murdered. Whichever way you looked at that crime alone, the method of removing them from the land of the living was lurid, unnecessarily blood-boltered and right over the top, the only 'excuse' possible being that knives are silent whereas firearms are not. But a silenced handgun would not have been heard beyond the walls of the barn. In my view whoever had done it had an obsession with knives, not to mention a thoroughly nasty turn of mind.

The victims' cars had then been discovered, burnt out, in a quarry. Subsequently, a coffin had been stolen, the body, that of the father of the man on whose farm the bodies had been found, having been substituted for something unknown but obviously valuable. Then another man, Horsley, had been found murdered in similar fashion.

'Who probably assisted at the first killings, and before that helped someone else, possibly the bossman, raid the undertakers', and could have been the van driver who met the Tanner brothers,' I said to thin air, having borrowed Carrick's office to do my thinking. 'He was then superfluous, someone who might prove awkward and had to be eliminated. He might also have demanded a share of the loot.'

If one was going to work along the lines of Brian Stonelake having been set up – it was wobbly to assume that the selection of his father's coffin as a hiding place was a coincidence but I was sticking with that for a moment – then only someone comparatively local could be responsible. As had been suggested before, whoever it was would know the lie of the land and the identity of neighbourhood villains.

I had thought it odd right from the start that the Manleys and Keith Davies had bought adjacent flats at the mill and that Davies was employed by the other two, for it was not as though the Manleys were elderly and unable to look after themselves. One got the impression that Davies had been their minder. To protect them from whom? The bossman? Others in a gang with which they had been involved? Whatever the truth, someone had caught up with them.

Known facts contradicted certain aspects of this for it appeared they had left home on that particular night of their own free will, got into their cars, and driven, independently, to the deserted barn in order to meet someone. They had then been overpowered and killed. Perhaps they had been promised a payoff or a share in criminal proceeds as a lure to get them there. That said, the coffin had not then been recovered so it was likely that none of the three knew exactly where whatever it was had been concealed.

And, the thought shot into my mind, *had* anyone yet shown the Tanner brothers a photograph of Peter Horsley?

I gazed around. Where was the file? I had a quick look and it was not with several others in a wire tray on Carrick's exceedingly tidy desk, so I went to see if I could find Lynn Outhwaite.

'The DCI might have it in his document case,' she told me when I found her.

'Where are the Tanners now?' I asked her.

'They've been released on police bail.'

'Has anyone shown a photo of Horsley to them to see if they recognize him as the man driving the van?'

'I'm not sure. I don't think so. Why don't you ask Carrick?'

'Any chance of a copy of the photo in case no one has?'

'Look, you mustn't go tangling with that pair.'

'Sergeant Outhwaite, I've tangled, as you call it, with far worse people than that pair of beer-bellied boneheads. Do I get a photo or not?'

She found one for me.

Obeying orders to the letter I went to the public library first and spent about an hour and a half researching shipwrecks in the South China Sea area, as I already knew that was where most of the wrecks had been found, making notes. I was torn as to whether I should contact Carrick with regard to the photo as failing to do so might result in a wasted trip. But better that than be forbidden to go in search of the bovine duo.

I reckoned that the Tanners would have gone straight back to work, for beer money if nothing else, so I walked back to the nick to get the car and set off for the quarry. It looked as if it might snow, the sky a leaden grey, the wind a bitter north-easter.

'They've gone and good riddance,' said the man on the gate, a different one, giving me the impression he would have spat in the road by way of a further comment had I been a bloke. 'Been given the boot.' He gave me a sideways look. 'You don't look like the sort of person normally to be asking after them.'

'I'm not *quite* the police,' I told him, not being yet qualified to carry a warrant card, if indeed, I decided to go that far, 'but nevertheless I'm checking up on them and the trouble they've got themselves into.'

'Try their home. Don't ask me where that is, though.'

'It's all right. I know where they live.'

Colliers Row, Hinton Littlemoor, someone had said.

On impulse, I showed him the photograph. 'Have you ever

seen this man hanging around here, perhaps waiting for the Tanners?'

He had not and I thanked him and drove away.

Colliers Row had probably been built during the Victorian heyday of the mining industry in the Somerset coalfields and was a terrace of limestone cottages with steeply sloping rear gardens set high above Hinton Littlemoor. One could reflect on the attitudes of those times: workers' homes were sited at this spot, open to the elements, because no one higher up the social scale would want to live here. Even today and with pine and fir trees planted on the stony ground behind them it was a bleak place.

There was one cottage out of the eight that appeared not to have been modernized, still with what could be an outside lavatory and the garden a sea of weeds and rubbish. This, surely, was where the Tanners lived. It was strange that two grown-up brothers continued to live together in what must have been their childhood home.

The road climbed from where I had paused and then curved sharply round before dividing at a little green in front of the houses, the right-hand fork providing access to them and then rejoining the road at the far end of the terrace. I parked by the unkempt cottage. The rotting gate moved only reluctantly on its rusting hinges but I shoved it open and banged on the front door: the bell did not seem to work. Almost immediately a woman put her head out of an upstairs window of the house next door.

'There's no one there, luv. The poor old dear's in a home now and it's going to be sold.'

'I'm looking for the Tanner brothers,' I said.

'Oh, they're right down at the end. Isn't this place a disgrace? My husband's trying to get something done about it. The council got rid of the squatters weeks ago but no one's come to clean up the mess the filthy little beasts made.'

I mentally apologized to the Tanners – whose names were Jethro and Vince, I had learned from the file – thanked her and walked down to the far end of the row.

This house too gave every appearance of being deserted,

all the curtains drawn, and again I rang the bell to no avail. Banging on the door drew no response either. A sixth sense telling me that someone was at home, I went down a side way towards the rear of the house. The path was host to quite a few motorbikes, some seemingly intact, others in pieces, a lot of oily patches on the ground, tools everywhere.

The back door, within a small ramshackle porch, was ajar but virtually barricaded off by a strange collection of items; an ancient wooden clothes horse, sundry garden tools and what Patrick would call a 'handrolic' mower. It occurred to me as I was forced to stop that they were arranged in such a fashion that the merest touch would send the whole lot crashing down. Was this, in effect, a makeshift burglar alarm?

I leaned carefully over and rapped on one of the glass panes of the door. Then, when nothing happened, took a hoe that was not part of the fortifications and pushed the door open wider with it, quite difficult as it was oddly heavy.

An enormous bundle of old iron weights, tied by their handles, crashed down from somewhere above it.

I stared at the hole in the kitchen floor in a kind of frozen horror for what seemed ages but it could have only been a couple of seconds for I had all guns blazing when two huge outlines materialized in the gloomy interior.

'Are you bloody well trying to kill someone?' I bellowed at them.

The brothers sidled like nervous horses.

'You got the other blokes with you?' asked one in what, for him, was probably a whisper but came out as a hoarse bark.

I tossed a mental coin. 'No,' I replied, adding tersely and sarcastically, 'You're quite safe.'

'What d'you want?'

I gestured towards the splintered boards and the iron-mongery – of the kind once used in greengrocers' to sell stones, if not half-hundredweights, of potatoes – which were slowly subsiding into the cavity beneath the floor. 'What's all this about, then?'

'Funny phone calls.'

'Don't tell 'er!' bawled his brother.

'Which one of you is Vince?' I asked.

'Me,' said the one who had answered my first question.

'Vince,' I said gently. 'You could have been on a murder charge right now. What funny phone calls?'

'Thought they might be from that bloke you were with who chucked the drill bit at us.'

'That's Patrick. He's my husband – and a copper. We were with DCI Carrick.'

He registered surprised. 'He looks like a hired killer.'

'Only when he worked for MI5 – or if you harm one hair of my head.' Nothing was actually lost by bunging that one in, I decided.

Jethro burst out with, 'Course he's a copper, stupid, he grilled me afterwards.'

Vince shrugged. 'I got Carrick. How was I to know?'

'Tell me about the phone calls,' I requested.

Silence.

'I only came out here to show you a photograph,' I wheedled. 'Please tell me about the phone calls. They're obviously threatening. You might need police protection.'

'Some geezer said not to talk to the cops – or else.'

'You don't have a lot of choice as you're already in trouble for digging up the coffin,' I told him impatiently, getting a bit fed up with talking to them across a palisade. These were, after all, the people who had desecrated the churchyard and so thoroughly upset my in-laws. 'We've found what should have been the rightful occupant, by the way.'

The pair moved a little closer to the door.

'You have?' said the other man, Jethro. 'Where?'

I produced the photograph and held it out. 'Buried in this man's mother's garden. Know him?'

It was snatched.

'No,' said Vince.

'The man who met you with the van,' I prompted.

'No, that wasn't him,' Vince said again. 'Not that we really saw his face. It was dark, like.'

'Tell me the truth,' I pleaded.

143

Pointing to the photo, Jethro said in strangled tones, 'That's the bloke who was fished out of the effin' river, innit? I wondered where I'd seen that 'orrible face before.' He drew himself up. 'Lady, I don't care if your man is handy with all kinds of hardware, we ain't saying no more.' He thrust the photo at me. 'We don't know nothing else. We didn't see who the bloke with the van was.'

'But it wasn't him,' Vince added.

'But if you didn't see his face how do you *know* that?' I bawled at him.

'He was older. He spoke, like.'

'Is it the same voice as whoever's making the threatening phone calls?'

But the pair had gone back into the gloomy interior, Jethro manhandling his brother out of the room to prevent him from saying more.

'Look, we can put a tap on the line and trace the calls,' I shouted after them, not about to follow. You do not corner grizzly bears unless well armed.

There seemed nothing for it but to go and fetch a big gun and I was not in the least squeamish about unleashing him on them. Then I remembered that Patrick was no longer permitted to take people apart, not even a brace younger than him and almost twice his size.

'Sod it,' I muttered and hurled aside the barricade.

The fanfare of collapsing impedimenta petered out as I went inside, and I found myself in a small kitchen. A short hallway led into a living room, probably at one time two but now knocked into one. That was where I found them.

A very, very old lady sat in an armchair on one side of the fireplace and on the other a young woman held a baby, her feet up on a battered sofa, sharing it with another woman who was probably about ten years older than me. Jethro and Vince stood nearby, propping up the walls. In the dim light, the curtains closed, the group looked like a peasant family in a Dutch painting.

'I'll arrange police protection,' I promised.

'Oh, the lads'll go for sure,' cackled the old woman in a

flat loud voice that suggested she was profoundly deaf. 'They'll do a runner and leave us women to fend for ourselves.'

'No, we won't, Gran,' one of the men bellowed at her, I was not sure which one.

'Well, your bloody useless father did and we never saw him again. What's different now?'

Lynn Outhwaite had reported to her boss the destination of my intended sortie. I did not blame or criticize her for this as it was her duty to prevent colleagues, even in the loosest meaning of the term, from coming to harm. There was yet another debriefing in Carrick's office but it immediately became clear that he had decided against getting really annoyed with me, not for the moment anyway.

'Did you find out anything useful at the library?' he enquired of me in a fashion that suggested he did not think I had bothered to go there.

'Quite a bit,' I replied, digging out the notes I had made. 'The librarian found me a book that told me everything I wanted to know. There was a full account of one of the wrecks, the *Geldermalsen*, which I took particular note of as the ship carried gold ingots. But, obviously, those were all accounted for at the time and safely auctioned off.

'I don't know how much you want to hear,' I went on, 'but it's all very interesting. In the eighteenth century, porcelain, and tea, were transported from China's hinterland to Canton and from there to Java in Chinese trading vessels where they were loaded, the china actually packed into the crates of tea, into ships belonging to the Dutch East India Company. Sometimes the trading vessels caught fire or were hit by storms and sank before they got there or, as in the case of the *Geldermalsen*, the Indiamen suffered the same fate on the way to European ports, usually Amsterdam. The cargo of porcelain, plus anything else that was in the hold, ended up being buried by a thick layer of sand and tea. There were six hundred thousand pounds of tea on that ship alone, plus a hundred and twenty-five gold ingots, eighteen of which were the very rare ones referred to as Nanking shoes. Several wrecks have been discovered since, including one known as the Vung Tau Cargo that went down off the Vietnamese coast at the end of the seventeenth century. We must find out if any museums or private collections have been raided within the past couple of years and what was taken.'

'How much did the stuff from the *Geldermalsen* fetch at auction?' Carrick asked.

'Over ten million pounds.'

'That is not peanuts.'

'It wasn't,' I agreed. 'The porcelain was just about as valuable as the gold.' /

'Thank you.' There was a little silence and then he went on, 'I understand you went to see the Tanners afterwards.'

'Yes, I did. I showed them the picture of Peter Horsley and they said he wasn't the man who met them with the van to pick up the coffin.'

'Do you believe that?'

'Yes, I think so. Vince was all for saying more but Jethro is the one really twitched by some phone calls they've been getting. He—'

Predictably, James interrupted with, 'They've received threats?'

'I was coming to that in a minute.'

'Sorry.'

'Vince thought the man they met was older than Horsley. From his voice. They both refused to say whether it could be the same person who's been making the calls, which have told them not to talk to the police, or else.'

'They could be making it up.'

'That crossed my mind too but I think you ought to ask someone to keep an eye on the house. Three women and a child appear to live there as well and Grandma thinks the men'll do a runner just like their dad did. Oh, and I was followed all the way there and back by someone driving a blue hatchback. I couldn't get the number – I think it had been partly obscured in some way, or muddied up.'

Patrick, who was present but so far had taken no part in

the proceedings, emerged from deep thought: or it could have been one of his most-systems-awake cat-naps that he perfected while serving as an undercover soldier. 'Where was this vehicle while you were inside the Tanners' place?' he wanted to know.

'I'm not sure. I only realized it was following me on the return journey. I mean, it's quite common for someone behind you to be going to the same destination on one leg of a journey. So I did a couple of small detours when I noticed it again on the way back and he, or she, stuck with me.'

'And when you turned into the car park here?' Carrick said.

'Just paused and then speeded off.'

'It was a pity you couldn't get the registration.'

'Did you get anything out of Brian Stonelake?' I went on to ask.

Patrick stretched his long frame. 'He came clean on the stolen horse harness and other bits and pieces we found in his tractor shed by the house. He admitted eyeing up places where he sold logs or hay, casing the joint as they say in old movies, and either lifting things there and then when no one was looking or returning during the night. A bloke in Gloucester usually took the stuff off his hands but he's apparently helping the police with their enquiries right now into something more serious and is on remand – he is, James checked – so Stonelake was stuck with the booty.'

Carrick said, 'But, according to him, he didn't steal the silverware and equestrian figures and was merely looking after them for someone else. For a consideration, of course. He gave us a name but it means nothing to me or the computer, so until he comes up with something better he's down for those thefts too. But as far as the murders are concerned, which of course we're much more interested in, he's still insisting he knows nothing about them and was not remotely involved.'

'If it is true that he's tricked his mother into changing her will so he gets everything, the sooner the place is sold and he can squirrel the money away somewhere,' I said, 'perhaps abroad, the better for him in case his sisters find out. The last thing he needs is a protracted murder investigation at the property.'

'I'd forgotten about that,' Carrick admitted. 'But we don't know if it's gospel that he's swindled his sisters out of their share. And, frankly, is it any of our business?'

'The police aren't the nation's conscience but upholders of the law,' Patrick intoned. 'No, it isn't any of our business.' He smiled sadly. 'Sorry, just quoting a lecture we raw recruits were given.' He leapt to his feet. 'That reminds me!' He headed for the door.

'Where are you going?' I called.

'To find out what happened to that dog!'

'There wasn't sufficient evidence of cruelty for a case to be brought against Stonelake,' Carrick shouted at the open doorway.

Patrick reappeared. 'No?'

'Apparently the RSPCA vet said that its fur was all matted and dirty and although on the thin side the animal hadn't actually been starved. It was a bit bruised on its back and one hind leg but that wasn't enough to prosecute the owner. They did interview Stonelake, who told them that he hadn't kicked or beaten it but it kept running back to the farm and he thought it had been hit a glancing blow by a car.'

'He was still going to shoot it,' Patrick said.

Carrick grimaced. 'Farmers shoot old dogs all the time.'

'I gave him twenty quid for it.'

'He doesn't appear to have mentioned that.'

'So what'll happen now?'

'Normally it would be put up for rehoming straight away.'

'But it isn't going to be?'

'No, it's got a problem with a claw that will mean a small op. And they'll neuter it at the same time as well as make sure its up to date with jabs so it'll have to stay in the kennels for perhaps a week longer.'

'I see.'

'I did tell them that you were interested in having it.'

Patrick came back into the room. 'I don't usually do things like this,' he said and gave Carrick a bear hug.

After all the difficulties this small episode was gratifying. For the moment, being followed by someone driving a blue car faded from my mind.

Eleven

The sense of relief was not to last for long. It actually existed for about five minutes and was extinguished by the arrival of the Area Crime Prevention Officer in the shape of an intimidatingly large superintendent from HQ at Portishead. Patrick and I were banished from Carrick's office with a dismissive flick of the great man's hand, the door virtually slammed on our heels. The ensuing grilling Carrick got on the progress of the murders-case investigation was absolutely nothing to do with the DCI being taken ill that night and admitted to hospital with a serious infection.

'It's in the exit wound where he was shot,' Patrick reported, throwing on his bathrobe. He had taken the call from Joanna and it was very early the next morning. 'The docs say it must have been brewing for ages and has never healed up properly. I shall go to the nick to do some brainstorming on the cases in hand and if that arrogant bastard who turned up yesterday arrives I'll interpret the "acting" bit of my title as permission to lop his bloody head off.'

'Patrick,' I said, to a breeze as he departed downstairs.

'Yes?' This came from somewhere out on the landing.

'You're in sole charge of the nick if he doesn't roll up.'

'Good, in the army I would have been permitted to command a soddin' *regiment!*'

Needless to say the crime, or crimes, did not get solved that day, Patrick having to take time to familiarize himself with everything else that was going on, things with which Carrick had not involved us. There were two phone calls from Joanna during the morning, relaying messages and information we ought to know about from her husband who, characteristically, was fretting about work. He was stable, she told us, but not yet responding to the drugs he was being given.

I spent most of the day in James's office, answering his phone and reading the case notes in the files on his desk. One useful piece of information did surface late in the afternoon when an email arrived from Interpol, obviously in response to an enquiry that Carrick had made. It related that just over two years previously, a dive boat working on the wreck of a Chinese junk that had gone down in 1746 in the South China Sea off Bunguran Island had been attacked by pirates, one of several raids on shipping in that area. A quantity of recently recovered gold ingots, probably around one hundred and fifty in number and including some of the rare Nanking shoes, plus several small pieces of gold-decorated porcelain had been stolen, the latter thought to have been snatched as souvenirs by the pirates as they escaped back to their boat. The Malayan captain of the dive boat had been killed and another member of his crew wounded in an exchange of shots as they tried to fend off the boarders. To the knowledge of the sender of the email none of the stolen goods had yet been recovered, although undercover sources suggested, tentatively, that criminals, fences, in Holland might have handled the gold en route to the UK.

I emailed back to ask about identification marks and also if, as the items had only just been raised from the seabed, there was a likelihood of tea still adhering to them – if indeed the cargo had been thus packed. An hour later I had my answers; there had been no time to clean it and it had left the dive boat in a wooden box where it had been tossed by the thieves together with sand, seaweed, no doubt a few small dead marine creatures and yes, tea. The pirate vessel had apparently been masquerading as a fishing boat that had, in hindsight, been shadowing the divers for days.

'That's one piece of good news,' Patrick said after I had told him. He had appeared with two mugs of tea. 'Can't we identify the gold any further – marks and so forth?'

'Yes, I've just received the answer to that question. There

are marks but they wouldn't necessarily be unique to the stolen ingots. We might get more information by consulting an expert.'

He seated himself. 'There's more to running a nick than meets the eye. One thing's certain though and most people have mentioned it: Carrick's been under par for a couple of weeks now. Don't forget that when we saw him last, before starting this lark, was when he was really weak and just recovering. He came back to work far too soon. And because this nick's still a DI light . . .' He reached for the phone. 'Bugger everything. I'm going to do what I would have done before landing in civvy street – raise hell.'

And he did. Listening to him, politely observing all the protocols, but acidly putting across his points to whoever was the superior officer of the man who had visited Carrick the previous day, I knew that he had found his feet.

'That's it,' Patrick said, having slapped down the phone. 'We're getting a temporary DI from Bristol CID as of tomorrow morning, someone whom apparently James knows.'

'That still officially leaves you in charge.'

'Only on paper. I'm to confer with him and to take orders if necessary.'

'If necessary!'

'I think that's meant as a substitute for pistols at dawn. But we've got to catch the murderer. Pronto. He made it sound as though it's a condition for my carrying on.'

DI Jonathan Bromsgrove was in his mid-forties, called Patrick 'sir' and asked him if he would care to carry on with the murders case while he himself dealt with other outstanding work, assisted by Sergeant Outhwaite. Patrick replied that that would suit him fine but we would consult with him should we need advice and if everything became manic. This arrangement got everything off on a very nice footing.

'I would like to tackle this in a less conventional way,' Patrick said to me quietly as we left Bromsgrove to get his feet under Carrick's desk on the grounds that that room was where all the general information was held, plus the DCI's computer for which we had asked James the password. He felt weak, he had told us in response to the second query. Lousy, in fact. Bloody horrible, no less.

It was Joanna who later told us that MRSA was suspected but not yet confirmed.

'Less conventional?' I repeated.

'Go sort of covert,' he whispered as though the walls might have ears and report the heresy.

'Find the gold, you mean.'

'We don't *know* that there is any gold. It's all guesswork.'

'We can't do as we used to and break into places.'

'It wouldn't matter if we broke into crooks' lairs.'

'Yes, it would. Because now you have to obtain evidence by above-board means.'

'OK. But the police do go undercover to try to buy weapons from illegal arms dealers. Or drugs from drugs traffickers.'

'Entrapment,' I murmured.

'Yes.'

'So you want to pretend to be a dodgy sort of antiques dealer asking around in the wrong places to buy Nanking shoes? Patrick, the gold, if it exists, might not be in criminal hands by now but belonging to perfectly innocent people.'

'This sting operation – I admit – rests on the supposition that whatever was in the coffin is still being hoarded by the ungodly. First though, before we do anything else, I think we ought to go right back to the beginning and return to Hinton Mill. That's where it all started. And then perhaps revisit the murder barn.'

In the ground-floor lobby of the mill we came upon an exceedingly tanned and smartly dressed elderly lady carrying in her shopping.

'Mrs Dewitte?' Patrick asked.

Laden, she turned with a slight frown. 'Yes?'

'Police,' Patrick said. 'Do let me take those for you.'

'Oh God, I haven't exceeded some ruddy speed limit or other, have I?' she cried.

'Not to my knowledge,' she was told.

He ended up by emptying the BMW's boot of shopping, mostly designer-label clothes and shoes by the look of the carrier bags, and carrying it all into the flat.

'You've no idea how ghastly it is to come back into this horrible weather,' Mrs Dewitte declared. 'I've left my husband out there. That's in the Drakensberg Mountains area of South Africa in case you don't know already. We've a house there. Alastair's older than me and not very well. But we've a buyer for this place so someone had to come home and deal with it. D'you want some coffee? I'm dying for a cup. I know I mustn't offer you anything stronger as you're on duty,' she finished by saying with a mischievous smile.

At nine thirty in the morning too.

The coffee was superb, freshly roasted and ground from a grocer's in Green Street, Bath, which she made a point of recommending to us. 'So handy, you've no idea. You can buy shotguns, lovely fish, the best sausages in the world and coffee all in about ten yards.' Then she laughed, a big masculine guffaw. 'So what's this all about then?'

'How long have you been back?'

'Since the night before last.'

'So you might not have heard that your neighbours directly above you have been murdered.'

She hardly batted an eyebrow. 'What, Mr and Mrs Misery? No, have they?'

'And their acquaintance across the landing, Keith Davies. We think they might have been involved in criminal activities.'

'Well, you don't have to be terribly intelligent to work that one out. I've never seen a more skulking, secretive bunch of no-hopers. Not even in Africa, and we had the Mau-Mau to deal with there when Alastair was in the colonial service. How did it happen?'

Patrick told her, not sparing details. He then followed it up with a short résumé of what had occurred since.

'But it's just like a ruddy novel!' she exclaimed. 'Oh, I know whom you mean by that farmer. He's the one who sells logs, isn't he? We don't have an open fire here but the Manleys

154

did – stored them in their garage and trailed all the bits of moss, twigs and mud across the hall and up the stairs. No, I caught farmer chappie trying to peer into one of my windows when he delivered some logs one day. Gave him a real piece of my mind, I can tell you and he took himself off at the double. Mr Brandon across the hall came out to see what was going on and backed me up.'

'Did you ever see any visitors the people upstairs had?' I asked. Stonelake had lied about that, then.

'No, it was like a grave up there, if you'll excuse the expression. Two of our windows are on the side where the cars are parked so one can't help but be aware of people's activities sometimes. I never saw them out there with anyone else who might be a friend or relation. The residents do tend to leave their cars outside in the bit reserved for visitors and not put them away and I suppose I'm just as guilty of that.'

'Do you know the people who live on the top floor?' I asked.

'Yes, sort of, but we are away a lot. Pascal and Lorna asked us up for drinks once when we were around. They seem a nice pair but you don't really get to know people at one meeting. I have to say I did find Pascal a trifle – what shall I say? – saturnine. But he might have just been having an off day. I met the other young lady, Tamsin, I think her name is, up there too. She's hoping to marry something in uniform. More coffee?'

We declined and prepared to leave, thanking her for her time.

'Oh, my pleasure. And people say nothing ever happens in the countryside! I hope you find the gold. Have you looked in all the garages?' She grinned at us. 'Where there's mucky logs . . .'

'They did, didn't they?' I said when we were back in the lobby.

'Not all of them. Carrick's team searched the Manleys' and Davies had rented his out to someone else but they didn't get warrants to look in all the others.'

We went outside, pausing in the parking area. A couple of inches of snow had fallen overnight and it was still very cold.

'Let's retrace their final footsteps working with what we know took place,' Patrick said. 'It's possible they didn't go directly to the barn but met up with others first. Peter Horsley, for example. By no stretch of the imagination was he Mr Big. Nor were the Tanner brothers, not that we've yet thought they were implicated in the murders. There was also the man who drove the van and met them to take possession of the coffin, an older man if one is to believe them. He might have been at the barn. Was he the person behind it all?'

'I still wonder why they took two cars,' I said. 'Davies often drove the Manleys around.'

'The cars were disposed of afterwards so I reckon someone suggested they went independently. It meant that no risks were run of being spotted by coming back here to collect the remaining one.'

'She didn't actually say so but Mrs Dewitte doesn't seem to have liked Pascal Dupointe when she first met him.'

'Mm, saturnine, she said. When we spoke to them he and Lorna disagreed about the time they'd come back from the pub on the night of the murders. We didn't check whether they'd actually eaten at the Ring O'Bells.'

'There might not even be a record of them having done so if they didn't book a table and paid cash.'

We had wandered while we conversed and ended up by the row of garages. There was absolutely nothing to see; all secured, all tidy.

Patrick sighed. 'Where to?'

'We're retracing the murder victims' last journey,' I reminded him. Afterwards I wondered if I had not needed to do so as the question could have referred to something else that was on his mind. Was it to ask himself if we would ever get a lead?

Daylight did the barn no favours, revealing years of dirt. Rubbish in the shape of old fertilizer and feed bags, coils of used barbed wire clogged with sheep's wool and bits of old fence posts were thrown into the farthest corners with abandon. The only tidy area was where all traces of the killings had been removed, the relevant section of concrete having been steam-cleaned and then spread with sawdust to absorb any remaining moisture.

We walked around, a little way apart, whether we liked it or not absorbing the indescribable deadness of the place. Indeed, when I spoke my voice did not echo as one might expect in such a large enclosed space but also was deadened, as in a tomb.

'Tainted ground,' I said, recollecting what Shaun Brown had said. Somewhere below my feet were the foundations of the old barn, a building that had also seemed to have been fated to be associated with death. Suddenly I could understand how people can be overcome with panic in places where horrible things have happened.

'I shall ask Dad to come and say a few words in here when he's stronger,' Patrick said, almost absent-mindedly. 'The Manleys and Davies *must* have known their killers, who suddenly took them unawares and overpowered them. Otherwise three people would have stood a good chance of getting away in a place this size.'

'Davies could have been taken out first,' I suggested. 'He was the only one with any real ability to fight back.'

'Yes, you're probably right. Shall we spend quite a lot of time looking for anything SOCO might have missed?'

I thought it probably a waste of time but did not wish to be negative and acquiesced as gracefully as I was able when Patrick suggested that we split up, divide the floor area into imaginary narrow sections and work our way along them. Nobly, he offered to tackle the side of the building where most of the rubbish was strewn.

It took almost the rest of the day and we did not even stop for lunch, just drinks of water, cupping our hands under a tap that was still working.

'Nothing,' I said, eventually subsiding, cold, tired, hungry and filthy, on to an upturned granite cattle trough. I looked at my watch; four fifty and getting dark. Patrick, judging by the sounds, was still ferreting through Heaven knew what muck and junk of ages over on the far side. Five minutes or so later he came over, pulling off the gloves we were glad we had had with us, and sat alongside me.

'Discounting farm-associated stuff I found one old penny, a rusty penknife and two dead rats,' he reported.

'A dented pressure cooker, a beer bottle, a ten-year-old knitting magazine, one dead rat and a photo of Elvis,' I said. 'I win.'

We sat for a moment in dejected silence.

'Beer,' Patrick said all at once.

'We can't go in the pub as dirty as this.'

'People have been going in the Ring O'Bells covered in the soil of honest labour for three hundred years. Besides, we didn't get around to asking questions there the other evening and can also check to see if Lapointe and Lorna Church really did have a meal on the night of the murders.'

As it was we thumped most of the dust off one another, had a wash of sorts under the tap and were reasonably fit to be seen when we crossed the threshold of the pub. Patrick and I are always treated with deference by the landlord, his wife and the local people, something that initially made me feel uncomfortable, but that is the way of rural England: the squire might have gone but the village parson and his wife remain, and in John and Elspeth's case are much respected.

Word had got around that Patrick had a new career and there was no need for him to show his credentials. The reservations book was immediately consulted and did indeed show that the couple had booked a table and eaten in the small side restaurant on the night in question. The landlord even remembered that they had left at just before ten thirty, one of the last to do so. He thought they had had a bit of a tiff on the way out.

'It's true, you can't do anything in a village without everyone knowing about it,' Patrick said, coming up for air from his pint.

We returned to the rectory at five forty-five.

'Is there time for a quick shower?' Patrick asked Elspeth around the kitchen door.

'You know I never expect people to eat if they're grubby,' she retorted. 'But please don't be long.'

I heard this exchange as I was on my way upstairs and also the strain in her voice. I went back down.

'What's wrong?' Patrick was asking his mother as I entered the kitchen. 'Is Dad OK?'

'Yes. Look, we'll talk about it after you've eaten.'

Her son seated himself at the kitchen table, immovable as an alp.

'Oh, all right, but I'm sure it's only a silly joke on someone's part. It might even be my fault and I'm going daft, senile or something . . .'

Elspeth then did something I had never, ever, in all the years I had known her, seen her do. She wept.

Sometimes even a wife and daughter-in-law can be an intrusion and I instantly moved to leave the room as Patrick shot to his feet and put his arms around her.

'No, please stay, Ingrid,' Elspeth sobbed. 'You're always such a great help to me.'

I really thought that we were talking of nothing more serious than something being mislaid and then turning up in a strange place, that she was physically and mentally exhausted after John's illness, or had had a very bad day generally. It happens to all women, whatever their age. I made myself useful and watched over the cooking.

Patrick sat her down in the chair he had just vacated and fetched her a glass of sherry.

'You know, it occurred to me the other day that we seem to rely on alcohol an awful lot in this household,' Elspeth said perfectly seriously after blowing her nose and taking a sip. 'I mean, something goes wrong and we reach for the bottle.'

'Only if it's just before dinner,' Patrick said lightly. 'Other times we call the doctor, talk about it or go to church. Just like a lot of other people. Please tell me what's worrying you.'

She seemed to brace herself, looked him straight in the eye and said, 'I found some tea.'

'Tea?'

'Upstairs. In my clothes drawer.'

I discovered that I had gone cold and shaky but managed to carry on with what I was doing. When I turned round again Patrick had seated himself and was holding Elspeth's hands across the table.

She cleared her throat and whispered, 'In with my underclothes, actually.'

Patrick looked at me rather wildly.

'Would you like to show me, Elspeth?' I asked quietly.

The pair of us went upstairs after I had removed a sample bag and gloves from Patrick's briefcase. Elspeth immediately sat on the bed and I noticed that she was shivering.

'Who's been here today?' I asked, putting on the gloves and opening the drawer she had indicated.

'Only some members of the PCC to see John. Oh, and it was my turn to host a committee meeting for the WI. There were only seven of us, the other three sent apologies as they're unwell or away.'

The tea, which to me looked exactly the same as that which we had found already, had been sprinkled evenly between the layers of undergarments. No rough handling seemed to have taken place which, in a way, made it worse. I looked carefully around me on the carpet but none seemed to have been spilled there.

'When did you find it?'

'Only about twenty minutes ago.'

'Have you looked anywhere else?' I enquired, placing a small amount in the bag.

'No, I couldn't bring myself to.'

'D'you mind if I do?'

'Of course not.'

I inspected all the other drawers in the room, including John's, and then, quickly, in the bottoms of the wardrobes and found no more.

I said, 'Elspeth, Patrick will have no choice but to ask a police photographer to take pictures.'

She took a deep breath. 'It would be silly of me to worry

160

that photos of the rector's wife's knickers will be in the *Bath Evening Chronicle.*'

'Not a chance,' I said.

She stood up. 'I must see to the dinner. It'll be spoilt.' The tears were ready and waiting. 'We don't tend to lock the doors during daylight hours, you know. We've prided ourselves on always being here for people, available. Perhaps we're fools.'

'No,' I said. 'You're not.'

'My dear, I don't think I can sleep in here tonight. Not in this house, really. Would it be all right if John and I went to an hotel?'

'You must do exactly as you please. Have you told John?'

'Yes, but you know what men are like. He seemed to think I'd somehow got some tea in with the clean laundry as I'd been making a brew while there was a pile of things on the kitchen table that I'd just taken out of the dryer. But, as you know, I don't make tea there but on the worktop by the side of the Rayburn. Who would lift a heavy kettle full of boiling water halfway across the room?'

Together, we went downstairs to find Patrick mashing the potatoes.

'I'm sorry, I can't eat anything,' Elspeth said. 'Perhaps the pair of you would serve up when you've had your shower.'

'And if I'd said the same to you in similar circumstances?' Patrick queried.

'I'm sorry, I just feel a bit – sort of violated,' she whispered.

Ruthlessly Patrick said, 'In the past I've arrived on your doorstep literally more dead than alive, bleeding like a pig and half off my head with pain. I didn't actually ever mention some of the things a group of Hell's Angels did to me. But I still made myself take the sustenance on offer. Please eat a little or some idiot will have won, hands down.'

'Put like that . . .' Elspeth murmured. 'Go on, away with you and get clean and I'll carve the chicken.' She finished her sherry in one and unsteadily sloshed some more in her glass. 'There you are, you see. Well on the road to ruin.' And laughed in a sobbing kind of way.

Patrick rang Manvers Street and a scene-of-crime officer and photographer arrived very shortly afterwards. They would be in the house for quite a while but there was no need for the householders to meet them if they did not wish to and the acting detective superintendent would be asking the questions.

'Please give me a list of everyone who was in this house on official business today,' Patrick requested of John when dinner was over. 'Names and addresses.' He had carried on behaving normally, deliberately adhering to family routines to avoid further upset but underneath, I knew, was raging at this latest development.

'It might mean a phone call with regard to the WI ladies,' Elspeth said. 'Hazel, the secretary, keeps that information, although I know where most of them live. Patrick, you *can't* think that –'

Patrick had found the phone book. 'We have to eliminate people from the inquiry, that's all. Any preferences?' he went on to ask her. 'For tonight, I mean.'

'What about tonight?'

'Ingrid said you'd like to go to an hotel. It's a good idea. I'll take you when we've filled in a few details.'

'It seems cowardly, running away.'

'You're not running away. Danny will be dusting for fingerprints and so forth for an hour or so yet in your room and it would do you good to have a change of scenery.'

'Go away?' John said, bringing a folder. 'What on earth for?'

'Because someone's been in our room,' Elspeth said. 'It's like being burgled and I feel horrible about it. Suppose whoever it is comes back?'

'You are sure nothing's been taken?' I said.

'Nothing,' she told me.

'Well, I'm hanged if I'm going anywhere,' John rumbled. 'Suppose I put the shotgun under the bed? That make you feel better?'

'No, much worse,' his wife said. 'It might go off or something.'

'While you're deciding,' Patrick said somewhat heavily, 'perhaps you'd be good enough to try to remember, both of you, which of those people who were here today were not under your gaze for the whole time.'

Briskly, John said, 'The PCC meeting was this morning at ten thirty and is always held in my study. It usually goes on for about an hour and a half and we have a break for coffee and biscuits at eleven fifteen. Your mother makes it and has it ready and I usually fetch it from the kitchen on a tray. But as I'm still not supposed to carry anything heavy yet Lawrence Fielding, the treasurer, came with me. No one but us two can have left the room while we did so this morning as we were only away for about half a minute, but someone did a little later. Visitors use the downstairs cloakroom.'

'Who was it?' Patrick asked.

'Vernon Latimer, the chairman.'

'And other than that you had everyone else in sight.'

'Yes.'

'The WI committee meeting was this afternoon,' Elspeth said. 'At three. I always have them in the dining room so people can spread papers out on the table. We have tea and cakes at about four and everyone's out of my sight while I organize it although someone usually offers to help carry trays.'

'Were there any visits to the cloakroom afterwards?'

'Yes, I think a couple of ladies went away for a couple of minutes but I couldn't tell you who they were as I was talking to Maggie Ruislip about our planned trip to London.'

'What about the rest of the day? Any visitors?'

'Only the postman with a parcel for John. Oh, and someone selling something he called peat-free, organic compost. I had some last year and it was terrible. It must have been made from unsterilized ground-up forestry waste – I had mushrooms and toadstools coming up in all my houseplants.'

'I think we're just interested in people who came indoors or might have done so when your back was turned,' Patrick said.

'No one else,' Elspeth said.

'Was the front door unlocked for most of the day?'

'Yes, it must have been. And the kitchen door into the garden. I'm in and out all the time.'

'It's very unwise when you think about it, my dear,' said John.

'But we're here for people, aren't we? That's what you've always said. Besides, I've never had a fortress mentality,' his wife retorted crossly.

John put a hand on her shoulder in a gesture of peace. 'Just within these four walls and no further,' he said to Patrick, 'I feel I must tell you that Vernon Latimer has a past that isn't quite – well – squeaky clean.'

'So how is he Chairman of the PCC?' Elspeth snapped.

'It happened a very long time ago, I understand.'

Patrick said, 'I'm afraid I do need to know your source of information.'

'Impeccable. The bishop himself.'

'Do you have any idea of the nature of this misdemeanour?'

'He served a prison term for fraud. But it wasn't in this country – out in Malaya.'

Patrick caught my eye. 'What was he doing out there?'

'Working, I understand.'

Master-minding pirates? I wondered.

Twelve

'What do you think of Latimer?' Patrick asked.

'He's an efficient chairman,' John said. 'Good organizer. Works hard. But you have to understand that I would never have him as treasurer – not that he's ever shown the remotest interest in the post. Which, as you know, are all voluntary.'

'And as a person?'

'He can be a bit bombastic. Arrogant, really. Doesn't suffer fools at all. To be honest I don't like the man and I don't envy you if you have to go and talk to him.'

'If he starts to throw his weight about I shall cart him off to the nick,' Patrick promised darkly. 'People tend to deflate after an hour or so in the cells.'

'Please be tactful,' his father begged. 'And I'm talking about everyone else who lives here. Something that people just shrug off in an urban area can have a dreadful effect in a rural community.'

I was listening to this, wondering if Patrick would go and see Latimer straight away and whether there was any need for me to tag along, when I had one of those bombshell ideas that are usually associated with my writing. Not so much an idea perhaps as a recollection.

'That large granite cattle trough in the barn,' I said to Patrick, interrupting him in the middle of assuring John that he would handle matters carefully, 'the one we sat on?'

He broke off, obviously irritated with me. 'What about it?'

'It was upside down.'

'That's why we sat on it.'

'When we were in there shortly after the bodies were found it was right side up.'

'Perhaps SOCO turned it over.'

'Why? Besides, it's huge, it must weigh at least half a ton.'

'Ingrid, it can't be important. It was probably in the way of getting vehicles inside the place.'

Sometimes I can just look at him unblinking and he really starts to listen to what I am saying.

'No, it was over towards one side, wasn't it?' he mused aloud, staring into space. 'The side you were working in.' The fine eyes focused on me. 'You won't rest until I've turned it over to see if there's anything underneath, will you?'

'No.'

'You couldn't possibly move a thing like that on your own,' Elspeth said.

'A few strong blokes with crowbars and a couple of Hi-Lift jacks should do it.' Patrick looked at his watch. 'Who the hell do the fuzz call in to do that kind of thing – the Royal Engineers?'

'Farmers with tractors and Land Rovers should do it,' John said. 'I'll give Roger a ring.'

'Are you both going out?' Elspeth asked in deceptively off-hand fashion when John had left the room.

'I'll talk to Latimer in the morning,' Patrick replied. 'Tonight we'll go and have a look under a cattle trough.' Realizing that she felt safer in his company he added, 'You can come with us if you like.'

'But surely it's confidential police work.'

'No, I'm just humouring Ingrid.'

'What do *you* think is under it?'

'A small pile of ten-year-old cow muck.'

The sliding doors of the building were as we had left them, partly open, and now we trundled them wider, the wheels squealing in dirt-encrusted channels, to allow a large tractor to gain entry. This did not belong to Roger, a local farmer, whom John had rung, but to his son, Steven, who farmed the high ground on a ridge above the valley in which Hinton

Littlemoor was situated. There, he did not have to contend with narrow lanes and was mechanized accordingly. He was only here now because he had come across several fields, his own property, from the main road, gateways having been constructed with the easy access of combine harvesters and the like in mind.

In the illumination provided by the headlights of the three vehicles – Roger, grinning delightedly, had felt compelled to attend – we pointed Steven in the direction of the granite trough.

'You don't want it bust, do you?' Steven called down from the cab above the roar of the engine. 'Those things go for a fortune these days.'

Patrick shouted back that we did not want it so much as chipped as it did not belong to us. It was suggested that we pile a lot of loose straw on the far side of it.

I was feeling very small already and preparing to vanish down a crack in the floor as soon as my silly notion was revealed for what it was. Even though Roger had told us that the tractor was brand new and Steven was itching to try it out on something I was asking myself how much fuel it had used to come here. What important jobs had the young farmer broken off from doing? No, in future I would confine myself to writing novels. And knitting dishcloths.

'I still loves yer, babe,' said a familiar voice in my ear as the bucket attachment on the tractor edged closer to the trough.

It was decided to hammer in some wooden wedges first at either end to avoid damaging the rim. This took a few minutes and I became more and more miserable. Elspeth, standing a little apart from where the action was taking place in case something nasty was revealed, sensed my mood and grimaced at me sympathetically.

Then, seemingly without any effort on the part of the machine, the trough had turned turtle and rolled over on to the straw.

Beneath it was a very small pile of straw and dried-up manure.

'I'm sorry,' I said quietly but my whisper was drowned

out by the tractor. Steven turned it off and Patrick went over and kicked at the manure in desultory fashion. His foot hit something hard, like a stone. He bent down.

I went over to see him unrolling a filthy rag. From the way he was handling the bundle it was obvious that whatever was inside was heavy for its size. Then, holding the rag by one corner, he tipped out the contents.

'Well, I never,' said Steven. 'Is that what I think it is?'

Five gold ingots lay in the straw. Even though I had seen pictures of them in the books in the library and they were not very big, some three and a half inches long by about an inch and a quarter wide, a photograph could not quite capture the wonderful lustre, the weighty, sensuous glow. I understood now how people could become crazed with greed for it.

Patrick straightened. 'Would you be good enough to keep this under your hats?' he said to Steven and Roger. 'Even coming over here tonight? Just for a while – until arrests have been made.'

We had been in a close huddle, having forgotten about Elspeth, and I was suddenly aware of her approach.

'It's not someone's *head*, is it?' she enquired with trepidation before peering over our shoulders. 'Oh, how lovely,' she murmured. 'So old, so full of history. I take it the Tanner brothers were lying and opened the coffin. They helped themselves to a few, sealed it up again and hid them in here under the trough using the digger they'd borrowed before taking the coffin to wherever they handed it over to someone else.'

'It's a brilliant theory,' Patrick said. 'You ought to be doing this job, not me.'

Before we left Patrick wrapped a few stones in the rag and then asked Steven to put the trough back how we had found it. After a bit of manoeuvring this was done. Patrick then gave the pair of them some 'beer tokens', as he put it, and the farmers roared away into the darkness together.

'The Tanners can't have done a runner yet or they'd have collected this little lot,' Patrick said, placing the small hoard in a sample bag he had found in the car. 'That's if they did

hide it here. We need to prove it. But having made everything look the same as it was before I'm reluctant to stake
the place out waiting for them to turn up or people might be
here for a month.'

'If they returned to retrieve it you'd have your proof,' I
said.

'I have to think about the cost of manpower. One could
still wait around for a very long time.'

'They'd never be able to sell it – they simply don't have
the contacts.'

'No, but they're stoopid, aren't they?'

'Nudge them into making a move.'

'Like what? A thunderflash down their chimney?'

It had been another long day. 'No, SILLY! They've been
getting funny phone calls. Give them a funny phone call.'

'Ingrid, you keep telling me to stick by the rules.'

'Who the hell'll know?'

'Are you going to tell James what's going on?' Elspeth
called from inside the car.

'Of course,' Patrick answered. 'Right now, in fact. Tell me
why I haven't inherited my mother's brains,' he continued
in an undertone.

Carrick, in a side ward, had been given special permission
to retain his mobile phone. Joanna answered.

'Yes, he's a bit better, but we still don't know whether it's
MRSA or not,' I just managed to overhear her say. 'He's still
feeling pretty rough, though. Is it important?'

'Tell him we've found some gold ingots,' Patrick requested.

Carrick came on the line straight away and there was quite
a long conversation of which I could only hear one side as
his voice was quite weak.

'Did he suggest anything?' I asked at the end of it.

'Yes, he said send a patrol car with all horns and blue lights
flashing to the front of the Tanners' house and give them plenty
of time to escape through the back door. You mentioned motorbikes so they'll quite likely do a runner on those. The plodding officers of the law will then pretend to lose contact with
them so they'll drop their guard and be feeling all cheerful

and superior when they turn up here. *If* they turn up here. If they don't nothing's lost as their descriptions can be circulated and we'll pick them up again anyway.' He got out of the car and continued, 'Please take Elspeth, and the gold, home. I'll stay here, fix up what James suggested and hide myself somewhere. Don't come back for if they're on their way here too and see the lights of the car they'll smell a rat and scram.'

'You can't arrest them on your own,' I said.

'No, I'll make sure the patrol car comes here quietly anyway.'

On the way to the rectory Elspeth said, 'How on earth would they turn the trough over again?'

'Pass,' I said. 'But they are built like elephants.'

She did not mention leaving the house for the night on the way home but when we arrived John was on the phone.

'That was Neil Makepeace,' he said to Elspeth. 'To ask how I was. I said we'd had a spot of bother with an intruder today and he's insisting we go over to their place for the night. Really insisting, I'm afraid. In fact he's coming over for us right away. It's very good of them, but—'

'Wonderful!' Elspeth cried. 'I'm dying to see their new house.' She dashed upstairs to pack an overnight bag.

Ten minutes later I had the rectory to myself and was feeling just the smallest, teensiest, smidgiest bit ignored. OK, everyone knew that some bug-eyed, tea-trailing monster wasn't going to come looming out of the night to slobber at the windows trying to get in at me, but . . .

I went out to the car, where the gold was safely locked in a secret cubby-box, found a map, returned to the house and, locking all the outside doors, pored over it. I thought Patrick was being over-cautious as the lanes around the Hagtop Farm area are always busy but respected his experience. I would walk back, across the fields.

During my explorations of the village in between writing I had discovered a public footpath that commenced at a stile set into the churchyard wall and crossed pastures in the direction of the next village, or rather hamlet. It went, if I remembered correctly, quite close to the barn.

I grabbed the map again. There was no point in taking it with me because I did not want to use any lights so I committed the route, actually much shorter than going by road, to memory. The only places where one was likely to go wrong was where the path met another in a spinney and at the point where I would have to leave it close to my destination. Everything like that would be obliterated by snow.

Enough time had been lost. Leaving the house, I ran.

The sky was overcast but because of the whiteness of the snow I found that I could see where I was going perfectly well, and, having crossed the stile, the only hazard appeared to be cowpats. There were some very hairy cattle being wintered in the field. The going was gently downhill and I jogged easily, quite enjoying myself but for the worry of Patrick being on his own awaiting men who would be desperate and possibly armed with shotguns. The Tanners would not worry about the consequences of opening fire, they would think only of the riches brought by something which, in reality, they would not be able to sell, and escape to a country where the law could not reach them when, in all probability, they did not even possess passports.

I had overlooked the fact that the path, little more than a dip in the snow, curved quite close to houses. But I did not want to leave it and strike blindly across country. Dogs barked, sending my heart into my mouth, and I almost ran right into a white cow – it was so large it could well have been a bull – that was lying down concealed by a hump of snow-covered briars. It jerked to its feet with a snort and thundered off, rousing a couple of pheasants roosting in a nearby tree which flew away, their clattering alarm calls loud enough to waken a sleeping army.

I slowed right down to give everything a chance to settle down, noticing with surprise that I was now only a matter of ten yards from the hornbeam hedge that formed the boundary of Hinton Mill. I could see that the lights were on by the row of garages and, on impulse, as quietly as possible, went closer. Some leaves still adhered to the hedge but it was fairly recently planted and although just above my head in height was quite thin. I found a place where I could see right through it.

Two of the garage doors were up, the spaces within a gaping blackness, and, as I watched, a woman, someone I did not recognize, came out of the nearest one carrying a package and went into the other, emerging moments later without it. She then closed and locked both garages and walked away.

I returned to the path and carried on running. A couple of hundred yards farther on I reached what I thought must be the copse but there were only a few trees and I wasted time trying to detect where the other path might be. Finally, I ran on, quite quickly coming to a much larger group of trees. It was very dark inside as they were conifers and I could see nothing at all. I had no choice but to walk around the outside and then strike across the field in the direction I thought the path might go.

Already, it seemed, I could be lost.

My feet were soaking wet by this time and becoming very cold, my trainers making squelching noises. The ground rose and soon I had to slow to a walk, conscious that I was puffing like a train. Then, quite by accident, I came upon a trail of footprints. Was this the path? It led in the right direction, uphill. Soon, I came to a fence and another stile, a detail I could not remember from the map. The field I found myself in was still down to autumn stubble, the tips poking through the layer of snow, sheep nibbling on what they could find. It was huge, crossing it seemed to take for ever and I slowed to a walk, not wishing to make them panic.

I crested a rise, left the sheep behind and ran again but after a while was going uphill once more and forced back to a walk. Once again I came to a fence and stile and another field with sheep, a few of which trotted off when they sensed my presence. A freezing wind met me: I was on open hillside, the ground flattening out, so I ran on. Then, on the wind, I heard the sound of a distant motorbike, seemingly over to my left but somewhere below. I stopped, crouching down in case I was silhouetted against the white background and gazed around me, breathing deeply.

If I had paused a few minutes previously I would probably have spotted my destination. There was no mistaking that brutal outline. I had come too far to the north and much higher up than I need have done and was probably in the middle of the last of the three fields that Steven had crossed in his tractor. No matter, this was better than plodding around somewhere below unable to get my bearings.

The single headlight of the bike came briefly into view as it flashed past a gateway and then there was only an intermittent glow as it travelled along the deep winding lanes. It was too soon to tell if it was heading for the barn. There was other traffic; a vehicle was moving slowly somewhere over to my left, going away from me, and on the other side of the valley the occasional lights of other cars went to and fro on a busier road.

I set off downhill and almost immediately came upon the fresh tracks of a heavy vehicle. This was more than I had hoped for and I jogged on. An untidy low hedge appeared ahead of me and a gate. This had to be a Hagtop boundary as the gate was rotten and literally leaning against the post at one end, the hinges having gone and been replaced with baler twine. Steven had obviously hefted it open but it was too heavy for me to lift so, carefully, I climbed over it.

There could be no mistake now: the bike was coming towards the barn.

I was actually standing in a lane. Steven must have had a problem turning the tractor to the right as the ground was thick with mud where the tyres had gouged into the verge. I followed the mud and churned-snow trail, slipping a couple of times, and then it turned left into a gateway set in a block wall. I had arrived at what no doubt had been bovine hell.

Coming to a halt, I peered around the edge of the opening in the wall. The gate was wide open, the area before me with not a scrap of cover before one reached the rear of the building. As I stood there the bike roared into view, made a complete circuit, two large figures mounted on it, and disappeared round to the front again. The row ceased but the light remained, moving. They were wheeling the machine into the barn to use it to see by.

Staggered by this blatant, if not downright idiotic, announcement of arrival I dashed across the open space towards a door, this just a small one for those on foot, with the idea of either observing what was going on from just outside or creeping in and concealing myself somewhere, coming to Patrick's aid if he needed me. Close to it was a lean-to, a homemade afterthought built of scrap wood and rusting corrugated iron. I deliberately went wide of the opening that led into the dark interior, mostly because such cobwebby places give me the horrors, and then paused by the doorway, a slanting oblong of light now thrown on to the ground near my feet.

Forgetting everything I had been taught.

I was swept off my feet from behind, a hand over my mouth, and borne bruisingly into the lean-to. Several spiders' webs later everything came to a halt and somehow, still off the ground, I was turned in the grasp until we were face to face. I did not need to see who it was, nothing was said and I had no intention of uttering a sound even though I could feel something small blundering around in my hair.

Patrick dumped me back down on my feet and then, like Macavity, suddenly wasn't there. I stayed right where I was, hardly even daring to breathe in case someone heard me.

Aeons went by and I could hear muffled voices and scuffing sounds coming from within the barn, the light flickering as people moved backwards and forwards in front of it. I remained motionless, but was eventually driven to carefully catch hold of the thread of a large spider as it abseiled past my face and wind it, very securely, around the handle of a nearby wheelbarrow I could just make out in the gloom.

It was obvious that they were trying to turn over the trough, a lot of gasping noises and swearing were emanating from the building, the occasional loud crack and exclamation suggesting the breakage of a piece of wood or something similar. Then, after a crescendo of grunts and groans, there was a heavy thud and someone cheered. Predictably, several seconds later when the horrible truth dawned, it was a different story and, predictably again, they suspected one another. They would not have noticed if the Camel Corps had marched in now, bawling accusations at one another, still less see the approach of the officer of the law.

'You're under arrest!' I heard Patrick shout, the kind of delivery that at one time would have withered with terror those under his command.

In the next moment or so there was the roar of a shotgun, both barrels, followed by a terrible screaming. The headlight of the bike went out and then the screaming stopped.

Choking with shock I crept into the barn on all fours. Then, outlined against the expanse of sky between the widely opened doors opposite, I saw a figure, fleeing, awkwardly, as though not accustomed to running. It was not one of the Tanner brothers. Or Patrick.

I risked all. 'Patrick?' I yelled. 'Patrick!'

'I'm here,' his voice said from somewhere or other. 'Stay where you are. Got your phone?'

'Yes. Are you hurt?'

'I'm not sure. Call in, get some people here.'

This proved to be unnecessary as moments later a vehicle swept into the yard, swiftly followed by another: police cars. In the illumination they provided I got to my feet and, ducking low, ran towards where I thought I had heard Patrick's voice. I found him half under the bike, which had fallen over, its light not out but covered by debris. I shoved this away with one foot in order to see.

'Someone got them from behind at almost point-blank range,' he said matter-of-factly, flat on his back.

I quickly glanced over to see the two bloodied corpses, finding myself praying that they were corpses now with such ghastly injuries and not going to suffer further.

Patrick pushed and I heaved at the bike and he emerged from beneath it. There was blood on his coat.

'I think I stopped a couple of pellets,' he muttered, sitting down on the floor after using his torch to check the two bodies for signs of life. 'But those poor bastards took the full brunt of it. God, who was it? Who could have possibly known what was going on?'

Carrick, apparently beside himself with a feeling of help-lessness, had called out an armed-response vehicle, just in case. The crew were from Bristol and had lost their way because, we discovered later, local youths had turned round a couple of signposts in the maze of lanes. Finally they had met up with the patrol car and arrived together.

Patrick, in his turn beside himself, but with bitterness and fury, refused to go to Accident and Emergency to have the four shotgun pellets removed (three in his left shoulder, one in his upper arm on the same side), and asked the paramedics to do it there and then, arguing that as his GP had done the same twenty years previously there was no reason why it could not be done now. Fortunately the pellets were not at all deep, a couple just below the skin. He thought they had ricocheted off the bike, which he had knocked over diving for cover.

Holding his hand, and he only swore once with the pain, I thought that another few inches the other way and he could have been blinded.

'Still angry with me?' I said quietly.

Patrick turned to me in surprise. 'I'm not remotely angry with you.'

'For coming back, I mean.'

'I had an idea you would. I heard you coming several miles away.'

DI Bromsgrove, he of the earnest brown eyes, arrived to assist and as he was obviously fully experienced Patrick put him in charge of the crime scene. By this time it was just after two in the morning.

'Right now I feel like kicking in Vernon Latimer's front door,' Patrick said. He had his arm in a sling, a temporary measure to help prevent more bleeding.

'But you've not one iota of evidence, so we'll politely knock on it in about seven hours' time,' I said.

'I could do that for you, sir,' suggested Bromsgrove, who

was busy writing notes nearby and had overheard. 'He's a suspect, I take it.'

'Only insofar as we're trawling through potentially iffy locals,' Patrick told him. 'I'll talk to him unless I'm on a life-support machine by then. And, Jonathan . . .'

'Yes, sir?'

'Not one word to the DCI that I've been winged – he has enough on his mind.'

'That might be difficult, sir.'

'Look, call me sir when anyone else is around but Patrick when we're working together. And if Carrick asks just tell him I hurt my shoulder a bit getting out of the line of fire.' He could have added, but did not, that after almost having had his leg blown off in the Falklands a few bits of shot were a mere bagatelle.

Latimer lived in one of a group of 'executive' houses in a close situated at the opposite end of the village to where the railway station had once been. John had told us he was retired, but I had expected an older man than the frowning individual who answered the front door. He was of medium height, and had an unhealthy sallow complexion and lumpish, pear-shaped figure. It occurred to me that he could easily be the man I had seen making his escape from the barn.

'This is not remotely convenient,' Latimer snapped when Patrick had introduced us and explained the reason for the visit. 'You'll have to come back later.' And he actually started to close the door.

Patrick stepped smartly on to the front step and winced as the door hit his shoulder. 'I don't think you heard me correctly. Two men were murdered last night and it would appear there's a connection with an existing murder inquiry. I'm actually investigating another incident at the rectory which we believe is also connected and should like to ask you a few questions about your own presence there yesterday.'

'I was there for a PCC meeting, for God's sake!' the other shouted furiously.

'I sincerely hope you were,' Patrick replied, annoyingly

taking the remark at face value. 'May we come in or do you want me to take you kicking and screaming to Bath police station in front of all your fascinated neighbours?'

'I'll have you know I'm a respected member of the community,' Latimer countered, boring to the last.

'All you have to do then is prove it.' This with a death's head smile.

Icily, Latimer stood aside to allow us to enter and we went through an archway into a large living room. Afterwards I could not remember a single feature of the decor, only that it was wishy-washy.

'Do you own a shotgun, Mr Latimer?' Patrick asked.

'Yes. I'm a member of the local clay-pigeon-shooting club.'

'May I see it?'

'It's in a cupboard in my study.'

'Lead on, then,' said my husband encouragingly.

Latimer stood there for a moment longer, seething, and then stalked from the room. We followed.

A woman wearing a dressing gown, of wishy-washy colour, was coming down a flight of stairs as we filed down the hall. She completely ignored the three of us, went into what I just glimpsed to be the kitchen and slammed the door.

The study appeared to be a euphemism for a storeroom, boxes piled everywhere, just leaving sufficient space for a computer standing on a cheap DIY unit, a chair, a metal filing cabinet and a sturdy steel cupboard. Latimer went to this, unlocked it with a key that was on a bunch in his pocket and opened the door.

'There,' he said. 'All properly licensed and stored. This safe cost me a damned fortune.'

Inside were two shotguns and an air rifle with telescopic sights. They were individually secured.

'Does your wife shoot?' I asked.

'Carol! God, no. She's useless at anything like that. The older gun, the Purdey, belonged to my father. I don't use it – it needs attention.'

'I should like to see them both,' Patrick said. Sans sling this morning, he went to put on forensic gloves and then gave them to me. 'You handle them, my left arm's a bit weak this morning.'

'I resent this,' Latimer ground out, sorting through his keys.

'And next you'll say that the Chief Constable is a personal friend of yours and you'll be making a complaint about me,' Patrick said. 'Go on, man, it's in quite a few of Agatha Christie's whodunnits.' After a short silence he went on, 'When you were at the rectory for the PCC meeting and left the room after coffee was it to visit the downstairs cloak-room?'

'Of course. Where the hell else d'you think I'd go?'

I am a reasonable shot and familiar with shotguns and it was John himself who had taught me how to use one. I removed the weapon nearest to me, the Purdey, from the securing device that Latimer had just unlocked and broke it while wondering why he did not have it repaired as they are just about the finest money can buy. It smelt of gun oil. I replaced it.

I took the second, examined it and caught Patrick's eye: it had been fired recently.

Thirteen

I gave the gloves and then the shotgun to Patrick and he took the weight of it on his right arm.

'Don't you clean it when you've used it?' he asked mildly, looking down the blackened interior of the barrels.

'Normally, yes, but I was in a bit of a hurry this morning and forgot.'

'Where were you last night, Mr Latimer?'

'Here, of course.' He flared up. 'Look, I'm not your bloody murderer!'

'It was bloody all right,' Patrick whispered. 'Why did you fire this weapon?'

'I went out into the field behind the house.' Here he waved wildly in the direction of the window. 'That one – and gave both barrels to some pigeons that have been eating my vege-tables.'

'That should be easy to check up on, someone must have heard you.'

'I didn't fire close to the houses. Over by that oak tree you can see down there.'

'So you crawled across the field?'

'No, I just walked very slowly along by the hedge.'

'I happen to know enough about country matters to be aware that pigeons are highly alert birds and would have flown off before you got into range.'

'Most of them did. I didn't hit any.'

Having just met the man I had to admit to myself that I could picture it. But I had an idea no creeping about had taken place, he had merely noticed the pigeons in his winter cabbages, snatched the gun, raced out into the field and let fly at the fleeing culprits. But that did not mean the weapon had not been used prior to that, in the early hours of the morning. In fact the recent firing could have been intended as a cover-up.

Patrick said, 'I shall impound this for forensic testing. You'll get a receipt. Now, when you left the rector's study yesterday and crossed the hall, did you see anyone else?'

'I did not.'

'Please think carefully. It's very important.'

'No, I didn't see a soul.'

'And when you returned?'

'The same. No one. Not that I can guarantee that I looked both right and left on each occasion.'

Patrick gave him a smile. 'Thank you. Tell me about the time you were in Malaya.'

Charm and then pounce.

Stonily, Latimer said, 'That is nothing to do with anyone, not even you.'

'And if I tell you that the cases I'm working on would appear to involve piracy in the South China Sea . . .?'

Latimer shook his head. 'My little spot of bother was in Singapore. Banking. Nothing whatever to do with pirates.'

I decided that more might be learnt elsewhere and excused myself from the room. The kitchen door was still shut but I did not knock. Who the hell knocks at kitchen doors? Who the hell closes them?

The woman whom we had seen coming down the stairs was within, giving every sign of being overwrought, drinking whisky neat, straight out of a small bottle.

'What the hell d'you want with *me*?' she shrilled, ramming on the top and shoving the bottle in a drawer. 'Shouldn't you be talking to that sanctimonious old fart in there?'

'Mrs Latimer?' I asked. I went to the window and looked out over the back garden. No vegetable patch. To make sure I opened the back door and went outside. There was nothing in sight that could be classed as edible, not by people anyway.

'Yes, I am,' she said, much more quietly. 'Why have you come here?'

'We're checking on legally held shotguns in case any were stolen and used in a serious crime last night.' This was not actually a lie as it is standard police procedure. I went on to introduce myself and then said, 'Who, or what, did your husband fire his shotgun at this morning?'

'God knows. Nothing, probably. We'd had a row and he just went outside and blasted off. He does sometimes, just to try to scare me.'

It appeared that he had succeeded: she had been crying and her reddened eyes were like those of a frightened rabbit. She had been attractive at one time, even beautiful, but self-neglect was now all-apparent.

'Was he here last night?'

'I don't know. We have separate rooms.' As she spoke she was twisting one of the free ends of her dressing-gown tie with fingers as tiny as those of a child.

'D'you mind telling me what the row was about?'

She sat down heavily on a pine bench. 'The same thing we always row about – his insufferable behaviour. Nice as pie outside this house, bending the knee in church, collecting around the village for charities, on the local council, this committee and that panel, you name it, Vernon's there wearing his best pious face. But underneath he's quite different – horrible to me – and I've got to the stage where I just don't know what's going on. He despises all these people really.'

'Despises them?'

'Yes, I think it gives him a feeling of power, you know, by pulling the wool over everyone's eyes. Sort of holding them in contempt while wheeler-dealering behind their backs to get his own way with things.'

'Is money involved?' I asked.

'It *could* be,' she replied dubiously. 'I've no proof but I've seen people come to this house who I know have put in planning applications – I follow it up and they always seem to get permission.'

I had an idea I had opened the wrong can of worms here but was prepared to press on anyway. Before I could say anything, though, Carol Latimer went on, 'You know, he's actually written to the bishop to complain that the rector's past it now he's been ill and we ought to have a younger man. Vernon doesn't like him for some reason, but it's probably because the Reverend Gillard's acute enough to know what he's really like and prevents him getting his own way all the time. Vernon's good on revenge. Oh, I don't know,' she said softly. 'Perhaps I've got it all wrong.'

'What do you mean, he's good on revenge?' I asked.

She bit her lip indecisively, and I wondered if she was regretting what she had said. 'Years ago Vernon got into trouble in the Far East – when he was a lot younger, before we met. Someone ratted on him – his words, not mine – on some slightly dodgy deal or other and he was sent to prison for two years. Vernon bragged to me that he'd got his own back but he wouldn't say how. And he got into a row in the Ring O'Bells one night. We'd gone in for a meal and someone was a bit drunk and obnoxious. Vernon reported him to the police because his tax disc was out of date. He gets his own back on me too . . .'

'Is he violent?'

'No, just – intimidating.'

I was trying to work out why she was still married to this man. 'Do you know who it was he had the row with in the pub?'

'Someone did say but I can't remember his name. I think they said he lives in one of the new flats at the mill.'

'Was it Keith Davies or Christopher Manley?'

'It might have been the first one. They were the ones murdered, weren't they? No, sorry, I simply can't be absolutely sure.'

I spotted the kind of wooden case that might contain chef's knives on the worktop and opened it. 'Who does the cooking?' I asked, surveying the very expensive and seemingly razor-sharp contents.

'I do now. Those are Vernon's. Once upon a time he cooked most of our evening meals but he's lost interest lately.'

'Do the names Jethro and Vince Tanner mean anything to you?'

'No,' Mrs Latimer replied without hesitation. 'But they might to Vernon. He knows loads of people.'

'Brian Stonelake?'

She thought for a moment or two. 'He's a farmer, isn't he? I don't actually *know* him but I think Vernon's had some dealings with him. Shooting rights or something like that. Vernon's a great one for shooting, it makes him feel like a real man.' This last comment was uttered in a flat, utterly bored tone. Then she fixed me with a surprisingly keen gaze. 'You know, I'm really glad you came here this morning. Talking about everything has made me realize that I've got to go and get myself a life before it's too late.'

Sweet revenge on my part, I supposed, if my presence had robbed him of hot dinners and someone to be nasty to.

'Do you have to repeat everything I've said to that officer you came with?'

'No, not the private bits,' I told her.

'You're really lucky working with a good-looking man like that.'

I would not necessarily tell him that either.

Patrick was just leaving as I closed the kitchen door after me and I relieved him of the shotgun.

'Anything?' he asked laconically when we were outside.

'Plenty that'll get Latimer run out of Hinton Littlemoor on a rail,' I said. 'But not much else other than a splendid set of chef's knives in the kitchen with none missing and the fact that Latimer's wife thinks he may have shooting rights at Hagtop Farm. It could have been Keith Davies he had a row with in the pub one night. No veg patch, by the way.'

'So he's a one-time fraudster, a liar and—'

'It's possible he's still on the make. His wife thinks he might be getting back-handers from people putting in planning applications – he's on that committee too.'

'Um. But as far as this case is concerned?'

'A blank. Unless the gun was fired twice.'

'Short of getting a search warrant and tearing the place apart looking for gold ingots . . .'

'Evidence *is* what we need,' I sighed.

'We'll call in at the rectory for coffee,' Patrick decided. 'See if Mother's got the list of the WI ladies. That'll eliminate them from the inquiry, another bloody box ticked.'

I caught the tautness in his voice. 'Is your shoulder hurting?'

'Yes.'

As far as the snippet of information about John was concerned I decided to keep it to myself for the present and let events take their course; to divulge it right now might do more harm than good.

The couple were only just back from their night with the Makepeace family, a short break that had obviously done Elspeth good.

'There!' she said, taking a folded sheet of paper from her bag and giving it to Patrick. 'We called in at Hazel's on the way home.'

Patrick thanked her and slipped it into an inside pocket of his jacket. Not the leather one he had been wearing the previous night, which was probably ruined.

'Had another run-in with roughs?' she casually asked him, noticing a telltale wince.

Patrick beamed upon her. 'No, I fell over a motorbike.'

'I hear there was a shooting at the barn last night.'

The police, in the shape of Inspector Bromsgrove, were yet to make any official announcements but word spreads like a winter virus in rural communities.

'A couple of aspirins with your coffee?' Elspeth went on to suggest before Patrick could make a reply and perhaps realizing that she was not going to get any more out of him right now.

'Thank you.'

'I do hope nothing's happened to Roger or Steven,' she said, going down with all guns blazing.

'No, they're alive and well,' Patrick assured her.

'We ought to have a word with them,' I said to him.

He met my gaze. Yes, his shoulder was giving him hell.

'Beer talks,' was all I said on the subject just then.

To Elspeth, Patrick said, 'If you see an unmarked car parked by your drive with one or two blokes sitting in it don't worry. I've asked that the rectory be placed under surveillance in case you get any more unwanted visitors. People coming here might be stopped and asked who they are, that's all.'

The discomfort was sufficient to ensure that when we were ushered into where Steven was doing paperwork on the kitchen table the young farmer received a severe fright. I do not think Patrick was rehearsing what he would do and say on the way to speak to him but when confronted with a possible security leak his resentment surfaced.

'What did you say?' was his opening question. 'What did you and your dad blab all over the bar? Or to the whole village? Or all of bloody north Somerset?'

The demeanour of the man before him was sufficient to drain the blood from Steven's face. 'N-nothing,' he managed to get out. 'We didn't say a word to anyone.'

'The Tanner brothers are both *dead*! When they turned up at the barn to look for what we found someone blasted them to hell with a shotgun. In the back. You were the only people who knew about it.'

'I – I swear to you we sat in a corner on our own and said nothing,' Steven said. 'OK, we might have whispered a bit to each other but there was no one who—'

'You whispered,' Patrick interrupted. 'Boy, you and your pa have voices like soddin' foghorns.' He flung himself out of the chair he had commandeered on the opposite side of the table and paced the room. 'Who was sitting or standing near you?'

'No one, really. As I said, we were sat in a corner. There was nobody that near to us.'

'The fact that you were in a corner would amplify anything you said and when you'd had a drink or three you wouldn't have realized that you weren't effin' whispering at all!' This last was an impassioned yell. He wasn't acting. And because he was shouting he wasn't really going to lose his temper either, which was nice.

I seated myself in the chair. 'Steven, do please try to

remember who the other people were, whether they were close to you or not.'

Steven said, 'The usual old codgers. Just the sort of folk you see in the public bar most nights. One or two young couples, a few strangers who had driven out from Bath. The only people I knew by name were the landlord, his wife, Sid Coles and his cousin Matt Leyton. Oh, and Spooky Sue and her boyfriend.'

'And who might they be?' Patrick wanted to know.

'I don't know her surname. She says she's a white witch or some such nonsense. He's a traveller, one of a bunch living in a lay-by on the Shepton Mallet road. They were knocking back scrumpy and all over each other.'

Grabbing the list that Elspeth had given to him, Patrick unfolded it and placed it in front of Steven with the blank side uppermost. 'There. Draw a plan of the inside of the bar. Mark the tables and then try to remember who was sitting at them. Don't worry about the ones you don't know the names of. Just write C for codger and YM and YW for young man or woman.'

'But I can't even remember how many tables there are!'

'Think! God above, man, you've been in the place enough times!'

'We'll go outside while you do it,' I said, giving Patrick a meaningful look.

We exited.

'He's not going to remember a thing while you're standing over him gnashing your teeth,' I said as we strolled in the yard. I had a sudden recollection. 'While I was on my way to the barn last night I passed quite close to the mill. The lights were on by the garages and the doors of two were open. A woman was going in and out of them but I didn't recognize her.'

'A visitor, perhaps.'

'If you remember, James's initial investigation discovered that Keith Davies had not used his garage but had rented it to another resident. It crossed my mind, that's all.'

'Damned if I can remember any more,' Steven reported sheepishly a few minutes later.

Patrick sat down and examined the plan. Taking up the pen he put in a few additions of his own. 'The door to the outside is there, the fruit machine is in that corner, a pillar with a dried-flower arrangement on a small shelf is next to it there and the archway to the restaurant is between that and the bar. And there's another small table under a window in that alcove. Who was sitting there? Anyone?'

'I don't know. Sorry, I couldn't see it from where we were sitting.'

'But that was actually the closest table to yours, just on the other side of wooden panel that acts as a screen. Didn't you see anyone when you first entered? They would have been in your full view as you crossed the room.'

Steven shook his head. 'No. I'm really sorry. S'pose Dad and I were a bit taken with what had gone on that evening.'

'Can you describe any of the people whom you thought were strangers, folk who gave the impression they were out for a drive and a bite of supper?'

But Steven could only remember the barest details.

Patrick pocketed the plan. 'It's OK. Sorry, I shouldn't have shouted at you. There's absolutely nothing to say that someone wasn't lurking outside the barn when we were all in there last night and overheard our conversation.' He stood up. 'I'll keep you posted.'

'I still feel responsible,' Steven mumbled.

'The murderer's responsible.'

Joanna phoned my mobile to tell us that James did not have MRSA but the infection was nevertheless a bad one and he was on the kind of antibiotics that made him feel truly awful. Another piece of good news was that he was being allowed to go home on condition that he took things exceedingly quietly. At least, I thought it good news: Patrick, for the DCI's own well-being, was convinced that they ought to keep him in hospital, chained to the bed.

'He'll be content so long as we keep him right up to date with the investigation,' I said, over a sandwich bought from a roadside snack-bar.

188

'So when's he coming home?'

'This afternoon.'

'We'd better call in, then. Or, as you say, he'll stagger into the nick in case everyone rats up.'

'Was Steven's plan of any use?'

'No, I don't think so. As he said, old village codgers, codgers-to-be and a few strangers, couples.' He delved into his pocket and drew out the sheet of paper, somewhat crumpled now. 'Here. This is a nice little job for you to do while I talk to the landlord of the Ring O'Bells to see if he can remember anyone sitting at that table during the time Steven and Roger were there. Please check up on the WI ladies. Drop me off in the village and take the car. Find out if they noticed anyone in the rectory who perhaps shouldn't have been there. Then we can both go and brief Carrick and soothe his fevered brow.'

'It'll take me most of the afternoon.'

'Surely not!'

I looked at the list. 'There's only half a dozen of them but you can't just storm in and out again. They'll be elderly and can't be rushed. And without wishing to sound pompous, I *am* Elspeth's daughter-in-law. I don't want to do anything that might reflect badly on her.'

'As you wish. Give me a ring then, when you've done.'

'Enjoy your pint,' I said, giving him an I-see-through-your-cunning-ruse grin.

It seemed to me that we were taking things too gently but the mundane checking had to be done. It was sensible to give Bromsgrove free rein at the nick and carry on ticking boxes, as Patrick had put it, especially while his shoulder was giving him a bit of trouble.

It quickly became obvious that I was behind the times. The first on my list, Miss Hannah Oldberry (a name suggestive of old lace, 4711 perfume and a cottage hung with roses), turned out to be a wild-looking female with long wavy red hair who was probably in her thirties. She lived in a rundown bungalow behind the village hall. Several wolf hounds in various stages of decrepitude which had been lying in the long grass of the front garden escorted me to the door, wearing expectant expressions.

Miss Oldberry apologized for the utterly revolting smell that wafted out as she opened it, going on to say that it was green tripe she was cooking for them in an old twin-tub washing machine. She removed from her shoulder a ginger cat I had not noticed as it exactly matched her hair and then banished the dogs to a pen. Several mostly bald hens exploded from it as she opened the door.

'Sorry, the place is always like a zoo,' said Miss Oldberry. 'All rescued, you know, even the chickens. So-called spent battery ones. Poor little buggers have never even seen a blade of grass until we rehome them. What can I do for you? You wouldn't like some hens, would you?' she added eagerly. 'They really do lay, you know, when they've got themselves back together again.'

I told her I would think about it and went on to explain the reason for my visit. It would become increasingly tedious, I knew, repeatedly to clarify my exact role as it was unusual for a policeman's wife to become involved in his work. I decided I would merely say that Patrick, who these ladies must know by now from Elspeth had a change of career, had requested my help.

'There was an intruder at the rectory?' Miss Oldberry echoed. 'How dreadful. Do you mind if we talk out here? The pong inside'll kill you.'

'I just need to know which of you ladies left the room where the committee meeting was being held to visit the cloakroom so I can find out if they saw anyone in the hall or on the stairs. Elspeth thought just two had but it might have been more.'

Hitching up a pair of men's trousers probably bought at a jumble sale she plonked herself down, with furrowed brow, on a low wall. 'Now then . . . Elspeth, our chairman – none of that politically correct crap with us, please note – served the tea and cakes, Maggie Ruislip was helping her and they had a natter afterwards about arrangements for the trip. I was talking to Joan and Cathy and none of us went to the loo, yes, I lie, Cathy did.'

'They would be Mrs J. O. Dutton and Mrs C. Southy?' I said, consulting my list.

'That's them. There were only seven of us at the meeting as everyone else was unwell or couldn't make it. That just leaves two to think about. Ah! Yes, there's a new member and she found herself volunteered on to the committee as she's had secretarial experience. Didn't seem to mind. I can't remember her name, though. Do you have them all written down?'

'It has to be either Mrs L. M. Brandon or Lady Rockley.'

'Oh yes, Marjorie. She was talking to Flo, she's Lady Rockley.'

'*Marjorie* Brandon?' For some reason with the different first initial I had not made the connection.

'That's right. I understand Elspeth went to see her recently as she'd been told she didn't know anyone in the village and was a bit on her ownsome.' Miss Oldberry's voice dropped to a whisper. 'And her husband's an old bore, or something along those lines.'

'Did she leave the room?'

'I really couldn't tell you if either of them did. I didn't notice. You'll have to ask.'

Which I did, and as I had predicted it took over two hours, especially as I tarried at Lady Rockley's historic and beautiful house. It turned out that she was a fan of my books, eager to ask questions and thrilled to meet the author. This is heady stuff when you write and makes up for those signing sessions at bookshops when only your agent, your husband and a traffic warden coming in out of the rain turn up.

Finally, I had the information I needed, although it was not conclusive, nor quite complete, as Marjorie Brandon was not at home. I had left her until last as she lived nearest to the rectory. Cathy Southey had indeed visited the cloakroom in the hall – she told me she saw no one else – but Elspeth had not been quite correct in her recollections as most of the women had helped carry the tea things into the kitchen when the meeting had finished and had then stood around chatting in various parts of the ground floor for several minutes. None of the ones I spoke to had seen anyone not connected with the group, had not even glimpsed John, but from what they said it was obvious they had not necessarily had each other in sight all the time. The latter fact was only important from a formal police point of view, of course: none of these people was a suspect.

This was the state of affairs as I sat making notes in the Range Rover, parked at the mill, while everything was still fresh in my mind. Then, having finished, I phoned Patrick, who following a request from Inspector Bromsgrove had taken a taxi to the nick, to tell him. I got out of the car: while I was here I would walk round to the garages and see if I could remember which ones I had seen with the doors opened the previous night.

It was very quiet and already getting dark as the sky was heavily overcast, everything dripping and sodden after sleety rain, the ground still slushy from the snow. I could not remember the last time the sun had shone.

The memory of the woman I had seen haunted me for some reason. She had been tall and assured but perhaps not young, the hair either blonde or silvery grey under the lights. Could it possibly have been Marjorie Brandon? Or a daughter? With regard to the former I dismissed the idea out of hand but then made myself think about it. I had only ever seen her in bed and because of her illness the impression had been one of frail weakness. I phoned Elspeth.

'Marjorie? Well, obviously, she's recovered now,' she said. 'She's very well, in fact.'

'What's she *like*, though?' I asked.

'Oh, vivacious, quite jolly, we're glad to have her.'

'How tall is she?'

'Around five feet eight or even nine, I should say. Just a little taller than me, come to think of it. Are you on your way here?'

I told her that I would be there shortly and rang off.

No one was about and there were no lighted windows at

the old mill, the place could almost be unoccupied. I expected the lights by the garages to come on automatically at my approach but they appeared not to be security lights and must be activated by a switch somewhere. This was lucky as I did not want to draw attention to my presence. I have a bit of a thing about not wishing to be suspected of snooping around, not a particularly useful trait for a would-be detective.

Everything was tidy and quite deserted. Gazing along the row I reckoned that those I had seen with the doors opened were the third along from where I was standing and the one at the far end. I strolled down and tried the third door. It was locked.

Although I was pretty sure I had seen the woman lock both doors the previous night the one at the far end was not. I hauled up the door and looked in, mindful of police procedures, the need for search warrants and all the rest of it.

Just a blue car. A hatchback. Nothing else.

Fourteen

'It's extremely tenuous,' Patrick said. 'You said you thought you were followed to the Tanners' place and back again by a blue car and then, in a garage at the mill that could possibly be rented out to the Brandons, you discovered a similar vehicle in the same shade of blue. You've found out that Marjorie Brandon was present at the rectory on the day someone put tea in Elspeth's drawer. It's possible William Brandon was in the pub and overheard Steven and his father talking but could he really have been in the one in Bristol and organized the mob that did over yours truly? You can't just snap your fingers and conjure heavies out of thin air, you know.'

I supposed I could feel happy that he was starting to sound like a real policeman. 'No,' I said. 'He would have noticed some half-drunk social misfits nearby and on the spur of the moment decided to slip them fifty quid to have a bit more fun.'

After telling Elspeth of the change of plan I had driven into Bath to pick Patrick up but it did not appear that he had finished for the day, reading through recent reports in Carrick's office. Bromsgrove was out on the job somewhere with Lynn Outhwaite.

'It's worth doing a little digging,' I argued.

'But dig where? Neither of them has a criminal record. And there are no grounds for searching their house and their own garage. Brandon's name isn't even on the list of licensed shotgun holders.'

Patrick was tired – he had not had much sleep the night before. His face was a little drawn, and I knew that his shoulder was still painful.

'You could interview them again.'

'There are no grounds for that either. But you have a good excuse to talk to Mrs Brandon. See what you make of her now she's better.'

I sat back in my chair. 'Do you have any theories as to the reason someone put the tea in Elspeth's clothes?'

'Only that whoever did it is arrogant and attempting to get at me personally.'

'What do the forensics bods say? Have you had the report yet? Is it the same kind of tea?'

'Yes, they think it is.'

'I'm convinced whoever went upstairs at the rectory is a woman. It's the kind of thing a woman would do. Nothing was disturbed. A man would have turned everything over, deliberately, to make his mark. Even wrecked the room. I don't think that was the impression the person who did it intended to make – it's deeper than that.'

'But still meant as a distraction to me. Shall we go and talk to James and get his views?'

He wasn't tired, he was exhausted. But I stuck to my guns. 'It's a threat too. I'm really glad someone's keeping an eye on the rectory, especially for when we're not there.' This, although true, was not really what I had wanted to say, which was that I thought the threat was to Patrick himself and that he had already met the killer. Why did I have a certainty that the murderer thought this son of the parish to be worthy of removal? Patrick would think I had taken leave of my senses if I said that he stank in someone's nostrils.

'I've beefed up surveillance at the rectory,' were James Carrick's opening words. 'I don't like that development at all.'

He was seated in an armchair, looking weak enough to melt into it and disappear. Nevertheless, he gave Patrick a hard stare. 'I understand from Derek Woods that you stopped a few pellets last night.'

'It's of no consequence,' Patrick told him. 'Just shallow flesh wounds.'

We should have realized that nothing escaped the good sergeant.

'Thank God for that. I don't know if you've heard, but SOCO have turned up a couple of details since we last spoke. It seems that the person who fired the shots might have concealed himself behind one of the stacks of pallets. I take it you didn't have a wander around inside the building before the Tanners arrived.'

'No, there seemed no need, mainly because I hadn't actually left the area after we found the ingots.'

'There was very little time then for the farmer and his son to have driven to the pub, someone to overhear them talking and then that person to go to the barn armed with a shotgun.'

'No, it's something that's been bothering me slightly. But I can't see how anyone else could have learned of the find. Roger and Steven would have gone straight there in Roger's Land Rover, leaving the tractor somewhere. And don't forget, the distances involved are fairly short.'

'How much time *are* we talking about?'

'Fifty minutes from the time Roger and Steven left, just after which I rang you, to when the Tanners arrived. Ingrid had turned up again by then – she'd come across the fields on foot. The killer has to be local. What evidence was found behind the pallets?'

'Some wool fibres from a sweater caught on rough wood. They could have been there for ages but forensics don't think so. And a dropped cartridge. There's a blurred thumbprint on it, in all probability not a lot of use. How d'you reckon this man got into the barn without you seeing or hearing him?'

'In the dark . . .' Patrick shrugged and then regretted it. 'I used no lights and it was virtually pitch black inside. I didn't go into the barn at all but concealed myself in a lean-to at the rear so would not have seen anyone approaching on foot and entering through the front doors. You must appreciate I was expecting people either in a car or on motorbikes, the headlights of which would have been likely to reveal anyone trying to hide in the interior.'

'That's true.'

'Whoever it was *must* have come on foot. I would have heard a car, even if it had been left out in the road.'

Had I actually followed almost in the murderer's footsteps or had they come from the opposite direction?

Carrick said, 'The killer crept up behind the Tanner brothers when you entered and were endeavouring to arrest them.'

'I sneaked in the barn while they were engrossed in trying to turn the trough over. The light from the bike was directed roughly at the trough, at right angles to an imaginary line between me and the brothers. Anyone to the rear of them and the trough would have been invisible.'

'I saw him running away,' I said. 'Just an outline against the night sky between the doors.'

'You mentioned the Brandons to me earlier,' Patrick said to me. 'Could it have been William Brandon?'

'The man I saw was going much faster than I would have thought him capable,' I replied. 'But he was a heavy sort of man, not used to hurrying.'

'But they're pensioners, elderly,' the DCI protested, adding to me, 'He was the one I promised you'd apologize to. Have you?'

'No,' I said.

'Are you sure you haven't got some kind of resentment thing going for this man?'

This was not a moment to go all fluffy or switch on the charm. 'Not enough to want to put him in the frame for murder,' I said.

'Ingrid hasn't been able to speak to her yet but it appears Mrs Brandon was at the rectory yesterday,' Patrick said, perhaps in an effort to draw some of the flak in his own direction.

'I rather thought half the village was,' Carrick argued.

'James, I was only mentioning points to Patrick raised during routine checking,' I said, getting exasperated. I went on to repeat all the other points buzzing around in my bonnet as well, including the blue car. Just for the record.

There was a little silence when I had finished speaking and Carrick looked at his watch. 'It's still only five thirty.

Ingrid, I think it would be a good idea for you to pop in and speak to Mrs Brandon on the way home. You can apologize to her husband at the same time.' After another, longer, silence he continued, 'You're part of my team right now and I won't tolerate rudeness.'

It was time to leave.

Fearing mutiny Patrick bundled me outside. 'Look,' he whispered in my ear just outside the front door, 'he's doped up to the ears. Tell yourself it's not James talking, just a handful of pills.'

I had not the slightest intention of calling in at the mill on the way home. 'If I'm going to have to do this it's in my own way. All right?' I said stiffly.

'Of course,' Patrick said. 'Don't make a such a mountain out of it.'

'I'd like to go to the rectory first.'

There, I changed my clothes, had a drink of water and raided Patrick's briefcase. He was in the shower by this time so I was quite safe as I removed his bunch of burglars' keys (he had not got round to handing them back to MI5), his tiny torch, which I knew had new batteries in it, and another couple of handy bits and pieces. When I found something else, something so unexpected, mind-blowingly wonderful and fantastic I clutched it to my bosom for a moment and then tucked it securely in my jacket pocket.

'I'm doing one last job,' I told Elspeth on the way out.

'Does Patrick know where you're going?' she called after me.

'Yes, just to the Brandons.'

'Oh, that's all right, then.'

I walked there and the happenings of the next few hours were only finally pieced together some time afterwards.

The last garage in the row was still unlocked. I pulled up the door as far as I needed to in order to duck inside, praying that the mechanism would not squeak, entered and then closed it behind me. All seemed to be just the same; one blue car, and nothing else.

There was a light switch but I dared not use it in case the door did not fit properly and slits of light gave away my presence: it would have to be the torch. I put on a pair of latex gloves before I did anything else and then carefully walked round the exterior of the vehicle. I had already noted the registration number. No tiny lights flashed on the instrument panel indicating that an alarm was set and as the torch beam moved downwards I saw that the keys were in the ignition.

The previous night the woman, Mrs Brandon or not, had left this garage carrying a package or something similar and taken it into the other one. It had not appeared to be particularly heavy. I was itching to open up the car but something held me back. An un-alarmed vehicle with the keys left in it in an unlocked garage, the owners of which might be, as the expression goes, dodgy? If the garage had been locked the previous night what the hell was different today? It could, of course, be ready for someone's quick getaway.

It was my MI5 training, a maxim along the lines of never go down the pathway that your adversary has strewn with roses, only a much pithier version not for use before the nine o'clock watershed, that finally caused me to leave the whole thing severely alone and, as silently as possible, leave the garage.

The handle of the other garage was not hot-wired, or anything equally unfriendly, and I used Patrick's keys to open it. Then, having felt the smooth click, I stood quite still, listening, for a minute or so. There were only one or two lights on at the mill but at this side of the building the windows were mostly small, presumably bathrooms and toilets, not the kind people would gaze out of, the glass probably frosted anyway.

It had started to drizzle, more like a heavy cold mist, and I was glad to get into the comparative warmth of the garage. Warm it was, and stuffy, a black Porsche cosseted from the winter dampness by a tiny heater beneath it. There was nothing else in there at all, not even the box or package I had seen the woman bring in. Perhaps she had put it in the boot of the car: nothing could be seen on the seats.

This vehicle was alarmed and I made sure I did not touch it. Doubt was now in my mind that either garage was anything to do with the Brandons, whom we already knew possessed an Audi, and could even be rented to people living elsewhere in the village.

The floor and walls at first glance appeared to have been swept clean. This was not the case I discovered after I had gone down on hands and knees; there was black dust, that might or might not be tea, and sand in all the corners. I carefully placed as generous an amount as was possible in one of the sample bags I had brought with me.

The drizzle had turned into heavy rain when I emerged and I put up the hood of my jacket. I was not disappointed by not finding anything as I had not expected to come upon a hoard of gold anywhere so obvious. It seemed unlikely that it would be stored indoors, in the flat, which was arguably even more obvious. Thieves and murderers do not usually entrust their loot to banking organizations and William Brandon did not have the physique for digging deep holes. That left more cunning options. I ducked around the side of the garages to explore what lay behind them.

Immediately, I came upon a stone wall about five feet in height, the continuation of the one that bordered the river from which the mill had originally obtained its power. There was no space worth mentioning between the wall and the rear of the garages. I had no reason to suppose that it did not go all the way along and decided it was preferable to climb over it here rather than risk being spotted walking to the other end and then be faced with the same obstacle.

I could hear the water flowing somewhere below the wall, managed to jump up and wriggle over the top sufficiently and shone the torch beam down. There was a grassy bank, but it was less than eighteen inches wide, the river probably two or three feet below that but obscured by reeds. The upright coping stones were digging painfully into my ribs by now so I squirmed myself over and swung down, my heart in my mouth for a moment as one of my shoes became jammed in a gap between them. I kicked it free and ended up in a heap on the ground.

Why the hell was I doing this?

Because I was surrounded by under-the-weather, if not downright sickly, blokes, who at the rate they were going would never get the job done.

I edged along the narrow bank. There was nothing to hold on to. If it was anything like the one on the opposite side – the river was about eight feet wide here – it was seriously undermined in places and I took care to tread as close to the base of the wall as possible. I jumped when, with a plop and a splash, a small animal of some kind bolted from almost under my feet and made its escape. A fox barked.

Pausing where I thought the third garage might be I examined the wall and bank carefully. An enormous dead thistle was there but nothing else. The rain was getting heavier. Then, my left foot slipped and I almost went in the river but I managed to grab a handful of vegetation that fortunately included a small sapling that took my weight and hauled myself back onto the bank.

I guessed I was now about halfway to the other end of the row and went more slowly. Then the bank became even narrower so I turned my back to the wall and sidestepped and this proved to be much easier, even where the bank for a couple of feet had been undercut almost right away. Nothing now though would save me if I slipped.

Only some kind of sixth sense prevented me from falling over the large stone that lay right on my route just before I got to the end of the building. It was more like a small boulder but I was able to step over it. Making my way, with difficulty, as there were other, smaller stones on the bank I stood on one of them and looked over the wall. Sure enough, I was a matter of a few yards from the hornbeam hedge.

Back on my side of the wall, the bank widened out and there was quite a large pile of stones of various sizes. I suddenly realized that they had been left over from building the wall. There was every indication that the big one I had come upon had been part of the pile until quite recently: the vegetation had been flattened where it had been rolled along the ground. I went back and had a proper look at it.

The stone was slippery from the rain and snow. I put the torch in my pocket for a moment and just about managed to heave it over into the river, the water plants preventing what might, in other circumstances, have been a huge splash. I dug out the torch again, switched it on and found myself gazing at the top of a hammered-in metal peg of some kind which had a thinnish nylon rope tied to it, the other end going over the edge of the river bank and from sight.

Everything was getting just a bit exciting. /

I knelt and groped down the rope. It was very taut as though it had something heavy tied to the other end, far too heavy, I quickly discovered, for me to pull it up from the position I was in. How deep was the river?

In the end I worked out that the reeds and rushes were not the kind of plants that grew in deep water and gingerly lowered myself in. Liquid ice spread up to my knees and busily proceeded to freeze me solid. I wasted no time, bent, hauled up what appeared to be a canvas bag and just achieved dumping it up on the bank before all my muscles gave up. Then I had to wade for a short distance before the bank became lower and, shivering, I was able to clamber out. All this I had had to do in the dark for fear of totally immersing the torch. Memo to Patrick: get a waterproof one.

It was an old, albeit small, army kit bag and the rope had been threaded through the metal rings in the top and then knotted several times. It took me what seemed for ever to untie them but I only broke two fingernails in the process and my reward was well worth it: the entrancing gleam of gold.

The little ingots had been roughly done up in bubble wrap and there did not seem to be enough to represent the entire haul stolen from the dive boat, thought to be around one hundred and fifty. This was not to say that Brandon, or whoever (I was forcing myself to keep an open mind on the actual identity of the person responsible), had bought or received all those plundered.

I would go and ring his doorbell. But first of all I spent a little while putting the gold somewhere else.

He opened the front door, eyed me narrowly and said, 'What the hell do *you* want?'

'Just a word,' I replied, my arms still aching from lugging the gold. 'With your wife.'

'She's not here.'

'D'you mind telling me where she is?'

'Yes, I do. Bugger off.'

It was then that I noticed the slick of fresh blood on his shirt sleeve. It was then, if I'd had any sense, I ought to have run like mad.

Brandon was looking at my soaked clothing.

'It's pouring,' I said. 'Do you own a shotgun?'

'No.'

'I'm sure you do. Was the gold a little private affair in an otherwise fairly routine life of crime and you decided to retire on the proceeds? Even though they might have helped you hide away the ingots you then had the problem of what to do with all the tedious hangers-on, especially the Manleys as you'd only hired him, through Davies, because you thought his security-guard insider knowledge might come in useful one day.'

'You're not being at all clever,' Brandon sneered.

'And you thought it was really neat to throw away the murder weapon in Brian Stonelake's tractor shed, being as you'd used his barn as a charnel house. He was the local bad boy and the police were bound to turn the whole place over when the bodies were discovered and find the knife together with all kinds of stolen property. But it was a pure coincidence that Stonelake's father's coffin had ended up being used to hide the gold. I bet you had a really good laugh with Davies about that. Where did that blood on your sleeve come from?'

'He must have brushed against the steak that's ready for grilling in the kitchen,' said a voice behind me.

I whirled round and the person I really thought he had just

203

done to death stood before me. Not a frail and gently smiling Marjorie Brandon but a wiry, ferocious-looking woman who then struck me with a fist, just like a man might do. Pain exploded in my face and then I was flat on my back on the marble tiling, my head having come into violent contact with a wall. She dragged me inside the flat by my feet, dropping them on the hall carpet. I heard the front door slam.

She was not finished with me and actually pulled me to my feet so she could hit me again. 'Stupid little cow!' she screamed at me, spraying saliva, as I lay on the floor. 'People like you are shit! And that husband of yours! If there's one thing I loathe it's holier than thou, Daddy's a vicar, I'm an army officer saving the world and raising money for charity SHITS!'

'You haven't seen Patrick on one of his bad days,' I told her.

This time she hit me so hard I passed out.

It was a surprise to recover consciousness and realize that I was still alive and not existing as some kind of shade hovering in the roof of the barn watching the blood drain from my lifeless body below. With an effort, for my imagination is formidable and has to be controlled sometimes, I did not decorate this sad little picture with grieving husband, family and friends but slew the whole bloody thing and concentrated on escape.

I was lying on my right side, still on the hall carpet, and although they had tied my hands behind me and my feet together I could feel the heavy lump that was the short-barrelled police-issue Smith and Wesson in my pocket. I had no idea whether they had removed the mobile phone from my other pocket.

These lovely people were having dinner, judging by the tinkling of cutlery on china, the smell of seared meat heavy in the air. I lay quite still, eyes closed, when I heard foot-steps approaching and someone walked close by, her, she kicked me as she went by, and went into the kitchen. I heard a bottle crash into the rubbish bin, the fridge door being opened and the distinct squeaky sound of the cork being drawn from another. Were they drinking themselves into a state where they could happily contemplate murder? It did not seem to me that she needed much, if any, artificial help. She was also firmly in charge of everything that went on here.

How long had I been away? How long did I have left? My fiendish imagination presented me with the rectory dining room, the three of them eating, my dinner drying up in the Rayburn while Patrick and his father discussed the village cricket team. I actually banged my head on the floor a couple of times to stop this flight of fancy, making myself nauseated with the pain. Truly, truly, I would stop writing novels and have a brain operation to rid me of this curse.

My sight was blurred but I twisted my neck and looked around. Nearest to me was a bathroom: the door was ajar and I could see inside and next to it another door, also not pulled quite closed. The toilet? If it was a really small room I might be able to . . .

Moving as soundlessly as possible I started to hump myself along the floor, pausing frequently to listen. They were still eating, talking in low voices. Then I achieved sitting up and, head spinning, reached the door and gave it a gentle push. Yes, a small loo. The door was still slowly moving and then the hinges squeaked.

There was a crash as cutlery was dropped on to plates and in the same moment I hurled myself into the little room, twisted round and kicked the door shut with my feet. Bracing them against it, my back to the toilet, I waited, shivering.

At that moment the doorbell rang.

Someone opened it and I heard Marjorie say, 'Oh, it's you, Teddy.' They then carried on talking in an undertone.

I really did not stand a chance. The door was suddenly rammed open and it was either move or have my legs broken. A thick-set individual hauled me out, backwards, by my arms and dumped me back down on to the hall floor.

'Who the hell is she?' he demanded to know.

'Daughter-in-law of the local vicar,' said Brandon, coming into my line of view, puffing at a cigarette. 'Playing policeman.'

'More realistically, from our point of view,' Marjorie said coldly, with a dismissive glance in his direction, 'she's the wife of the rector's son, who I understand has just started a police career at senior level. He's working on the investigation of our little escapade in the barn.'

'So we just wring her bloody neck. What's the problem?'

'Teddy, you really must stop thinking you can solve everything with violence. Someone must know she's here.'

'Do they?' the bull-necked moron shouted at me.

'Of course.' My own voice surprised me, slurred and faint. 'Where's your car?'

'I didn't bring it.'

I thought for a moment that he might resume where Mother had left off but his fists dropped back to his sides. 'We'll clear out for a while until the heat's off.'

Marjorie appeared to count up to ten. 'Teddy, you're not in the US now. The heat, as you put it, won't go off and –' her voice rose – 'everything would have been perfectly in hand if you hadn't come back and interfered!'

Teddy gave his brain cell a quick trot around his cranium and grabbed the cordless phone from a small table. 'Here, you,' he said to me. 'Ring your old man and tell him you won't be home for a while. Say you've been delayed.'

Marjorie groaned. 'This is not some country plod you're referring to but a man who used to work for MI5! His mother told me and she should know!'

'You'll have to untie my hands,' I said encouragingly to Teddy.

'Tell him you've had an interesting lead that you're following up,' Marjorie said after a pause. 'Say there's no need for him to become involved and you'll be back shortly. Say that, nothing else, or I shall kill you. Right now.'

Teddy took a flick knife from his pocket and sprang the blade, smiling at it. I was looking at the murderer.

I was in no shape to outwit even a bunch of fourth-rate crooks. It took a few minutes to massage the circulation and feeling back into my fingers, during which time the execrable Teddy walked up and down the hallway, thrusting the knife

206

into the woodwork, farting at intervals and carrying on a shouted conversation with the other two discussing where in France they would go for a couple of months when they had collected the gold, there having been a change of mind on Marjorie's part. At last, I could delay no longer and the three of them grouped around me as I sat on the floor.

I rang Patrick's mobile number.

'Gillard,' said the man I had known for most of my life.

I repeated the message, word for word, not taking any immediate risks by adding any of our code words or changing the tone of my voice. The gun was still in my pocket – I could not imagine why – but I simply did not trust myself to use it there and then against the three of them. My mobile was in my other pocket, I could feel its slim shape against my side with my elbow.

I obeyed all the instructions but after I had rung off everything went black.

Fifteen

On two previous occasions, when Patrick and I worked for D12, I have woken up in hospital to see him, and James Carrick, sitting by my bedside, looking worried. This time though I immediately knew that something was different and it probably had something to do with the fact that, for one shocking moment, I had not been able to remember who these two men were.

'How do you feel?' Patrick asked quietly.

Yes, I reminded myself, he was my husband, but it seemed that I was looking at him for the first time or from a new perspective. He was actually very attractive, I decided, and it was mainly the eyes that did it: grey irises flecked with gold, a darker band encircling them. His black wavy hair tinged with grey could do with a trim but then again it always turned me on when it curled down on the back of his neck like that.

They appeared to be waiting for me to say something. Oh, yes, how did I feel. 'I don't know,' I heard my voice say.

Carrick was still not well but soldiering on in the way Scots do and right now was gazing at me in a direct sort of way. 'Why were you walking along the main road, Ingrid?' he asked.

'I don't know,' I said.

'Can't you remember?' Patrick enquired, alarm in his tone.

'I can't remember being anywhere near the main road.'

'You were hit by a car.'

'No,' I said. 'I wasn't.'

'There are four witnesses,' said James. 'A couple in the vehicle that hit you and a mother and daughter in another car coming from the opposite direction.'

'Was anyone else hurt?' I asked, dreading his reply and now aware of the dressings on my head and chin. My mouth felt strange, my head fit to burst.

'No, nothing really serious. The man's wife has a minor whiplash injury where he braked hard to try to avoid you – you really have him to thank, he really only bumped you over – and naturally they're shaken up. Ingrid, there are no street lights along that road and you were walking along the middle of it wearing dark clothing. That's just asking to be knocked down.'

Patrick said, 'You phoned me, said you were following up a lead and I needn't bother myself with it, but rang off before I could suggest you came home first as we were about to eat. Do you remember doing that?'

'How long have I been here?' I asked. Yes, I did have a vague recollection of doing that, it was part of the blur of events in my mind. Some of this had to be real, the rest perhaps just a lurid dream I had had after the car hit me.

'About twelve hours.'

I now saw that my left arm was in a sling.

'Do you remember phoning me?' Patrick repeated.

They were both furious and had lost patience with me and had not even told me how bad were my injuries.

'Go away,' I said, closing my eyes. 'I don't know what I remember. I don't even know if *this* is real or not.' The things that were swilling around in my mind were preposterous. Marjorie Brandon, a different woman altogether to the one I had met, had hit me? They had a thug of an accomplice, probably their son, by the name of Teddy? I had found the gold? I had been hit by a car after walking along the main road in the dark? The last was the only thing of which I had no recollection at all.

'Brandon's made an official complaint,' Carrick said, getting to his feet. 'In writing, this time. Do you remember going to his place and bawling him out, accusing him of the murders, of leading a life of crime and just about anything else you could think of?'

'Oh, yes, I can remember that bit,' I said.

'I thought I told you to *apologize* to him.'

'Go away,' I said, knowing tears were trickling down my face. 'I'll talk to you again when you're off those bloody pills.'

The DCI went, shaking his head sadly at Patrick on the way out.

'If you loved me—' I began.

'I do,' he interrupted, pulling his chair up closer. 'Nothing's going to change that.'

'But I took the gun, broke into the locked garage, confronted Brandon . . .' My head hurt so much I felt sick. I had to stop talking for a moment.

'It was still in your pocket and would have taken a bit of explaining away if I hadn't been issued with a permit. Brinkley arranged for me to have it.'

'Why?' At least no one had made off with it.

'You and I are still on several terrorist organizations' hit-lists. Ingrid—'

'I know, you've been given the boot and it's all my fault.'

'No, I haven't. But your position's a bit iffy now. Don't worry about it.'

'Go away,' I said.

'I was going to suggest I take you home, to Devon, when your wrist's been put in plaster.'

'I've broken it?'

'Yes, they're waiting until the swelling goes down.'

'What else have I done to myself?'

'Hasn't anyone told you?'

'Patrick, I've only just woken up.'

He smiled to himself in infuriating male fashion. 'Not quite. You've been telling the doctors and nurses you found a big bag of gold. Other than the wrist you're only very badly bruised. And you've two super black eyes.'

'I think I did find the gold, actually.'

'What, the ingots? Where?'

'In the river.'

'But—'

'I can't remember what I did with it afterwards.'

The pig actually smiled again, patting my arm. 'It's all right. Don't worry about anything.'

'Go away.'

'OK. I'll come back later.'

'Don't bother. Just ask Elspeth if she'd mind bringing me some clean clothes.'

By the door he paused. 'Did you find anything in the locked garage?'

'What locked garage?'

'You just said you broke into the locked garage.'

But it had gone, I had no memory of it.

I must have slept, for when I next woke up the late-afternoon sun was shining across the bed. The sun. When had I last seen the sun? How wonderful. I moved the hand not in the sling and from which someone had removed the drip attachment while I slept into the bright light and could feel the warmth. It was a part of emerging from my bad, dark dream.

The events in my mind were much more in focus now, at least, everything but walking along the main road. This was not to say that most of it could still be a dream and I was merely recollecting it more clearly. What I needed was proof. The main problem with obtaining that was the men who would have to go and find it for me, were the same ones who thought me deluded, suffering from amnesia, or whatever, after being hit by the car. The infernal imagination had survived unscathed, however, and now presented me with a neat little scenario of white-coated experts discussing with James and Patrick what was wrong with me, utilizing all the very latest psycho-babble, the whole boiling lot's heads going up and down like nodding donkeys.

I tried to get my thoughts in order but I ached and throbbed all over. It seemed logical, that until proved otherwise, I should regard everything I could remember as having actually taken place, no matter how bizarre it might appear. One problem was the dreamlike quality of my memories, the colours over-bright, lurid, the people stagey, almost grotesque caricatures of themselves. Not to worry, I would ignore that as well and put the phenomenon down to medical reasons.

Elspeth arrived, took one look at me and embraced me like swans' down.

'It's that bad?' I asked. 'I haven't dared look in a mirror.'

'You're not badly hurt, that's all that matters and the rest will mend. There's no one around – do you need me to come with you to the loo, or anything? I've brought your sponge bag and dressing gown.'

A quarter of an hour later, having washed myself, one-handed, as well as I could, including the areas that actually appeared to be going black and blue as I watched – I had thought for a moment that the mirror was faulty – I was far more comfortably back in bed.

'He's completely at sea,' Elspeth said, smoothing the covers. 'Patrick, I mean. He simply doesn't know what to make of this.'

'It's because I have a reputation for a vivid imagination,' I said. 'Even I can't separate fact from fiction right now.'

'You could relate it all to me and I could write it down. Would that help?'

'I could try but it won't make any difference. Patrick, and more importantly James Carrick, still won't believe it. In his eyes the Brandons are OAPs and that's that.'

'All this happened to you because you called on the Brandons? How incredible!'

'I've no real evidence to back it up. Only the gold, if I really did find it.'

Her eyes glowed.

'Only I can't remember what I did with it,' I added.

Elspeth rummaged in her bag for pen and paper. Then she paused. 'What a dreadful woman you must think I am!' she cried. 'I haven't even asked you if you want anything to eat or drink.'

'Tea,' I pleaded. 'And something sweet to give me energy. I must have missed all the mealtimes.'

She went away, muttering about neglectful husbands and absent NHS staff.

My arms ached as though I had been weight-training with far too heavy weights. Come to think of it they had ached like this when I had entered the mill, crossed the hall and rung the . . .

There was a box of tissues on the bedside table and I snatched one and cried a little into it. I was starting to remember. My arms ached from hauling the gold out of the river in the old kit bag, I could feel the rough, sodden canvas under my fingers even now. I looked down at my hands. Two of my nails were broken from picking at the knots in the tight nylon rope. After succeeding in opening the bag to discover the ingots bundled up in bubble-wrap I had dropped the undone end of the rope back in the river and rolled another stone over the hammered-in end of the metal spike to make everything look just the same as when I had found it. Then what?

Just a blank until I had returned to the mill.

Returned? Where had I been? Where had I gone, no doubt hugging the bag to myself as it was much too heavy to carry one-handed?

Elspeth came back with the tea and a large iced bun with a cherry on top.

'You're bound to be upset for a few days,' she said consolingly when I had dried another few tears.

'No, it's just that Patrick and I always have sticky buns at the nick,' I gulped. 'It's turned into a little ritual, a joke between us, really.'

She cut it into small pieces for me as my mouth was very swollen.

'If you're going to tell me what you thought happened someone else should be here,' Elspeth said solemnly. 'As a witness. This is bound to end up in court.'

'You won't believe what I think happened either,' I told her.

'Try me.'

Elspeth was helping me drink the tea as even my good hand was too shaky to hold the cup. I said, 'Marjorie Brandon appears to be the brains behind a career in crime the pair of them have had. She hit me and dragged me into the flat by my feet where she hit me again. They have a yob helping them who might be their son called Teddy who arrived shortly afterwards.'

'I know about him. Edward, she referred to him as. He works in the States and she made him sound very grand. Oh, my *dear*.'

I had dissolved into tears again. My imagination did not seem to have hijacked my brain after all.

'I'm going to call Patrick,' Elspeth announced when I had been persuaded to eat something. 'He ought to be here with you anyway.'

Patrick arrived about twenty minutes later – he had been working at Manvers Street – and brought with him a witness in the shape of Lynn Outhwaite and a tape recorder. It was all official and Elspeth did not have to write anything down. I thought for a moment she would be asked to leave and prepared to protest but Patrick solemnly gave her permission to stay.

There were still holes in my memory of what had happened and as I spoke I could see the doubt on their faces, especially when I said I had found the bag containing the gold, but I carried on talking, dredging up every smallest detail I could remember, for a little while longer and then asked for a short rest.

'How about the locked garage?' Patrick prompted ruthlessly, but stopping the tape. 'Are you sure you still can't remember that bit?'

'No,' I said, carefully sipping another cup of tea, unassisted this time.

'Yet you can remember going in the unlocked one first that contained the blue car.'

'I've just said so, haven't it? Oh, that's right, the alarm wasn't set and the keys had been left in the ignition. I had an idea it might be booby-trapped in some way so I didn't touch it.'

'Whatever made you think *that*?' Lynn asked incredulously.

'I was trained by MI5,' I told her. 'It makes you twitchy.'

When we recommenced and that new recollection had been inserted for the benefit of the tape I went on to say that I could not remember what I had done with the gold and began to relate, again in as much detail as possible, what had happened after I had rung the Brandons' doorbell. Here open scepticism surfaced among my audience and when I spoke of how they had cooked and eaten dinner while I lay, tied up, out in the hall Lynn started to become restless. Even Elspeth looked doubtful and once again I began to doubt myself.

'The Brandons are adamant that they didn't even let you in after you'd confronted them at the door,' Patrick said at one point.

'I'm sure some of my DNA is on their carpet,' I retorted. 'Are they still there, by the way?'

'So far as I know.'

'Only they were talking of going to France until things settled down again.'

Patrick shook his head. 'I'm fairly sure they're still there. But you're ahead of yourself. This man Teddy – he's their son?'

'I only guessed he was their son, from the way Marjorie spoke to him.' But I could not remember the exact words she had said.

'I know I'm probably not supposed to say anything,' Elspeth suddenly interposed, 'but if Ingrid put the gold somewhere after she found it and they looked for it in the place they left it and it wasn't there they're not going anywhere until they've recovered it, are they?'

Or got their hands on me again to make me tell them where I'd hidden it. I shuddered. Perhaps I would go home to Devon after all.

Patrick smiled at his mother in acknowledgement of this and said to me, 'Go on. What happened after he arrived?'

'They made me phone you. Marjorie said she would kill me there and then if I did not exactly repeat the message they gave me. I felt too awful to try to resist. He had a knife.'

'But you had the gun in your pocket.'

'My hands and feet were tied together and they all stood in a ring around me as I sat on the floor. They undid my hands so I could phone.'

'Then what?'

'I don't know. I passed out again. I think Teddy must have hit me. He was standing nearest to me then.'

Lynn said, 'But why didn't they remove the gun from your pocket, or your mobile phone? Surely both posed a risk to them. I'm ignoring the skeleton keys, by the way.'

'I've no idea.'

'But you're saying that these people are hardened criminals.'

'Brandon's attitude was that I was just the rector's daughter-in-law playing policeman and Marjorie was far more worried about Patrick. They probably didn't search me.'

But there had been something else in my pocket. I said, 'May I have another break while I try to think about something?'

Patrick got up to stretch his legs. 'And we haven't even touched on why you then walked up the main road.'

'You still don't believe me, do you?' I stormed. 'They must have loaded me in a car, driven up there, and then, when presumably I'd come round sufficiently to be mobile, left me in the road hoping I'd get killed!' What had been the other thing in my pocket that they could have regarded as a risk to them?

'What, and risk someone else at the mill seeing them?' Lynn scoffed.

'It's not that I don't believe you,' Patrick said. 'You were knocked unconscious more than once and that affects the mind. You get vivid mental pictures, strange dreams. I know, when I was blown up in the Falklands I dreamt that I was a boy again and walking along Plymouth Hoe having a long conversation with Dad about the birds and the bees.'

'Really?' said Elspeth. 'What on earth did your father say?'

'I don't think I ought to tell you,' he said with a grin.

'More tea?' Elspeth asked me, going a bit pink.

'Tea and sand,' I murmured. 'In the garage. I took a sample. Plus a black Porsche. It's probably Teddy's.'

'Marjorie did say he had a good job,' Elspeth said eagerly.

'A pound to a penny he's just out of a US penitentiary,' I said. 'He's too thick to have a good job.'

Lynn was getting impatient. 'There were a couple of sample bags in one of your pockets but they were both unused. How many did you take with you?'

'I don't know,' I told her. 'I just took some from Patrick's briefcase. They must have removed it.'

She was having great trouble staying polite. 'Sorry, I simply can't believe they'd take that – surely they wouldn't have had a clue what was in it – and leave behind your mobile and the revolver. Sorry again, Ingrid, but I honestly think you lost your temper with Brandon – he is a rather obnoxious old man – then had an idea about something else after they'd refused you entry, phoned Patrick and then set off to wherever you were headed and got knocked down. As Patrick says, the rest is hallucinations brought on by being hit by the car.'

'You've only got to check the garages,' I said. 'And find the stone I rolled back over the top of the metal spike that has the end of the rope tied to it.'

Patrick and Lynn exchanged glances and it was the kind of look that sent humiliation rolling over me in a clammy wave. This man of mine was now a policeman, I reminded myself again. Here was another person and the magic of our previous working relationship had gone.

Patrick brought the interview to a formal close, switched off the tape and there was a short silence.

'Ingrid didn't previously know that the Brandons had a son,' Elspeth said defensively. 'I never mentioned him to her until she spoke of him today.'

'He might have answered the door when she got there,' Lynn said, rising to go. 'There's no knowing exactly what took place and we probably never will. Now, if you don't mind, I've still got work to do. Shall I take the recorder with me?' she finished by saying to Patrick.

When it had been handed over and she had gone Elspeth said to Patrick, 'You owe it to Ingrid to check up on some of the things she's said. Surely it isn't that difficult.'

'I'd need a search warrant for the garages,' Patrick said. 'I don't think I'd get one. You have to have really good reasons, a certain amount of evidence, before they're issued.'

'But can't you issue one yourself? I thought you were an acting superintendent.'

'I'm nevertheless a probationer and not permitted to do some things.'

Elspeth shot to her feet and made for the door. 'This doesn't sound like you talking at all.'

'It isn't the same now, Elspeth,' I said, hating that I was responsible for something coming between them. 'He had carte blanche before.'

She turned and snapped, 'Well, I suppose it all boils down to priorities and how much he wants the job.'

Patrick and I were left on our own and for several seconds neither of us spoke.

'What now?' I whispered.

He appeared to gather his thoughts. 'Later on they're going to have a look at your wrist and if the swelling's gone down it'll be put in plaster. You're to have more blood tests to confirm you haven't suffered damage to your liver, spleen and things like that. If all's well you'll probably be home tomorrow morning.'

Which had not been the question I had asked and well he knew it.

By this time I was practically convinced that Lynn Outhwaite, in her blunt but well-meaning way, was right. It was a relief for it meant that I could go home, tell myself that I was made of unsuitable stuff for police work, carry on working on *A Man Called Celeste* and keep my nose right out of Patrick's new career. Nothing was actually lost, I told myself, the only resentful party being a miserable old devil who objected to being harangued by demented female novelists.

I was not resentful for, obviously, if I had been walking along the middle of the main road I deserved to be hit by a car. At this stage I was not really asking myself what I had been doing there if the Brandons had not been responsible, for if all the rest of what I had said was pie in the sky and no one was taking any notice it did not matter, did it? The only slightly worrying thing about it was that if one stuck to this theory, I had set off along the road *before* the car hit me and I should be able to remember, even in garbled fashion, what this fantastic lead was all about.

At ten the next morning Patrick collected me and I managed to get to the car, slowly and carefully, under my own steam. He was quiet and I assumed that his shoulder was still hurting. We made a good pair.

Never assume.

'Well, I broke all the rules,' he said when we were having coffee at the rectory, Elspeth and John out somewhere.

'What do you mean?'

'I applied for a search warrant, first to Carrick and then to Bromsgrove's boss – Bromsgrove was all for it by the way, he seems to have taken quite a shine to you – and was turned down, flat, by both of them on the grounds of lack of evidence. Apparently Brandon's now written to the Chief Constable. So last night I went down there anyway, had a look in the end garage, no car, broke into the third one along, no car, no sand or tea. Then I walked along the river bank behind the garages, just the same as you described. No stone, no metal spike, no rope, no sign of anything like that ever having existed there.'

I could only gaze at him, utterly appalled. 'But you could see where the grass was flattened where the stone had been rolled from the heap,' I said.

'It was all flattened, as though a herd of cows had got in there.'

I gripped my hands together to try to stop them shaking.

'And of course I owned up,' Patrick went on. 'I had to.' He paused. 'I'm suspended, as of an hour ago.'

'I'm so terribly, terribly sorry,' I moaned, shaking like a whole forest of leaves by now.

He leaned over and kissed me. 'But I'm fairly convinced that what you can remember actually happened.'

'You believe me!'

'It was just the way you described. The big thistle, then, farther along I could see where your foot had slipped and you'd grabbed the handful of grass and the little tree. The place where the bank had all but gone. It's all there. You couldn't have dreamt that up.'

'I could still have gone along there and not found the gold.'

'You said you'd broken two fingernails undoing the knots in the rope. Did you nibble off the broken bits and spit them out?'

'Probably.'

He produced a tiny plastic bag. 'I didn't bother to show this to anyone at the nick but that is the rather violent orange varnish you've got on now, isn't it?'

'I can't understand how, even with a torch, you found these in the dark,' I said, looking at the minute scraps of fingernail.

'One was on the wall and I spotted the other quite by chance. They reflected the light like ladybirds, only they're not around during the winter months.'

'But you're suspended,' I agonized. 'It's all over.'

'No, it's not. I'm going to nail these people who punched you in the face and hoped to kill you. Nail them to the wall.'

Sixteen

After a hot bath heavily laced with some kind of 'rural remedy' (Hinton Littlemoor is very keen on this sort of thing), one of several items intended for emergencies that Elspeth had procured for me from somewhere, and then taking two strong painkillers with a brew of special herbal tea from the same source I found that I could at least walk and not hobble. The plaster on my arm, just to the elbow and leaving my fingers and thumb free, was lightweight and there was no longer any need for a sling. I then lay down for a while with an icepack on my face, actually a bag of frozen peas, and when I looked again my swollen mouth was definitely less puffy. Nothing could be done about the contusion on my forehead and the black eyes but I've always thought it a waste of good steak anyway.

I had no idea what Patrick was doing, only aware that he had departed, driving with more speed than normal down the rectory drive. His shoulder must be better, either that or he was ignoring it.

Thought about cold-bloodedly, what had happened was inevitable; sooner or later the pair of us would have run head-on into officialdom and the perceived correct way of doing things. It was just as well, perhaps, that it had happened now. That is what probation periods are all about, I told myself. We would just have to write off the whole episode as experience: it was not as though Patrick had badgered the police to let him in.

Quite shortly afterwards he returned. 'We're leaving,' he said, finding me in the living room. 'Please start packing – I'll help you in a minute.'

221

He disappeared and I made my way out into the hall and surveyed the flight of stairs down which I had laboriously journeyed some two minutes earlier. Perhaps if I went up backwards on my bottom . . . No, that was badly bruised too. I was still standing there, working out tactics, when a whirlwind arrived and I was borne aloft in a fireman's lift, this, I assumed, on account of the temporary weakness of one of his arms.

'You weigh a bit more than you did on our wedding day,' he said, tipping me down, but reasonably gently, on to the bed.

'I felt one hell of lot randier than I do right now too,' I observed crossly. 'What's the plan?'

'We leave here making more noise than usual. Say cheerio loudly in the pub and things like that. Candidly mention that we're going home, as the police isn't for me. It also makes sense not to expose Mum and Dad to any more possible danger. I shall then take you home, but I'm going to come back tonight. Live rough, or at least undercover, and watch these characters at the mill. If – and I'm not for a moment saying you didn't find the ingots – if they still haven't recovered the gold themselves it's fairly certain they'll go looking for it. I shall be there too, shadowing them.'

'Hoping they'll find it and you can alert Carrick?'

'Yes, or incriminate themselves in some other way so I can fix it that they're arrested while, say, loading the stuff in the car. We still need hard evidence.'

'If *only* I could remember what I did with it,' I fretted.

'How did you manage to get the bag over the wall?'

'I just heaved it up and dropped it over, having checked that no one was around.' This took me by surprise, up until now everything I had done regarding the ingots had been a blank.

'And then what?'

'I climbed over by jamming a toe into a crevice.'

'Go on.'

'I think I can recollect picking up the bag again. It's a

wonder I didn't put my back out, and then I sort of cuddled it to myself and started walking. I was really worried someone would see me.'

'Did you walk far?'

'Too far, my arms were killing me – they still are. But I don't know where I went. Sorry, it's all a fog.'

'What was going through your mind, though? Had you decided where you were going with the stuff when you left the mill?'

'No, I don't think I decided in advance. I just walked until something presented itself.'

'Did you go across fields?'

'Probably not. I wouldn't have been able to manage fences and things like that.'

'I'll do a reconstruction if the Brandons don't show, try to follow in your footsteps from the garages utilizing a lot of guesswork. Tonight, when I return.'

'It would be far more useful if I could be here too. Then it might all come back to me.'

'I agree, but there's no time to wait for you to recover a bit. I dare not leave it any longer or they might search the village from end to end, find what they're looking for and get away.'

'They could have already done so.'

'No, they're still there. I managed to climb a fir tree across the field behind the mill just now and had a good look at the place through binoculars. I could only see Mr and Mrs, though, no Teddy.'

'He went off in the car, perhaps.'

'He'll be back – he'll be the one poking around in hedges.'

'This is all supposing that they're sure it was me who went off with it.'

'It's a straw they'll clutch at – it's all they have.'

'If you don't mind I'd prefer to stay with you.'

'But, woman, you can hardly move!'

'I'll be all right, I'll take the pills I was given.'

He surveyed me dubiously.

'The last assignment,' I said.

'OK, please yourself. I'll go and buy you a jerry-can of tonic wine as a bracer.'

I ended up relying on another item in the rural remedies kit, an 'Essence of Flowers' that apparently the President of the Mothers' Union swore by when she took her fox terriers to Crufts. Whether she gave it to the dogs or drank it herself I never discovered.

We departed about three-quarters of an hour later, without even telling John and Elspeth that we were not actually leaving the district. We told them no lies either, Patrick emptying his wallet of cash and leaving it on the kitchen table, as he usually does after a visit, and promising to return in a few days. Elspeth did not ask any questions and diplomatically made no comments but I knew she was very disappointed by the suspension. She might have been feeling guilty after egging him on.

From MI5 days there was still the bag in the car packed with changes of dark, practical outer clothing; thick, warm tracksuits that fitted either of us, underwear, a first-aid kit, this more comprehensive than another in the glove compartment, washing gear and emergency rations. We also carried the usual waterproofs and boots.

At the moment however we did nothing more controversial than stopping at a pub high on the outskirts of Bath for an early lunch. Afterwards we drove to a quiet lane, parked, reclined our seats and slept for longer than we intended to, waking into a gloomy late afternoon.

I made Patrick strip off his sweater to check the dressings on his shoulder and the wounds had bled again a little so I changed them.

'What on earth's that?' he wanted to know when he saw me taking a swig out of the 'Essence of Flowers' bottle.

'A herbal pick-me-up that Elspeth gave me. It tastes rather nice.'

He took it and gingerly sniffed, pulling a face. 'It says on the label to take two or three *drops* in water twice a day.'

'Only boring people read labels,' I said.

* * *

We listened to the radio until it was almost dark and then drove back in the direction of Hinton Littlemoor. Patrick had already found somewhere to park the Range Rover out of sight, a narrow track that led into a field near where he had climbed the tree in the morning. No one would need access to it at this time of day.

'Where are we going to watch the mill from?' I said as we walked down a bridle path towards the village centre, just able to see where were going in the deep dusk. I had taken as many painkillers as possible this side of an overdose and, ye gods, *something* was coursing through me zapping all the aches and pains. I had an idea it was the rural remedy, the little green bottle of which was safely in my pocket.

'There's a house for sale opposite with an L-shaped flat-roofed extension down the side and partly at the front. It's empty, we can keep watch from up there. No one'll see us, there are no street lights until you get to the corner.'

No, but there were the exceedingly stylish exterior lights of the mill itself, resembling Victorian street lamps, which I thought illuminated the house across the street beautifully. Patrick did not hesitate, leading the way through the gate and around to the rear of the house so we could get on the roof out of sight. He gave me a leg-up on to a water butt, which fortunately had a piece of broken paving slab across the top and not a plastic lid, and from there I stepped on to the flat roof.

'Down!' he urged. 'Flat on your front, wriggle on your elbows, don't even crawl.'

Just to think: I was in hospital not many hours previously.

Side by side, we eventually lay on our stomachs near the edge of the roof. There was a good view of the main entrance and parking area of the mill when one parted the fragile branches of an overhanging birch tree, which Patrick assured me in a whisper would screen us completely from a distance.

Cars and people on foot went to and fro, Pascal Lapointe left the building and walked in the direction of the centre of the village, returning several minutes later with what could have been a bottle of wine tucked beneath one arm. A car drew in and Tamsin Roper got out, presumably returning from work. Then Lorna Church arrived and also went within.

'We'll have a while to wait,' Patrick said softly. 'They might even leave it until the early hours of the morning.' He then exclaimed under his breath as John came into view, going for his final twice a day prescribed half-mile walk. Seeing him, something jolted in my memory but nothing came of it.

We took it in turns to watch while the other rolled over onto their back for a rest. We ate the bars of high-energy food in our pockets, played I-spy in whispers and heard the church clock strike the hours.

Midnight.

Patrick groaned as the final chime faded eerily away into the chill mist that had descended. 'May a thousand curses rain down upon their scabby heads,' he said faintly.

At two, pain having got me back in its grip, I had a good mouthful of 'Essence of Flowers' and almost freaked out a few minutes later when my fingertips started to burn and my hair felt that it was standing on end. The sensation gradually faded but then I suddenly felt that I was floating a couple of inches above the surface of the roof.

'What's the matter?' Patrick asked after I had looked under my chest to check.

'I just feel a bit odd, that's all.'

'You've overdosed on that bloody elixir.' He chuckled. 'Probably going to spontaneously combust.'

'Don't be so *beastly*.'

'I'm going to give them until three. Then we'll reconstruct your movements of last night but without going into the garages, see what that brings and then come back again tonight.'

Three a.m. arrived and still there was no movement over the road, all the windows in darkness. Then we heard a car approaching and, moments later, a black Porsche swept in, tyres squealing, and went from sight in the direction of the garages. There came the distant sounds of a garage door being opened, the car driven in and various doors slammed shut again.

The stocky figure came into view, walking quickly, hunched into his jacket, took a key from his pocket and let himself in.

'That's him,' I said.

'He moves like a real bruiser – and in a bad temper too. Good, that affects judgement.'

'He's not exactly overburdened with it already.'

It was a wonderful moment when, just a short while later, the three of them emerged, stood talking in low voices waving their arms in various directions for a minute or so and then went off towards the garages.

Patrick sat up. 'Will they return this way or start climbing over walls and going though hedges from that end?' Answering the query himself, he went on, 'No, I reckon, being as they think it's you who made off with the loot, that after another quick look round down there they'll assume you came this way and stashed the bag somewhere easy, a front garden or shed. We'll wait.'

Brandon junior came back almost straight away, gazed about and then wrenched a couple of lower branches from a small tree, pulling off the side shoots and breaking off the thinner ends, scattering the debris, ending up with something the size of walking sticks. He went off with them.

'Well, he's got an ASBO coming to him at least,' Patrick said. 'I suggest we get down while they're away and conceal ourselves behind the hedge down there.'

This we did and although I still felt a bit floaty it proved to be of no help whatsoever in getting down off the water butt. Patrick had to assist me and we both finished up in an untidy heap.

'God, I'm really glad I'm not staying in the police and Carrick isn't here,' he muttered.

'You've only been suspended,' I pointed out.

'Only!' There followed a few almost inaudible epithets.

We crouched down behind the front hedge and it was nice

to assume a different uncomfortable position. Then we froze as we heard voices. If it was the Brandons they were not bothering to speak quietly now, actually arguing. Bad temper is catching, I thought, remembering Teddy's arrival.

Which was all in our favour, of course.

They crossed the road and came right towards us and I jumped as a stick thwacked into the hedge close to my head. In the next second Patrick had placed a steadying hand on my arm. We stayed quite still.

'You really screwed this up, didn't you?' Marjorie's voice said in a sibilant whisper, the pronunciation as I had last heard it, the vowels flattened, definitely not the refined manner of speaking she had put on when I had first met her. 'What a damn-fool place to hide it! That little cow must have sneaked it away before she came round. I hope she's dead.'

'I heard an ambulance or police siren a bit later on,' said Brandon senior. 'She's not dead, though. Someone was talking about it in the pub. This bloke said they've gone home, he's chucked it all in.'

'Teddy, you should have killed her there and then,' Marjorie said poisonously, 'not just shoved her out of the car.'

'It was you who said it was too risky and I wasn't to kill anyone else!' he protested. 'Too scared stiff of that smart-arse husband of hers.'

'He's the sort to behave outside the law,' Marjorie countered. 'Before we'd have known where we were he'd have paid one of his old army cronies to put bullets between our eyes.'

As I had noted once before, the woman was amazingly perceptive. No money would have changed hands, though: Patrick is owed quite a few favours.

They moved on, the sounds suggesting a poking and prodding of the vegetation at the side of the road. I felt that they had provided us with rather a lot of evidence against themselves and while I was enjoying feeling vindicated I was wondering what the outcome of this night would be. Patrick, I knew, was armed. What was he planning? I hoped it was not a burning-of-all-our-boats scenario along the lines of

Marjorie's predictions. The auspices were not good. In the past, those who had laid hands on me had ended up mostly dead.

Cautiously, we emerged from hiding and Patrick peered around the gateway. He beckoned to me and we went out into the street just in time to see the Brandons disappearing around a bend. Had they been drinking? Could I really smell alcohol in the air? It would explain their bad temper and lack of caution.

Conversing was out of the question now, we just trod silently in their wake. When we reached the road junction with the high street, where there was a lamppost, we stood in the shadows behind a nearby phone box, able to observe our quarry for a couple of minutes as they wove their way down in the opposite direction to the village green and church. No, I thought, I had not gone that way, I had been out of breath while carrying my burden.

Dogs began barking as three increasingly desperate people tried side gates, peered in porches and doorways and rummaged in litter bins. Then the penny appeared to drop that if what they were after had been left anywhere so public it would have already been found. They headed off towards open countryside.

'It's not down there,' I whispered.

'It isn't?' Patrick said in surprise. He had been preparing to move off.

'I *think* I went up the hill.'

He pondered. 'We might wait for a long time while they poke their way through every ditch and hedge bottom. Damn.'

'It's not gospel. I could be quite wrong.' Inwardly, I was still agonizing over whether I had really found it. I could have broken my fingernails climbing back over the wall.

'And those who start work early or have a long way to drive will be stirring at around five. We've an hour and three-quarters left at the most.'

Then we saw them reappear, walking quickly and purposefully back up the road towards us.

'Plan B,' Patrick said under his breath. 'This is more like it.'

We backed into a hedge that ran behind the phone box, emerging after they had passed us, heading uphill. They were not talking now but I could distinctly hear William Brandon puffing and panting as he struggled to keep up with the others. We had no choice now but to trail them in the open, ducking into gateways and behind any piece of cover. We were fortunate: they did not turn round and look behind them.

'I'm worried now,' Patrick said in my ear as we paused in the village shop doorway. 'There's no reason to suppose they believe we've left, despite what old Brandon said. Are they heading for the rectory?'

'You mean to force their way in to see if it was only a rumour and if I'm there, grab me, or anyone else for that matter, to try to find out where I put it?'

'It's quite possible. Look at them, they're not searching anymore. They've made up their minds to take action.'

'There should be people watching the rectory.'

'Probably just a probationer on their own at this time of night who'll be no match for that lot.' He dived out of the doorway, going back in the direction we had come. But only for a few yards, turning sharp right down a narrow passageway between the houses, risking using his torch here as it was very dark. We ran. Well, I seemed to be running.

After fifty yards or so we turned right again and were then in a wider unmade lane. It was full of potholes forcing us to slow down again. After another short distance there was a left turn and we climbed a stile on to a narrow footpath, fenced on either side, that wended its way quite steeply uphill between what was probably back gardens. After coming to another stile I found myself on one side of the open space that was the village green. It is quite large with a cricket pitch in the middle. Patrick switched off the torch and ran on. Not for the first time I marvelled at how mobile he is, considering, the result of constant hard work on his part since his devastating Falklands War injuries.

I simply could not keep up with him now.

The dark outline of the church spire loomed up ahead and over to the right, a lumpy rectangle in the foreground was the rear of the Ring O'Bells. We headed for it. Gazing around I almost fell over a low chain-link fence that borders this part of the green to prevent cars being parked on the grass. Still able to see Patrick ahead of me I crossed a side road, moved in the lee of the pub's side wall and then there was no choice but to cross another section of the green where it narrowed at one end. The church was straight ahead now, the rectory drive to the right of it but Patrick did not go that way, bearing round to the left where the road curved so we could cross out of sight of anyone coming from the other direction. There was a pedestrian access to the churchyard I had not known existed, where he waited for me, and we went through it and then were following an inner path by the high wall. We took shelter under the roofed lychgate, listening. We had seen no vehicles that would point to police surveillance.

I could hear but not see Brandon senior gasping for breath and had an idea the three were stationary close by. Patrick pointed and then I spotted them, just the tops of their heads showing above some bushes as they stood in the road about thirty yards away. They then moved on again, coming towards us and the rectory drive entrance.

Patrick turned and went down the main pathway to the church door and then around the side where a little picket gate allowed access to the rectory garden, a relic of the days when there was a right of way across it from the Grange next door.

In my slightly other-worldly, and if the truth were known, slow-witted, state it was a shock to realize that war was about to break out but, unlike in the past when we would have neutralized the threat and asked questions afterwards, now, in order to make a case against these people, we would have to wait for them to make any first, illegal, move. I hoped this truth was also going through Patrick's mind but when it comes to threats to his family he was quite likely to mow the lot down before they got to within a yard of the door.

Utilizing the little side paths in the garden Elspeth had created to make weeding the wide beds easier, we went through the garden. Entry to the small courtyard at the rear of the house was gained though an archway in the wall, which would conceal us from anyone standing by the back door.

It was then that Patrick encountered someone else, sort of enveloping them as an octopus might its prey, and I nearly tripped over the pair of them as they sank to the ground. Something was whispered and half the dark shape on the ground stayed where it was.

There were thumps and bangs as someone tried to kick in the back door.

I walked into a low branch of a shrub and received a stinging, and wet, slap across the face. When I had fought my way free Patrick had gone and I was just in time when I peered around the corner of the archway to see a large shape hurtling backwards through the opened doors of the garage. I made all available speed and was just in time to meet William Brandon endeavouring to come out again. A hand flat on his face I whispered, 'Sorry about being rude,' and shoved him over backwards. Grabbing the doors I shut them, shooting the bolt across. One down, two to go.

No sign of Patrick.

A shotgun roared out from somewhere at the front of the house and the security light came on. My feet were suddenly and unaccountably leaden but somehow I carried on. A woman started to shriek, not in pain, but as she might whilst watching a boxing or wrestling match, something similar, I saw when I arrived, to what was taking place in the drive. She had her back to me and was poised to dart forward, a rock she now snatched up from the ground held high to smash down on Patrick's head.

Another woman shouted out, only in warning, and I had just enough power left in my legs to tackle Marjorie from behind and the pair of us thumped on to the gravel. I wrestled the rock from her hand and knelt on her, taking disgraceful pleasure in boxing her ears when she struggled to rise.

'Hit him, Patrick!' Elspeth shouted from an upstairs window, pounding the ledge with both fists. John was there too, his shotgun still at the ready.

Patrick did not disappoint her, Brandon the Younger practically doing a backward somersault on to the lawn. Patrick then bent over, gasping with pain, holding his shoulder, which had just taken the full force of a fist. 'No handcuffs,' he managed to say in my direction.

Elspeth had the answer to that: plastic tree-ties.

James Carrick came into view down the drive in a fashion reminiscent of a Western, on foot, not rushing, not able to, a kind of inexorable but deadly patience emanating from him. His gaze came to rest on the prisoners whom we had garnered together by tying a length of washing line around them a few times and guarded by the one-man surveillance team we had come upon in the garden whom Patrick had told to provide any necessary rear-guard action.

'Margo Kadović,' he said quietly, going right up to her. 'Fancy meeting you again.'

I thought for a moment that the woman was going to spit right in his face but she refrained, staring straight through him instead.

The DCI moved on. 'William Kadović,' he said. 'And you . . .' He paused by Teddy. 'Out of the same pig pen, by the look of you.'

'Edward Brandon,' said Teddy. 'I don't know these people. I'm going to press charges for assault.'

'You were just passing?' John said derisively. 'Didn't try to force your way into my house?' He had insisted on keeping an eye on the trio as well, with his shotgun, and they had not even blinked.

'He's our son!' Margo raved. 'This was all his idea! He's ruined our retirement with his murderous schemes!'

'Shut up,' Carrick said. 'The pity of it is that I didn't interview everyone at the mill myself straight after the murders or I'd have recognized you then. Take them away,' he added to a waiting Bromsgrove and Lynn Outhwaite. 'Charge them with attempted breaking and entering – that'll do for a start.' He watched them being led away. 'That woman, she's one of the worst I came across when I was with the Vice Squad in London.'

'You'll want us to give statements,' Patrick said.

'I take it you were acting in a private capacity in order to protect your parents,' Carrick said stiffly.

'Only insofar as we got here, fast, when we realized they were heading in this direction. We'd been tailing them through the village as they looked for the ingots, which, strictly speaking, wasn't up to me right now.'

'Not in any manner of speaking,' Carrick said.

Determined to see this through but forced to take some more of the 'bloody elixir', only a sip this time, I said, 'It was something anyone might have done if they'd spotted the suspicious way they were behaving.'

'Did anyone find any ingots?'

'No,' Patrick said.

'Your whole rationale rests upon the existence of a substantial haul of stolen property.'

Patrick then pointed out to him that it was his, Carrick's, case as well. Things might have become heated but both broke off early hostilities when they saw me going down the drive and hastened after me.

'Where are you off to?' Patrick asked, sounding concerned. I could read his mind: the woman's reached breaking point and flipped like a pancake.

'Ingrid,' James said, arriving to hook an arm through mine, 'I didn't mean to sound so off-hand. It's late and everyone's tired. We'll talk about it in the morning.'

'Are you still on those wretched tablets?' I enquired truculently.

'Yes, just for one more day.'

'Then we won't talk about it in the morning, we'll talk about it another time, when you're back to normal. Meanwhile, I'll find the gold.'

For some reason he did not argue. Patrick then held my other arm and my resolve took the three of us forward. We reached the road.

'Stay here,' I said. 'I must do this alone – you're a distraction.'

I went down the road for a little way and stopped. The village was waking, lights on in one or two homes and through the open lighted window of one early bird I could hear a radio. The church clock struck five.

It had struck the evening before last, six.

And something else. Another memory.

I remembered. I had seen John, returning from his walk. I had seen him enter the church, check that all was well as he usually did, the lights switched on for a minute or so, and lock up. Then when he had gone from sight around the side of the building, making for home, I had continued on my way.

I went up the hill, past Patrick and James and entered, for the second time that night, the lychgate. My arms had been breaking so I had dumped the bag down on the low stone wall that ran down the centre, a place traditionally where coffins were rested on their final journey. I paused there now for a moment and then went on. I could hear the men walking behind me.

On the last occasion I had seen the hiding place that I had decided upon but the mist was thicker than ever just here and from where I stood it was invisible. All I had to do though was follow a path that bore off to the left and when I reached the tiny shed where grass-cutting and other tools were kept, the key hidden under a stone by a grave, everything was clear in my mind. Elspeth had once asked me to fetch a pair of shears from here as hers were blunt.

The key was beneath the stone, exactly as I had left it. I unlocked and opened the door, went in and moved aside some plastic bags that were used to collect dead flowers and wreaths from the graves and with which I had concealed the canvas bag. Then my legs gave way and I sat down very suddenly.

I was removed from the shed and seated gently, if hastily, on the wet grass, immediately soaking me right through to my knickers.

'How the *hell* did you carry this on your own?' Patrick said when the pair of them had lugged it out between them.

Seventeen

Whether I liked it or not there was a meeting the following morning, at ten thirty, at the Manvers Street police station. It was held not in Carrick's office but in an area I had never set foot in before on the top floor, in a small conference room. Having spent quite some time the previous night writing a report on what had taken place, I had not actually expected to be asked to attend. Patrick, having taken a clinical look at my dilated pupils, had poured the rest of the Essence of Flowers down the kitchen sink saying, 'You know what's in this, don't you? Home-grown poppies,' so I was having to stick to conventional medicine.

We sat there in an otherwise empty room, waiting.

I eyed up James Carrick when he eventually entered and concluded that even if one ignored the business of his pills the recovery of possibly several million pounds' worth of stolen ingots had not necessarily made this a golden morning for him. With him was the burly superintendent from HQ – I still thought him a real roughneck – who had been introduced to us as a Crime Prevention Officer, something I was now beginning to doubt, and another man wearing uniform loaded with the kind of insignia that suggested he was this individual's god.

Who next, I thought sourly, Master of the Queen's Musick?

They all sat across the table to us.

'This is Assistant Chief Constable Judd,' Carrick said. 'You've already met Superintendent Norman.'

Yes, you virtually kicked us out of Carrick's office, my mutinous thoughts went on.

I glanced sideways at Patrick. He alarmed me a little,

237

exhibiting a mixture of boredom and amusement. Then I realized that actually I was immensely proud of him: he was not overawed by this lot. How mean I had been to think that he was a different person now he no longer worked for MI5.

'I understand you said to Detective Chief Inspector Carrick that you would have preferred to enter as plain constable,' was Judd's opening remark to Patrick, without bothering with any good mornings or sympathy with regard to the piteous state of his partner.

Carrick then, had relayed everything that had gone on and been said, everything.

'Yes, it would have been far preferable,' Patrick answered quietly.

'Why?'

'I'm of the opinion that it's a very clumsy way of doing things. It has a potential to cause resentment among established officers.'

'It's only a pay scale.'

'I'm aware of that. Rapid promotion for suitable candidates would be better, especially as by then they would probably have moved on.'

'Is that the reason why, as far as you're concerned, the experiment failed?'

'No, of course not. Anyway, it hasn't failed.'

He wasn't calling him 'sir', though.

'But you've been suspended.'

'For all I know you've decided to suspend everyone on the scheme who oversteps the mark to see how they react. I've never got results by sticking to petty rules.'

'I'm sure it's been made clear to you that working for the police isn't the same as MI5.'

'Yes, it was. I had practically free rein then.'

Judd shook his head. 'That's anarchy. And very dangerous.'

'I had a very dangerous boss.'

'Would you work directly for me?' Norman enquired, eyes narrowed.

'No, you're not remotely dangerous – nor sufficiently senior.'

I nearly let out a rude whoop of joy.

'To whom exactly did you answer?' Judd said, with, did I imagine it, a hint of a smile?

'I'm not going to reveal his name even though I'm pretty sure he's retired. He's a nobleman, a knight and I respect him tremendously. But he had the authority – reporting directly to the PM – to have me shot if I got it seriously wrong.'

'I find that very hard to believe,' Norman said.

'Only on paper. He sometimes had me done over to remind me who was in charge.'

'And you were happy with that kind of working environment?' Norman said sarcastically.

'Perhaps I should have said *tried* to have me done over.'

'You were very successfully beaten up behind a pub in Bristol.'

'Oh, glory be,' Patrick whispered. 'Drugs Squad volunteers, were they? They looked filthy enough. They lied through their teeth too. We left six of them on the floor or flushed down toilets and walked away.'

'We?' Judd said blankly.

'Ingrid and I. Mostly Ingrid. She's really evil with a bog brush.'

So no one had put that in their report, *either*.

Carrick coughed. 'I understood we were to talk about the murder cases first, sir,' he said.

'Yes, we did,' Judd agreed. 'I've familiarized myself with the gist of it. Bring me up to date.'

The DCI gestured in my direction. 'Miss Langley has the details. I'm still officially on sick leave and Inspector Bromsgrove is carrying out more investigations at Hinton Mill.'

As arranged with James I had been exceedingly well briefed by my colleague seated alongside me prior to climbing the stairs. Without waiting for permission I began, 'We have three suspects under arrest, William and Margo Kadović, and Edward Brandon, her son by a previous relationship. I'll quickly give you some background information. William

239

Kadović is of Serbian origin, entering this country as a juvenile. His parents lived on the proceeds of crime and he soon joined the family firm, becoming involved with vice rings and protection rackets in London. Later, he met and married Marjorie Brandon, a one-time actress, also known as Margo, and together they ran a racket that involved bringing girls from Eastern Europe to the UK on the pretext that good domestic jobs were waiting for them and then forced them into prostitution. That is how DCI Carrick came to hear of them. By this time Brandon had Keith Davies, Christopher and Janet Manley working for him but the exact roles of the latter two, at the moment, are unclear. They can never have come face to face with the Brandons so whatever they did the orders must have been given over the phone. Their furtive behaviour at Hinton Littlemoor suggests Brandon had some kind of hold over them and ruled them by fear. We're assuming Davies provided physical back-up and organized any intimidation that was required.'

Norman butted in with, 'Are the Brandons talking?'

'Yes, as it's difficult to explain why you were trying to kick your way into a country rectory they all admit to being involved with handling the stolen gold. That came from an underworld crony who was implicated in thefts of other antiquities and desperate to get rid of it as it was "hot" – murder had been committed in order to get hold of it. The Kadovićs say they'd been drinking, were drunk even, last night and decided to try to get it back. There's a chance they'd already rehearsed what they were going to say if they were arrested as they're all insisting they thought I was just a meddlesome villager, no connection with the law, out to steal what they'd paid good money for. That's a lie, they knew perfectly well who I was.'

Carrick looked up. 'As of last night we have a signed statement from a man by the name of Paul Keen, who's been in trouble on more than one occasion for poaching. He saw a woman being pushed out of a car two nights ago on the main road just before the Hinton Littlemoor turn-off. The car drove off. Before he could go to her aid she had been knocked down by a car coming from the opposite direction. Another car stopped so he reckoned he was superfluous and went home. He probably had the added incentive of a sackful of dead pheasants with him. He did get half the registration number, it was a silver Audi. We have the Kadovićs' car, a silver Audi that has that same registration. There are very small bloodstains on the back seat, samples of which have been sent for DNA testing, together with a sample from Ingrid to see if they match. There was also an unlicensed shotgun that had been fired quite recently hidden in a secret compartment in the boot of the car.'

'They're denying the murders?' Norman wanted to know.

I said, 'Individually they are. Edward is saying he's only just back from the States and his mother and William had already carried them out. That's a lie too as he's been in prison over there and was recently deported, arriving in the UK before the murders took place. Apparently he has a record of extreme violence when under the influence of alcohol. I think it was his idea to raid the rectory either to look for me or to see if I'd hidden the gold there. I'm sure he was behind the murders, or at least, the vicious manner in which they were carried out. He gets it from her.'

'That's just your own opinion, though,' Judd said.

'Yes, formed after she'd punched me three times,' I said. 'Why else d'you think I bled on the back seat of their car?'

Patrick fluttered his eyelashes at me. We have our codes. All right, I thought, I won't be too corrosive and mess this up for you. Despite what you said just now I rather had the idea it was already messed.

'And the motives for all these murders?' Norman asked.

'It's another of my opinions,' I admitted.

'Go on.'

'Last night Margo shouted at Teddy, Edward, that he'd ruined their retirement. I think he has. He's aggressive, stupid and dangerous. I have an idea that his mother and her husband had retreated to the mill, using her maiden name, with a view to waiting quietly until they could recover the gold, which as you know had been concealed in a coffin and buried in the churchyard. They recommended that their one-time employees do the same. When the gold was recovered and a fence, or even genuine private buyers, found for it they probably planned to sell up, the properties almost certainly having increased in value by then. But Teddy – and on reflection this morning I think it was him the Manleys and Davies were terrified would turn up again – came back and turned it all into a bloodbath. He wanted in. Why should all these other people have a share?'

'And I take it it's too early to know whether wool fibres found at the scene of the barn murders are compatible with any clothing belonging to those detained,' Norman said.

'I understand that when arrested Edward Brandon was wearing a woollen sweater with a hole torn in the sleeve,' I replied. 'But yes, we await the results of tests on that and the fibres.'

'The – er – counterfeit notes found in Keith Davies's flat?' Patrick floated into the room at large.

Carrick shrugged. 'A little souvenir of the bad old days?'

'Did the bag containing the samples of tea and sand that Ingrid found in the garage turn up?'

'Yes, it did,' Carrick replied. 'She must have dropped it in the garage where the Porsche was kept. That too has gone for testing. Another point I must mention is that some pieces of decorated Chinese porcelain were found at the Kadovics' flat, in a box that had sand and tea in the bottom.'

There was a short silence.

Norman said, 'Am I to understand that a search of the garages was carried out *before* Superintendent Gillard conducted one himself without a warrant?'

'Yes,' I said. 'Just before I found the gold in the river. Did you miss that bit in the report?'

He obviously had. Neither, for a moment, did he know how to react. Then, to me, he said, 'We shall have to wait until after further questioning and enquiries to know whether your theories bear fruit.' He would have continued but there was a knock at the door and before anyone could say anything it opened and Commander John Brinkley came in.

'Sorry I'm late. The trains are all to hell this morning.' His gaze came to rest on me. 'Ingrid! What's the world been doing to you?'

'Most unfortunate,' Norman put in quickly. 'But at least it would appear we have the perpetrator.'

Then, for several minutes, the three 'resident' police officers briefed Brinkley on the cases we had been working on. He had changed. It was not just that he had put on a little weight: here was a man who exuded self-confidence and fulfilment and dressed accordingly, with style and at considerable expense. Obviously, the world was good to him. He smelt like a gigolo.

The briefing reached the point at which Patrick had been suspended and four pairs of eyes fastened on him.

'Well, frankly,' Brinkley said, 'I would have been disappointed if you hadn't got into hot water.'

'Would you be less or more disappointed if I now walked out?' Patrick enquired. 'My question after that is how much longer is this pettifogging charade going to continue?'

'Patrick,' Carrick said earnestly, 'I agree. It's gone on for too long and personally I want to apologize. But you must have realized that everyone on the scheme has been tried and tested – in your case to see how you behaved when placed under stress and treated with less deference that you were used to in the army.'

He had risked getting into trouble for saying this and I waited for Judd to explode. I was looking in the wrong direction.

'Was that the sole reason for my request for a search warrant being refused?' Patrick asked in a dead kind of tone.

Judd nodded slowly.

'You don't seem to have hoisted in exactly the kind of people we've been dealing with,' Patrick told him. 'I'll jump through hoops in role-play sessions until the end of the world but had I known you'd extend silly-bugger tactics into the real job I'd never have agreed to take part. And, for the record, I was not used to being shown much deference except when actually in uniform and junior ranks were required to salute. I suggest you research your subject next time. You could have even come along to the dinner where all the senior officers serve everyone else if the bloody government hadn't binned the regiment.' He added a couple more sentences which I will not repeat, grabbed my hand and we left the room.

Outside in the long corridor I finally succeeded in slowing the pace at which he was going and then brought him to a halt. He was breathing hard and then turned, unseeing, tears of anger in his eyes.

On tiptoe, I kissed his cheek. 'I'm really sorry. This is all my fault – I've wrecked it for you. I kept telling you to do things by the book and then went off and did exactly the opposite.'

Brinkley was hurrying to catch up with us. 'That man Judd has handled everything appalling badly,' he said. 'Look, Patrick, I really do need you. The Met are giving me a small branch of my own. I want you for a department of it. Undercover stuff, just your line of business. You'd practically be your own boss.' He chuckled in a phoney kind of way. 'Sort of a branch of a branch.'

'That sounds more like a bloody twig to me,' Patrick said. 'No, sorry, John. I'll fill in the questionnaire and post it off to you.'

'But, man, you're not even at the end of your probationary period!'

'No, but you're at the end of mine.'

We left him standing open-mouthed, trying to think of something to say.

'They'll make James a scapegoat,' I said when we were driving away.

'They might try. I have every intention of writing a letter to the bod who contacted me in the first place and copying it to quite a few other people.' Patrick glanced at me quickly. 'Are you feeling bad?'

'About the job? Yes, I've just said so – for your sake.'

'No, you, yourself.'

'I could do with the rest of the day in bed.'

'Then home, eh?'

'Heaven.'

I had my rest, sleeping for most of the time, and when I finally decided it was time I showed my face downstairs at just after eight the following morning I found everyone having breakfast. Tea and loving kindness flowed, followed by bacon and eggs, and I soon felt almost restored to normal.

'Lorna Church rang,' Patrick said. 'She'd tried to get hold of me at the nick but was told I wasn't there so tried here. She was worried because she'd forgotten to tell me something. Apparently Janet Manley had given her a small porcelain bowl as a present when they were invited up for drinks one night. Janet said it had been in her family for a long time but I reckon it had been one of those the gang grabbed along with the ingots and she'd kept it in that box.'

'And that's how the tea got in there,' I said. 'I had wondered if there were a few more ingots on the loose. Will she be allowed to keep it?'

'I've no intention of telling her or anyone else it might be stolen property. Anyway, as far as I'm concerned it's all purely academic now.'

'You've really decided to give up?' Elspeth said.

'I've not given up,' Patrick told her. 'Just decided I can't work the way the law does.'

Could not stomach working for the plumped-up and fragrant Brinkley either, I had already surmised. Ironically, Carrick had been perfectly correct in his original judgement.

'We must contact James,' I said.

'I already have. As we'd suspected, he's been under huge pressure to act unfriendly – the powers that be thought he might carry me in the job and give an undeserved glowing report. It was the reason he didn't initially want to have anything to do with it. I got the impression that after we left he virtually told Judd and Norman to sod off back to HQ and let him and Bromsgrove get on with the work in hand. It looks as though Bromsgrove might stay though, he'd asked for a move to Bath as he lives in Oldfield Park.'

John looked up from the crossword. 'Vernon Latimer's resigned from the PCC,' he said. 'He told me he found your questioning of him quite unwarranted. The fellow seemed to think I'd set you on him in future if he put a foot wrong.'

Had he actually written that letter to the bishop complaining that John was no longer fit enough for the job, I wondered, then received a less than sympathetic reply? We would probably never know.

'Good,' Elspeth said. 'I never liked him.'

'His wife's left him,' John went on. 'And he's having to sell up – leaving the district by all accounts.' His gaze rested briefly on Patrick and me. 'You two do make waves, you know.'

'I want to know if you really must rush home,' Elspeth said to us, hands clasped at her bosom.

'Why?' Patrick asked.

'I'd love a few days on Sark. You know, we stay with our old friends the Framleys who used to live at the grange next door. They've a massive garden and a while ago decided to sell part of it to someone to build a house. Your father and I used some of our savings to buy the plot – I have to say they let us have it very cheaply – and it seems such a lovely thing to do at such a miserable time of the year to go over there and talk about plans and architects—' She broke off, eyes shining, hugging herself.

'Do go,' I said. 'Go for as long as you like. Patrick and I can take it in turns to house-sit.'

'There's the dog too, but only for a week or so.'

'Which dog?' Patrick said.

'Whisky. The RSPCA phoned and asked, as you'd expressed an interest in him, whether we'd have him here for a short while. In fact, they sent an inspector round to make sure the place was suitable.' In response to our blank looks she went on, 'Sorry, I must have forgotten to tell you but it only happened the day before yesterday. Vera Stonelake is going to live with one of her daughters and wants to take the dog with her. It's hers, after all. The daughter's got to have the garden fenced or something first. I was told Vera's a lot better since being looked after in the nursing home and with her daughter's help is contacting her solicitor to check up on her will. Isn't that good news?'

'Wonderful,' Patrick said warmly.

It was not until a fortnight later to the day that Patrick and I would be at home together and when he came in the front door he had a smile on his lips.

'Remember the blue car?' he said.

'The one I saw in the garage that disappeared?'

'Yup. You were right, it almost certainly had been booby-trapped when you found it. Traffic police became suspicious yesterday about a vehicle that had been parked in a side road for a while, and even more so when they saw liquid of some kind dripping from it that seemed to have killed all the grass nearby on a verge. They ended up calling in the bomb squad. It was acid. It wasn't actually set to go off but was a crude device that would have squirted anyone who opened up the car unless something was disconnected first.'

'William Kadović?'

'A bit of an inventor, he himself bragged. He'd done it with us in mind. Yes, I spoke to Carrick, went to the nick, in fact. After apologizing all over again he told me he has a good case against them and they're tacking that charge on for good luck.' He looked around. 'Where are the kids?'

'They should have just come down the drive and be waiting outside for you.'

'Can't they come in?'

'No, because the present we've bought you is too big to go through the door.'

The present, Katie's hand on his velvet nose in the hope it would prevent him whinnying, had been secreted in one of Lydtor's hidden lanes by the excited children a few minutes previously, Matthew holding Vicky. Justin was part way up a tree with strict instructions to watch the road and report when Patrick turned into the drive. For this reason I had asked him to ring me when he left Exeter so I could roughly calculate the time of his arrival.

George was dark bay in colour and had been described as a medium-weight hunter in the advertisement but was, I had been pleased to see on inspecting him, on the light side of that and at sixteen hands was ideal for Patrick's height. With slight trepidation I had ridden him out on Dartmoor myself the previous day. The words 'hunter' and 'wide-open spaces' can add up to make an explosive equine handful. But George was a perfect gentleman and had cantered off steadily when asked. However, he had at the moment a very light person on the other end of his lead rope and had towed Katie over to Patrick's car where he was busily scratching his chin on the radio aerial.

'That's George,' I said. 'He came well recommended by knowledgeable friends.'

'That's a very good horse,' Patrick murmured. 'Wow.'

'I got a pretty massive advance from the States for the screenplay,' I said. 'Go on, we tacked him up for you.'

Mounted, he said, 'I still don't have a job.'

'No, but the vegetable garden needs digging, the apple trees will have to be pruned and a length of gutter has fallen off the cottage. Oh, and the woodstove chimney of the barn needs sweeping.'

'I quite like the idea of being a kept man,' he said as he rode away, jeans, leather jacket, ordinary shoes and all.

This ambition was thwarted a few days later when a letter arrived from John Brinkley when he humbly proposed a new offer; would Lieutenant Colonel Gillard consider a position that would involve his being called upon to help the Metropolitan Police as an independent adviser on cases of 'great sensitivity' where his expertise could be utilized to the greatest advantage?

'He hasn't mentioned you,' Patrick commented.

'As always,' I said. 'Two for the price of one.'

'Do we consider?'

'When they've given us a few more details?'

'That's a good idea – play for time to give us a chance to think about it.'

'And you could go and ask George.'

Patrick went riding.

Sending rescued chickens in all directions in the drive.